CHASING GRAVITY

Tempeste Blake

Pocket Acorn
Press

Copyright © 2017 by Tempeste Blake

All rights reserved. This book or any portion thereof may not be reproduced or used in any manner whatsoever without the express written permission of the publisher except for the use of brief quotations in a book review.

The characters and events in this book are fictitious. Any similarity to real persons, living or dead is coincidental and not intended by the author.

Printed in the United States of America

First Printing, 2017

Cover design by Nancy Smith
Interior design by Catherine Trizzino

ISBN-13: 978-1544648408
ISBN-10: 1544648405

Pocket Acorn Press, LLC
11392 East Indian Lake Drive
Vicksburg, MI 49097

www.tempesteblake.com

For those who help, in ways large and small.

One, remember to look up at the stars and not down at your feet. Two, never give up work. Work gives you meaning and purpose and life is empty without it. Three, if you are lucky enough to find love, remember it is there and don't throw it away.
—*Stephen Hawking*

ONE

Saturday, April 4th

THIS was the last place Dylan expected to find himself on a Saturday morning. He should be parked in front of a bowl of Cocoa Pebbles, browsing through the sports section, feet up, Bugs Bunny chomping a carrot in the background. Instead, he was on a bogus mission, here to pacify a woman whose inner soundtrack might well have been Warner Brother's inspiration for Looney Tunes.

The house reeked of curry, scratchy wool blankets, and forced heat. Sexy lamp on a side table. Beads, bangles, and some sort of sparkling carpet spanning one wall. Helen was the definition of eccentric and certainly skirted the rules when it came to calendar ticks. Didn't look a day over sixty, but according to Dylan's calculations, she had to be at least eighty.

He walked the length of the living room and rearranged sheer curtains at a side window, his gaze landing on the bungalow beyond a thick hedge of bushes. A house both familiar and strange to him now. His ex-girlfriend's house. Only now she was married. To his brother.

"Did you call Finn?" he asked Helen, taking his time to turn back to her. "If your friend's really missing, a police report should be filed." Dylan had no idea why Helen had contacted him in the first place. He assumed that in her book, he ranked somewhere between an IRS auditor and Kim Jong-un.

The old woman flashed a panicked glare. "The police won't give this top priority. I *need* a private investigator."

Private investigator. The ink on his license was barely dry, and he had only worked a total of two cases. A woman trying to find out if her husband was cheating. He was. A man who suspected his son was on drugs. He was. The job was almost too easy in Riley's Peak. A town where the anonymous part of AA was anything but anonymous.

This he knew firsthand.

"Tell me again what—" Dylan started.

"Elyse showed up here last night, a day early. Leticia, that's her daughter, is coming to be with us for our annual Soul Cleansing Weekend. I haven't seen Leticia since she came home from Iraq. I couldn't be prouder. Anyway, she's coming up from Savannah." Helen stopped, stared past him with a near-startled expression. "So much to look forward to. Now Elyse is gone."

"Maybe she went out for a toothbrush or milk or something." Or maybe some extra soap for the "cleansing."

Helen pursed her lips in a sour pucker. "We don't do dairy." She shook her head defiantly; tips of dangly, mismatched earrings brushing her shoulders. One feathery. One all beads and stars.

"But her car is gone, her purse," Dylan pointed out. "It seems like she left on her own. Whatever the reason."

Helen pointed to a half-empty glass of red wine on the end table. "Elyse would never do that. She'd finish it, or she'd wash out the glass. This simply isn't her style."

So this friend left without cleaning up after herself. Bad manners. Not a crime. Dylan was ready to tell Helen to call him if she had a real problem when her eyes lined with tears.

"The cards don't lie." Helen moved to the coffee table and spread five large tarot cards in a wide arc. "Someone wants to kill her."

He'd never put much stock in cards, tea leaves, or people reading the cream in their coffee. "Do the cards say who?"

Helen swiped at her wet cheeks, straightened. "I know

skepticism is your strong suit, sort of your signature, but there are powers in this world you and I will never understand." She motioned to the table; her fingertips lightly touching a card featuring a scythe-swinging skeleton, and then tiptoeing to one with a star. "If you'll indulge me, this represents you. Hope and inspiration."

Hope and inspiration? He'd never been anybody's hope or inspiration. She needed a new deck of cards. "Where were you when your friend left?"

"I was out."

"Out?"

"I had plans with Stanley. At his place. We alternate. I came back a little after six this morning. As I said, Elyse was a day early. She didn't want me to cancel my date even though I told her I could see Stanley anytime. But she insisted she'd stay here while I went out." Her hands clasped together twisting, twisting. "She insisted."

He'd heard Helen was more "active" than most her age, maybe legendary. "Let me get this straight—"

A rap at the door interrupted him, and Helen ran to open it. A woman in a black leather bomber jacket and those pants that look air-brushed on gripped both sides of the doorjamb in a pose that was anything but casual. Freckles sprinkled her nose and marched in opposite directions toward perfect ears. No make-up. Dark hair scraped into a loose ponytail. A straight line of bangs nearly eclipsed what appeared to be her best feature. Her eyes. She certainly wasn't out to win any beauty pageants.

And yet she could.

Without waiting for an invitation, she stepped into the house, and Helen folded her into a hug.

"Aunt Helen, it's been too long!" The hint of a southern drawl worked its way through an attempt to downplay it.

Helen's niece?

"Leticia, I'm so glad you're here."

"It's Tish." Her tone instructive. You will call me Tish.

"I'll try, but Leticia is so ingrained."

"Mom's not here yet?" She unzipped her jacket. "I've been

trying to call her since I got off the plane."

Dylan's first impression of Leticia, Tish, whatever, the pretty face with a figure to match, was swallowed by her military precision, the way she barked out questions in a caps lock voice.

Tish spun toward him as though realizing for the first time he was in the room. "Who are you?"

At least she didn't ask for rank and serial number. Stepping forward he offered his hand, "Dylan Tierny," and let it drop after a few emasculating seconds. Okay, no handshake.

"As I said before, Tish." No last name required. Like Beyonce or Kesha, he guessed. She stared at him a penetrating moment before she returned to Helen.

Helen's fingers crept to her mouth and dropped to her chin, rubbing, deliberating. "I don't want to worry you, but Elyse is gone. She was here last night, but now ... something is very wrong."

"Did you try RJ?" Tish asked.

"I've called cell and home a hundred times. No answer." Helen turned to Dylan. "RJ Corman is Elyse's common-law husband. She didn't want to marry again after her dear Frank passed. Of course, that was years ago, but—"

"Are you sure she didn't just run out?" Tish interjected. "Maybe to the store."

"I suspected the same," Dylan said.

Tish zeroed in on him now. "Excuse me, Dylan, is it? I don't mean to be blunt, but this is a family matter."

Most cases were. He didn't need to be told. His morning routine was calling him back, and maybe it made sense to leave and let Tish here help Helen find her crystal ball. But the urge to stay and see how this turned out trumped his compulsion to walk away—this might be far more entertaining than the Saturday cartoon line up.

"Why don't you start at the beginning, Helen," Dylan heard himself say. "Don't leave anything out."

Tish closed the space between the three of them and assumed an authoritative stance; legs shoulder width apart, hands on hips. Almost masculine. Almost. Who was she trying to kid? She oozed female from her haphazard ponytail to her shiny black boots.

"That's not necessary, Aunt Helen." That drawl pulling at the edges of her words again. Then to Dylan, "Seriously, I've got this."

He felt the corner of his mouth involuntarily lift in a smirk before he barked out, "Dismissed!"

"A military crack?"

"Just speaking your language. But I'm a private investigator not some private in the marines. I don't take orders from you."

"Army." Her gaze floated over him. "I was in the army. Listen, I'm not sure why Aunt Helen called you—"

"Please." Helen spread her arms in a referee's T, indicating unsportsmanlike conduct.

Dylan conceded. For Helen's sake. Plus, he might enjoy tooling on this one. He knew the type. Bitter. Felt like she had something to prove.

"A picture of your friend would be helpful, Helen." He watched as the muscle in Tish's jaw did a little hop skip before he went on. "Do you happen to have a recent one?"

"I do!" Helen clapped her hands together. "Elyse and I went to see the Spirit Gourds of Native America Exhibit in Allentown last fall. It's quite a drive, but we generally do something special on Anne's birthday. She was Elyse's mother and my dearest friend. I drove so Elyse could work. Don't know why she needs to switch from gadget to gadget like that, but it was still—"

"No need for a picture," Tish broke in. "I know what my mother looks like."

"I'd love to see it," Dylan said to Helen.

She moved to the bookcase, selected a framed photo. "Lovely, isn't she?"

Helen and a tall woman stood side-by-side, silhouetted by a fog-capped lake. Charcoal smudged eyes, high cheekbones on mocha skin, she had a beaming quality, like she'd just won a prize. Her arms, crossed in a prove-it pose, broadcast her confidence. Beautiful. Like her daughter.

"Helen, is anything of yours missing?" Dylan asked.

"As I said—" Helen started.

"Now you're calling my mother a thief?" Tish made no attempt to mask her accent this time.

"That's not what I meant."

"Well the question sure sounds like an accusation."

"Yes!" Helen belted out. "Something very important is missing." She waited until she had their full attention. "Elyse."

✌ TWO ✌

TISH struggled to channel her inner warrior, not the worrier bombarding her with "what ifs." There had to be a logical explanation for Elyse being MIA.

Still, why would her mom tell Tish to meet her at Helen's this morning if she hadn't planned to stay? This visit had been on the calendar for weeks. Elyse had even surrendered a generous chunk of frequent flyer miles for a first class seat from Savannah to Pittsburgh. Despite a delayed take off, thanks to some dog-tired executive begging for the laptop he'd left at the gate, she'd made it to Helen's in record time. Now it was almost noon, her stomach was demanding food, a hammer pounded her temples, and she desperately needed to pee. But full bladder or not, Tish refused to leave until she knew what the hell was going on.

This Dylan chump was running his hand along the windowsill while Helen clung to him like lint. Private I? Did he think this charade was paycheck-worthy?

She tried not to notice how his goatee stippled the contours of his chin and how the pale green of his eyes reminded her of the Spanish moss dripping from the oaks back home. Real private investigators don't look like this. She wouldn't be surprised if he'd ordered his license from the back of a cereal box, bought a gun in a dark alley, and advertised his services on the local library's corkboard. Why had Helen called him anyway? Was her sixth sense working overtime again?

As if eavesdropping on her thoughts, Dylan stopped what he was doing and shoved his hand in his jeans pocket. Jeans that gloved his body like he was a walking advertisement for Levis.

Stop! The last thing she needed was to think about getting sweaty with this small town, detective wannabe. Not that she wouldn't benefit from a little hot and heavy. It had been a while. Fraternizing in the army had been off-limits. Anyone else she met on the outside turned tail and ran as soon as they found out what she did for a living. As if wearing camo and toting a gun cancelled out any chance of intimacy.

"I don't believe anything's wrong but—" Dylan parked himself uncomfortably close, so close his breath warmed her cheek.

A knock at the door, simultaneous with his words.

"That must be Elyse." Helen ran to the door and swung it open. A man wiped his feet on the mat, stepped inside. "Saw your truck," he said to Dylan. "Everything okay?"

"Helen thinks her friend is missing."

"I don't think, I know." Helen moved to the newcomer and admired him like a prized thoroughbred. "This is Detective Finn Tierny. My neighbor."

Tierny. Did all the good-looking men in town have the same last name?

"I didn't want the cops," Helen said. "No offense of course." A flash of something flickered on her face, the drift of her warming thoughts apparent. "However, since you're here, maybe you can assist."

Tish nodded to Finn. "You don't need to get involved. My mom probably got inspired in the middle of the night and rushed home. It's hard for her to take a weekend off. I'll drive to Crestwood and find her up to her elbows in paperwork."

"No. I'm certain she didn't leave on her own," Helen said. "Certain as tomorrow's sunrise."

In her mind, Tish was already on her way to Crestwood, but Helen's brow, knitted in her patented expression of concern, made her whip a U-turn. Eccentric or not, Helen was the spunky old lady version of Gorilla glue, holding delicate family ties together, forcing connections where they might otherwise fall apart. If she felt reassured by the local cop and his P.I. brother, it was worth a few minutes delay.

But Helen's recounting of stories, the way she took the circuitous route describing every detail, was tantamount to verbal water torture. Drip ... Drip ... Drip.

"Helen, do you mind if I fill Detective Tierny in?"

"Please do. And don't leave anything out."

"Ms."—Dylan swiveled in her direction—"What's your last name?"

The slant of his eyebrow, which she was certain he intended to be inquisitive, was downright sexy and it took all her willpower to pull her gaze away.

"Duchene."

"Ms. Duchene here is career military so I'm sure her retelling will be spit-shined."

"If you think you're better equipped to explain," she said, "by all means ..."

Utter frustration registered on Helen's face. "If I didn't know better, I'd think you two knew each other in another life or were having a lover's spat in this one, the way you're sniping."

Tish felt the sting of the verbal slap. "I believe my mother got here last night at approximately 1900 hours. Helen left soon after." She glanced at her for confirmation, and Helen nodded.

"You left?" Finn asked.

"Well, yes, Elyse didn't want me to change my plans just because she came early. There's still a good portion of juice left in this old lemon, you know." Her smile faded as her lips began to quiver. "I'd planned a nice brunch for us. For this morning, when Leticia, Tish, arrived. I intended to try a new recipe, quinoa salad with beets and kumquats." She scratched her forehead. "At least I'm fairly certain we discussed that."

Tish imagined the conversation. Elyse multi-tasking, phone to ear, jotting notes. Helen's finger zig-zagging over the recipe. It was like a grown-up version of the telephone game where the final message mangled the initial intent.

"When Helen arrived this morning—"

"At six," Helen interjected.

"When Helen arrived at 0600," Tish continued, "my mother was gone. There's no way to pinpoint what time she left."

"What about leaving a note?" Dylan asked. "Or calling?"

Tish pictured her mother's face scrunched in an earnest grimace, eyes blinking slowly as she calculated the next wonder drug. Another image blipped, a dark highway, a car crashed into a tree. She elbowed the thought away.

"Where does Elyse work?" Finn asked.

"At Saycor with RJ. They met there," Helen chimed in. "Oh it took some time for them to get together, but it was in the cards all along."

"Saycor Pharmaceutical?" Dylan asked. "In Crestwood?"

"I remember reading about how the CEO bought a villa in Tuscany," Finn said.

"The company does well." Tish gave the shortest possible response. A redirecting tactic learned from her father.

"And your mom?" Dylan asked.

She felt her jaw tighten. "I'm not sure what you're asking."

"Just curious if she does well too."

"How is her income relevant?"

Helen pressed her fingertips to her cheeks. "Someone must be after her money."

"I know you're worried, Helen, but there's no evidence of forced entry," Dylan said. "No sign that anyone else was even here."

For the first time, Tish agreed with Dylan. They were flying blind, investigating a non-existent crime.

Finn wrapped an arm around Helen. "I'm sure everything's okay, but I can keep an eye out for her. What does she drive?"

"I'm not a car person," Helen said. "But it's one of those fancy ones with a cat name . . . Cheetah?"

Tish would have laughed if it weren't for the mind-numbing aggravation. "Jaguar. Which I'm sure is back at her house or in Saycor's parking garage." She extracted keys from her purse. "Helen, I'll call you as soon as I can." She jutted her chin to each of the men in turn. "It was nice meeting ya'll."

Dylan's mouth pulled to the side.

This yahoo could make fun of her stretched vowels all he

wanted, but it was time to go.

After Finn left, Helen sidled up to Tish. "Something's radically wrong. I feel it"—she clutched her elbow—"in my bones."

For the first time Tish saw vulnerability in one of the strongest women she'd ever met. She knew any reassurance she could give would be little salve for Helen's fears, but she tried anyway. "I'll find her and call you the minute I do."

"Go with her," Helen implored Dylan. "Don't let her out of your sight."

He opened his mouth to speak, but Tish lobbed him a look. *Humor her.*

They made for the door like two kids responding to the fire alarm, two unruly kids whose shoulders collided when they didn't exit single file.

"After you." Dylan splayed his hand in a magnanimous gesture.

This was no time to be noble. Tish charged out onto the porch.

"Wait!" Helen scurried toward the kitchen and yelled over her shoulder. "This will only take a minute."

Tish did as Helen asked even though she was starting to feel like she didn't have a minute to spare. Not one split second to waste on this P.I. dude. Once they were on their way, she'd lose him like a bad habit.

Speaking of which; her hand traveled to her pocket, and she fingered her daily allotment. How she looked forward to the smooth effect of that lone cigarette, the nicotine sailing through her system.

It was stupid. She'd quit before she enlisted. But the army had a way of shining a floodlight on all your inadequacies. A floodlight that eventually brought her to her knees; then prostrate before her failure to do the most important thing.

She slid her finger along her last smoke. She needed to buy more. Needed the assurance of that single slice of peace each day. Only a couple minutes of calm, but she'd take it.

⁂ THREE ⁂

The Previous Night, Friday April 3rd

RJ Corman dropped four small cubes into a tumbler. The ice diluted his scotch perfectly. Plus, he liked the symmetry of four. He reached for the Balvenie, filled the glass, swirled it, and took a sip. The first taste transported him, sweeping him away to a land of kilts, bagpipes, and lazy afternoons. The Scottish Highlands, part of "Elyse and RJ's Champagne Bucket List." A plan that had taken years to talk her into, mainly because she couldn't ever imagine not working. A plan switched to an accelerated track now that he'd made the decision to leave Saycor.

Shit timing, but the company would weather the recent storm and come out with little more than a scratch on the hull. A death in a trial would be a deal breaker for most companies. Saycor, on the other hand, could get through anything with Philip Kelrich at the helm. The biggest casualty here might be Philip and RJ's friendship. Hopefully it ran deeper than company waters.

The salary and stock options at Clark Newman were too good to pass up if he and Elyse wanted to retire early, and in style. Twirling pasta under a Tuscan sunset, seeing a giraffe up close on an African safari, so close you have to roll your head back to scan her endless neck, kneeling beneath the majestic Kamakura Buddha on a side trip from Tokyo, all required a substantial nest egg.

He'd made the right decision. He just had to find the best time to break it to Philip. But he'd think about all this later. Tonight he was checking out.

RJ grabbed the Balvenie and headed for the back deck. He hated fighting with Elyse. Not only was her temper hotter than August in Arizona, she always left before they could resolve things. Always.

They'd fought about his sister, Annabeth. And as much as he hated to admit it, Elyse was right. Time to cut the cord.

Drinking alone on a Friday night. Wouldn't be the first time, and likely not the last.

But he wasn't exactly alone. Nutmeg, their sheltie-mix, lounged by the hot tub, chin on forelegs, droopy eyes mirroring his own emotions, a poster dog for empathy. He'd never seen an animal demonstrate such human expressions.

He reached down, scratched behind her ear. "Looks like it's just you and me tonight, girl." He shed his slippers and stepped into the tub, settling the bottle and glass next to him. His stomach growled, a reminder he hadn't eaten. Maybe he'd drink his dinner. He located a jet, positioned his back over it, and closed his eyes.

Pink's "Just Give Me A Reason" blared from the outdoor speakers. That woman's voice could hypnotize the pants off a skeptic. And there was only one way to listen to it: loud. The neighbors had stopped complaining about his deafening music after he'd landscaped the large lot's perimeter with a few rows of evergreens creating a generous buffer zone between the houses.

There were other changes too. When Elyse moved in with him five years ago, she'd put her stamp on the five-bedroom colonial: her vintage green pottery collection and a few well-placed decorative pillows added splashes of casual comfort to the space he'd spent years perfecting. Those things meant more to her than heated tile floors, Bose speakers throughout, and a massive media room with theater-style seating. Enviable landscaping, complete with a dream pool and hot tub nestled under a waterfall glowing in amber lights, had completed his Shangri La. But it was her touch that made this house a home. Her touch made everything right.

Taking another slug of scotch, he felt the burn in his throat, the buzz in his nasal passages, and he surrendered his head to the stone tiles.

"Comfy?" The word pierced the piano refrain.

RJ nearly shot from the water.

"You're a jumpy SOB." Philip stepped into the light. He looked out of place on the pool deck. Did he actually think removing his cufflinks and pocket square could make a Canali suit look Friday casual?

"Don't you own a pair of jeans?" RJ asked.

Rhetorical question. RJ had known the man for nearly four decades. Long enough to be familiar with his wardrobe, his disdain for late night talk shows, even his preference for Sumatran coffee beans. They'd met in a high school wood working class, and though they didn't have much in common then, they grew on each other. Philip had been the one who started calling him RJ because a guy named Reynold didn't have a snowball's chance in a heat wave of getting laid.

Given Philip's reserved seat in the principal's office and stack of detentions, no one thought he would amount to much, but he'd proven them all wrong. And he took great delight in shoving it in their faces year after year with hefty donations to Grover Cleveland High.

Saycor Pharmaceutical was Philip's third trip down money-maker lane. His first two companies had sold to big pharma, and Saycor was on the same track, despite the recent unfortunate incident in the clinical trial.

RJ finished his drink, refilled. "I should have never given you my alarm code. What if I'd been in the middle of something?"

"Or someone. By the way, where is Elyse?" Philip dropped into a chair. "And it wouldn't hurt for you to get a little more creative with the code. Hell, the mailman probably knows it."

RJ ignored his query. He wasn't feeling particularly social. All he wanted was a little solo time. But if he was completely honest, he didn't want to be alone, alone. He wanted Elyse. "Grab another bottle. I'm about to kill this one, but there's a Macallan in the bar."

"Do we have something to celebrate?"

"Since when do we need an excuse to crack open a Macallan?"

As Philip headed for the French doors, he threw a "ha" over his shoulder. Not a that's-funny laugh, but a you're-full-of-shit laugh.

"When I get back, you can tell me what you two are fighting about."

Nutmeg followed Philip inside and RJ imagined her scooching under the coffee table, out of the line of fire for the night. She was like one of those truffle-sniffing dogs, able to rut out tension even if it was deep below the surface.

Philip knew the drill. Whenever Elyse's temper reared its ugly head, she'd take off. Then after she'd had time to cool down, she'd return begging forgiveness, bribing RJ with backrubs and praline pie.

They'd all been working together for years—Philip the financial wizard, Elyse a brilliant biochemist and doctor, and RJ who could sell smart TVs to the Amish. But when RJ had started dating Elyse, it seemed to irk Philip. Concern about their business relationship, or flat out jealousy? RJ had caught him more than once looking at her. Really looking. Of course, a man would have to be blind not to. Who could blame Philip for appreciating more than her skill set? Wandering down that path stimulated RJ's frontal lobe and he imagined a romp between the sheets, on the kitchen counter, the sunroom floor, Elyse's legs coiled around him like insatiable vines. And though it made him feel like a jerk to even think about it, the make-up sex almost made their fights tolerable.

Philip rattling around the bar inside brought RJ back to the problem at hand. Maybe he should go ahead and get it over with, tell him he was leaving Saycor. This tension, however subtle, wasn't doing anybody any favors. What once passed for friendship and admiration was now overshadowed with suspicion capped with a hint of contempt.

Elyse needed to get her gorgeous ass back here. No way RJ could broach the subject of his resignation without her by his side. Plus, whether they were fighting or not, everything always seemed better when she was around. It all sounded like a sugared-up Hallmark card, but every bit of it was true. The woman was everything to him, and though he didn't want to wish his life away, he couldn't wait for those golden years, retirement and spending all day every day with her.

Finally, Philip returned with a tumbler of ice and a bottle of Macallan Ruby. This one had been a gift from Elyse, and they had been saving it for a special occasion. RJ's new job certainly qualified. What the hell, he was popping it anyway. It wasn't his nature to be vindictive, not even in the remotest part of his molecular structure, but DNA never told the complete story, did it? This rogue architect known as life was perpetually busy reworking the blueprints and sketching new patterns into his psyche.

Philip took a seat at a small metal table near the hot tub.

"Get lost in there?" RJ asked.

"Took a detour to empty the tank."

How much of that detour included snooping around? RJ emerged, put his slippers on, shrugged into a thick cotton robe. Booze didn't usually make him feel paranoid, anything but. All this change was harshing his buzz. And not having the balls to just tell his best friend he was moving on made him feel like he needed absolution, not Absolut. But then, he was more a Goose or Belvedere man nowadays. Either the heat or the scotch was messing with his lateral thinking. He needed to play the game though and not let on that he was losing it. "Hungry? I can't guarantee the identity of the heat ups in the fridge"—he sat next to Philip—"that would take a trip to the lab. But I could order a pizza."

"Nah, I'm good." Philip leaned back in his chair and intertwined his hands behind his head. "What's going on?"

Paranoia reared its jittery head again. Had Philip seen something inside? Something about Clark Newman? Or was he still talking about Elyse? RJ decided to go with the latter. "Nothing. She's got a girls' weekend thing."

"Everybody needs time away, but somehow the wandering heart always finds its way home."

Maybe this was about Elyse. But maybe not. RJ never discounted Philip's ability to hide knives inside his words.

"Well, she's only wandering as far as Riley's Peak," RJ said. "We had a stupid argument so she left straight from work. Didn't even bother to come home and pack. You know Elyse."

"I do." Philip's expression said he'd been on the receiving end of Elyse's zero to sixty temper more than once. "You left your Roadster out."

"It'll survive one night outside." He'd been on his way to move it into the garage when Elyse called, tanking the rest of his evening.

Philip's phone buzzed, but he declined the call. When it rang again, and then a third time, he answered, listened, his exasperation evident. "I'll call you back."

"Someone's got you fired up," RJ said with a laugh.

An almost imperceptible hitch in Philip's demeanor suggested this wasn't a laughing matter. "Minor upset." He emptied his drink, eyes narrowed to slits. "You know all about dealing with curveballs though, don't you?"

The question rose like a specter, pointing an accusing finger right through the ragged edges of a snootful of scotch.

RJ tightened his robe, suddenly feeling cold. Exposed.

❦ FOUR ❧

Saturday, April 4th

THE calendar announced *April*, but winter held Riley's Peak in a death grip. Crisp air teased through Dylan's thin flannel shirt as he and Tish waited on Helen's porch. He hadn't bothered with a jacket this morning. This was supposed to be a quick in, out, and back to the news so he could gloat a little more about the Pirates sweeping the Cardinals. But no, this actually might be turning into a real case.

The chill emanating from Tish didn't help. He tried to ignore her as his mind filtered through what he knew, or thought he knew. Elyse could have split as soon as Helen left last night, or bolted early this morning. Her arrival could be a figment of Helen's overactive imagination. Boiling it down, he knew squat.

The door whooshed open, and Helen waggled two brown bags at them. "For sustenance."

Wow. When was the last time someone packed a lunch for him? Dylan quickly buried the answer along with the image of his name written in curlicue next to a smiley sticker on the lunch sack.

Tish gave Helen another hug and scurried down the steps. Dylan hesitated a beat too long, and Helen side-stepped, blocking his escape. Her eyes loomed large behind glasses covered in brightly painted flowers. "Remember what I said. Stay with Tish. Find Elyse. Whatever it takes."

"Whatever it takes."

A pledge he hoped he could keep. He'd already left a trail of broken promises in his wake.

Tish was half way to her car, a green Sebring convertible, top up. Of course it would be, this one wasn't the carefree, wind through your hair type. He wondered if the rental place was out of jeeps, or Humvees, something more utilitarian. "Wanna slow to a dead sprint so we can talk?" he called out.

She pivoted, cocked her head, and her eyes skewered him like he'd asked her to get naked. Which under different circumstances . . .

Contention lay between them like a force field.

"I'll keep Helen posted," she finally said. "And I'm sure she'll contact you if necessary."

Chain of command. Dylan repressed a salute. Tish might not want a joint mission, but in his mind, it made sense to team up. "I'll follow you."

Before she could object, he started toward his truck. His Timberlands scraped to a halt as he followed the trajectory of her sight. The faded red paint, almost pink in places, bleached white in others, and rusted-out fender gave his ride character. At least he thought so. "Don't judge her on appearance, she's as reliable as they come."

"Good luck with that."

Did he really need another person, a stranger at that, reminding him he needed a new four-by?

He hopped in, slammed the door, and barely got the key in the ignition when the Sebring flew past him. If she hadn't had to stop for a distracted kid crossing the street, plugged into his phone, she would have been long gone. Dylan rolled down his window and warned the kid to be careful. Catching up with Tish, he stuck close as they wove their way through Helen's neighborhood toward the highway. Tish turned right, he turned right. He thought about gunning past her, or turning around and heading home, but Helen was counting on him.

At the first stop light, Dylan fiddled with the radio, tried to look anywhere but at the car in front of him. The light turned green, and his truck sputtered. Then . . . stalled. He flipped the key, which resulted in a grinding noise, then silence. He banged the steering wheel. The driver behind him honked. Hanging his arm out the window, he motioned the car around him. Tish slowed and U-turned as he watched his day slide from a pain in the neck to a sharp spike in the ass.

She stopped and strolled to the truck. "What's that you were saying about not judging her on appearance?"

Dylan climbed out and raked a hand through his hair. "I've got to get her off the road. Help me steer."

"How can I resist when you asked so nicely."

Her sardonic smile made him want to leave the damn thing in the middle of the street. "Please."

Tish maneuvered past him, grabbed the steering wheel.

"Go ahead, get in," Dylan said.

"I'll help push."

"I just need you to . . ." He tried to keep annoyance from his tone. Arguing with her was about as productive as a woodpecker pecking on a tin roof. He trudged to the back of the truck and got into position. Tish put it in neutral, and they pushed it across the right lane and into a parking lot.

Dylan took out his cell and punched in a number. "Hey, Durwood, my man. Need your help again. Ace Hardware . . . I know, I know. I need to let her go."

He reached into the passenger's seat. "Can't forget my *sustenance*." He grabbed the sack lunch and headed for the store. Might as well have a look around while he waited.

"What will you do?" Tish asked to his back.

He turned. "My buddy has a whole yard full of junkers just waiting for an adventure. Don't worry, I'll catch up later."

Her face momentarily muddied by a landslide of contemplation, then she pointed to her rental car. "I guess you could ride with me to Crestwood."

Suspended between options, he decided it wouldn't pay to be stubborn. Plus, as much as it ground his nerves, Helen was his only paying client at the moment. He headed for the Sebring, climbed in, and redialed Durwood's number. "Change of plans, man, no loaner. Give her a tow, and I'll settle with you later."

Tish ripped off her jacket, threw it in the backseat, and shoved the key in the ignition. After adjusting her rearview mirror, she revved the engine, and started tapping an address in the dashboard GPS.

"I know how to get to Crestwood," he said.

She pivoted. "Look, we're sharing a ride, but as far as this operation—"

Operation? This was probably about Elyse forgetting her toothbrush, along with her common courtesy. He knew the brainy, inconsiderate type. Why the hell hadn't she called anyone? He reached for the door handle, started to tell Tish this wasn't going to work, but before he could say or do anything, she threw the car in gear and left a line of rubber that would make a NASCAR driver envious.

All right then.

"On the other hand, that GPS lady's voice gives me the all-overs so lead the way," she said.

"The all-overs?"

"Heebie jeebies, jim-jams, willies."

Well maybe his voice didn't agitate her. Not yet, anyway.

"Hang a left here," he said before he turned his attention to the sack in his hand. "Wonder what's in a Helen goody bag." He pulled out an apple, rubbed it across his shirt, took a bite. After a few chomps, it was gone, and he found something else, popped it in his mouth, fought the reflex to spit it out, but choked it down. "That's the nastiest cheese I ever had."

"That's because it's tofu."

Dylan stuffed the rest into the brown sack and crumpled it into a ball. He motioned to the Riley's Burger ahead. "Whip in there. Food's all I can think about." Not exactly the truth. He'd been considering sweeping her hair out of the way for a better look at those eyes. He'd been thinking about how those skinny jeans must have been a bear to squeeze into and the way she curved in all the right places.

Tish fell in line behind an SUV with a "My Kid Beat Up Your Honor Roll Student" bumper sticker.

When they reached the intercom, a pep squad voice sprang

from the blue box. "Would you like to try a Riley's Burger Supreme Combo today?"

Dylan leaned toward the open window, stalled. He hesitated a minute or an hour, he couldn't be sure, while a hint of Tish's perfume anchored him in place. "Double Riley Delight Combo . . . no onions. Coke to drink."

"Oh, hi Dylan!" A girl hung out of the drive-through window ahead and waved frantically.

"Hi, Shelby." Now he remembered why he'd been avoiding this place. This girl didn't let up. Didn't seem to notice he was twice her age. Or maybe that was the point.

Tish glanced briefly in his direction before she ordered. "I'll have the same, but with extra onions and a triple chocolate shake instead of a Coke. And onion rings instead of fries."

"Lots of onions," Dylan said.

"They keep the bugs away." Tish unfurled a twenty from her pocket.

"Bugs?" Dylan handed her a twenty.

"In Iraq. Don't you have anything smaller?"

"Just pay for all of it with that."

"I'd rather pay my own way."

Dylan rooted through his wallet and produced a five and five singles. "Does this make you happy?"

"Ecstatic."

She paid for the food, pressed some change into his hand, and turned onto Lexington, finding a gap between a pair of motorcycles and a minivan. Balancing her food in her lap, she switched lanes again and tailgated a bread truck while she ate.

"Guess I shouldn't have let my life insurance lapse."

Before she could respond, his phone made a mini jackpot sound announcing a text. Two seconds later, a different tone came from Tish's cell: Chimes.

"Helen." Dylan read the text. "She wants to know if we have any news."

"It hasn't even been twenty minutes."

A smile passed between them that seemed to ease the tension. Maybe it would be a good time for a little conversation. It was hard, though, to think of things to say, apart from the crisis at hand. He measured a mile of silence from mile marker forty-two to forty-three before he finally said, "So, you're from Savannah?" He let out a slow whistle in his head for coming up with such a brilliant question.

"Yup."

"Peanuts, peaches, and well, I can't think of anything else Georgia's known for."

Tish stopped mid-chew. "A killer St. Paddy's Day bash, pirate ghosts, and kudzu."

And apparently beautiful women. Maybe he'd head south one of these days. But weren't Southern belles supposed to be just as sweet as the tea they peddled?

"Savannah's a long way from the 'Burgh," he said around a mouthful of burger.

"Are you investigating me too?"

He pressed on, past her snark. "What does your mom do at Saycor?"

Tish closed her eyes, took a long, savoring draw from her shake, and Dylan had a brief "I'll have what she's having" moment.

"Chief Medical Officer. Oversees drug trials and that sort of thing."

"Like those experiments where one group gets a placebo and the other gets the real deal?"

"Basically."

"Or they all get a sugar pill and the consumer gets duped."

"Cynic much?"

"Let's just say I'm not a big fan of the pharma industry."

Tish didn't respond.

"Anyway, sorry you made the trip all the way here and ended up dealing with this."

A nod. That was something, he guessed. And in a way he felt for her. She would probably prefer to be soaking up the Georgia sun instead of coming to Riley's Peak to "scrub her soul."

The Peak wasn't such a bad place though. Of course, the union soldier outside the bank had a mustache that was more purple than bronze thanks to kids with nothing better to do on a Friday night.

And the décor in the only Chinese restaurant in town did have kind of a Mexican flair. Food did too. What would you expect with an owner whose name is Santiago Juarez? But the brick buildings dated back to the early 1900s and benches out front invited passersby to take a load off. Overflowing flowerpots every few feet spruced up the view. And there were flags. Lots of flags. Old fashioned street lamps. Parking meters.

Dylan ground through the rest of his burger and started on his fries. "Sure beats tofu."

Tish made a slow transformation from at attention to at ease. "Helen means well."

"I noticed you called her aunt, but Helen called your mom a friend."

"Is everything about what you noticed, Sherlock?"

So much for at ease. "Look, I don't know who pissed in your OJ, but if I find out I'll send him your way."

A few long, painful seconds dragged by before she said, "Sorry. This whole situation has got me . . . Helen's one of those family friends that's as close as a relative."

"How do you know her?"

"She and my grandmother were neighbors. Friends."

"Anne."

Her thoughts seemed to veer to a past that she clearly wanted to keep there. "Helen was a Rockette. Grandma needed work, and she happened to be a fabulous dancer. Helen tried to get her in . . ." She paused, flicked at the straw in her milkshake. "But they turned her down. Helen quit. After sharing her quiet opinion on diversity of course."

"I can only imagine Helen's *subtle*, respectful resignation." Dylan balled up his burger wrapper. "A Rockette. Somehow, that makes sense. And doing what she did, quitting and all to make a point, that sounds like her."

Tish slurped an onion from the last onion ring like a wet noodle and popped the breading into her mouth. She wiped her hands on a napkin.

"Here's the highway," Dylan said. She veered right. "And this boyfriend, RJ?"

"He's Saycor's Chief Commercial Officer."

"What's he like?"

"He's a good guy." Tish clenched her hands tighter on the steering wheel. "My mother wouldn't be with him otherwise."

A muscle in her jaw began to twitch and she slammed the accelerator, zipping around a slow-moving Prius. She threw him a sideways glance, telegraphing a message he read loud and clear, "Enough grilling."

Thirty minutes later, they cruised onto the Crestwood exit; a forty-five minute investment on a good day.

Downtown Crestwood came into view: a string of boutiques, a bank on every corner, and a public square with a gazebo. Two bars and a church. Bars always outnumbered churches. There must be a rule somewhere. His life would have probably been a helluva lot easier if the reverse were true.

Dylan shook his head as they turned down a side street. "When I look at these houses, all I see is a whopping utility bill."

They came to a stop in front of the most impressive one. A skyline of evergreens stood guard over a massive brick house with a high-pitched roof, the kind he hated to shingle after he'd turned in his police badge for a carpenter's hammer. A four-car garage, the adult equivalent of a toy box, made him wonder what was inside.

Walking up the driveway, Dylan ran his fingers across the hood of a black Mercedes Roadster. "Sweet ride."

"It's RJ's."

"He doesn't keep it in the garage?"

Tish climbed the porch steps, rang the doorbell, and heaved a sigh at the massive inconvenience of answering him. "Their dog has issues. She won't get out of the car if it's in the garage, and RJ takes her everywhere. He moves it into the garage at the end of the day."

Dylan joined Tish on the porch, and she rang the bell again.

A series of sharp barks came from the other side of the door.

"Nutmeg," Tish said by way of explanation.

She grabbed the brass doorknocker and gave it three loud taps, which made Nutmeg's yelps go from nuisance to ballistic.

"Maybe nobody's here," Dylan said.

Tish glanced at the Mercedes. "RJ is."

A large van pulled into the driveway, the image of a soaped-up dog and the words K9 COUTURE painted on the side. A man got out, wearing a jacket with the K9 COUTURE logo on the back. A shock of wavy hair rising above his receding hairline flopped in the breeze as he made his way to the porch.

"Take a number, huh?" The guy checked his watch.

The barking on the other side of the door, now punctuated by a few high-pitched whines, continued.

Color drained from Tish's face as she pressed her fingertips to her forehead.

The K9 COUTURE man spoke first. "Are you all right?"

"Something's wrong." Now she slapped wildly at the door, twisted the knob. "Nutmeg doesn't bark like this. She's afraid of everything. She hides under the bed when the doorbell rings."

"You know, I think I'll come back later." The groomer scurried from the porch, tripped over a dimple in the sidewalk, and mumbled, "Shoulda stayed in vet school."

Seared by the panic on Tish's face, a sick feeling claimed Dylan, and he briefly thought about the Glock in his boot. "Let's check 'round back."

They circled the house to a privacy fence. Music vibrated through a thudding backbeat.

"Elyse? RJ?" When no one answered, Dylan took out his ValueMart card and slid it into the gate latch until it clicked open.

A medium-sized, rust-colored mutt, smaller than the big fuss it was making, was inside, jumping against the sliding glass door. The words of the song throbbing distinctly now, Adele's throaty ballad: "Set fire to the rain." Not exactly at odds with the gruesome display before them.

A man floating face down in the hot tub.

Tish stood rooted to the patio, a horrified look darkening her face before she visibly crumbled. Her knees buckled, and Dylan rushed to catch her. Pushing him away, she raced for the hot tub and frantically felt for a pulse.

A fruitless effort—this guy was long past dead.

Dylan didn't need to ask. Tish's reaction made it clear this was RJ. To keep his insides from lurching, Dylan always tried to imagine the vics alive, doing what they might have been doing before the life was sucked out of them. RJ would have been relaxing against the brick ledge, hair perfectly spiked, fingers around a glass of scotch. At some point, he'd placed the half-empty tumbler on the pool deck and something had gone terribly wrong.

"He's dead." Her tone clinical.

Tish rounded the hot tub and shot through the sliding glass door, shrieking her mom's name. They raced through the house, dog at their heels, combing the main floor, up the winding staircase. At the top of the stairs, Tish flung open the French doors, scanned the space, then searched the walk-in closet, pushing back neatly hung clothes and shoving a small ottoman aside.

For a moment she froze, locked in a trance. Her breath quickened, eyes shot wide. He reached for her, but she jerked away. Backing against the bedroom wall, she slid down, pinched her eyes shut, and crossed her arms as if suddenly cold. As she shivered uncontrollably, the dog nuzzled into her lap. Dylan grabbed a blanket from the end of the bed and wrapped it around her shoulders. Where had the fierce woman in head to toe battle gear gone? She seemed so helpless and small, and protecting her instantly became his main priority.

A strange new thought forced an involuntary chill across his shoulder blades. Elyse could have had something to do with this. It certainly wasn't out of the realm of possibility. He'd watched enough episodes of Snapped to know that wives, even mothers, lost it from time to time. Hell, he had firsthand experience with mothers taking off, leaving people to wonder, to suffer.

Hyperaware of time passing, Dylan shifted into overdrive. The last thing they needed was to be dragged in as witnesses or worse yet, suspects. *Let the cops deal with this, I've got a live one to locate.* Tick tock. His asset's dead boyfriend upped the ante. And to think he'd doubted this case would measure up to a Saturday morning devoted to Cartoon Network. He grabbed a cordless phone off the nightstand.

Tish's eyes snapped open. "What're you doing?"

"Calling 911. Then we're outta here."

✺ FIVE ✺

TISH forced herself to her feet. *Acknowledge. Wait. Action. Repeat. End.* She rattled through the steps in her head, singling out *Action*. The rest would have to wait. She dashed for the stairs, Dylan and Nutmeg close behind. She tried desperately to remember where they kept the dog's leash. Forget it. She scooped her up, burst out the front door, the quivering animal clamped under one arm.

When she reached for the Sebring's door handle, Dylan stopped her with a hand on her shoulder. "Listen, we called 911, that's all we're obligated to do. If we open ourselves up for inquiry, it will do nothing but slow us down. I don't know the cops around here. We might get stuck with some guy who doesn't know Jack Shit, but he'll shoot his mouth off like he knows Jack Shit intimately and his estranged cousins, Joe Shit and Bob Shit, too. So let's find out what we can about the dead guy on the patio first."

Tish jerked from his grasp and jumped into the car. Nutmeg squirmed in her lap, unsure of her footing. Dylan vaulted over the hood and into the passenger door like a Hollywood stunt double. Not exactly what she had in mind, but the whir of sirens closing in made it clear she had no choice. She shot from the driveway and rounded a corner. After two quick turns, she veered south and headed for the highway.

Caught in the chaos and intensity of the moment, she heard Dylan's cacophonous objections roar, an angry tirade that broke through her concentration. "Wanna tell me why you're bolting like you're trying to outrun a suicide bomber?"

"Feel free to get out or shut the hell up. Take your pick." Her words were met with a high-octane anger, it radiated from him, unrestrained, and she pushed back with a flammable rage of her own. "And by the way. That 'dead guy' has a name: RJ." She was desperately trying to beat down the panic that had been bubbling up inside her all morning.

"Pull over." Dylan pointed to a Shell station. "There's not enough room in this car for me and the monster-sized chip on your ego."

The Sebring screeched to the curb. "You can't handle a woman in the driver's seat."

"I'm all for women running the show. I voted for our governor . . . a woman. It's just that going off half-cocked with your my-way-or-the-highway-frying-pan-into-the-fire tactic that pisses me off."

"Think you could have worked maybe one more idiom into that sentence?" Frustration boiled through her, but his little speech was intense and committed, and though she hated to admit it, slightly charming. And this was no time for a debate. Her mom was missing. *Possibly dead.* And she didn't want to face any of this alone. "I'll play nice if you stop second-guessing me."

Silence stretched. "Fine. Where to?"

"Philip Kelrich's. Saycor's CEO. Elyse is a workaholic and nobody knows a workaholic better than her boss."

Dylan's phone buzzed in his pocket. "What's up?" Then after an extended pause, "Thanks bro, call me the second you get anything else."

Whatever it was, it was bad. Dylan didn't have much of a poker face.

"They found your mom's vehicle."

"And?"

"It was on the side of the road off Route 51. Flat tire. The trunk was open with the jack next to the car. Looks like she tried to fix it and—"

"Tried to? My mom never met a challenge she couldn't handle."

"There's more."

The urge to throw up pricked at the back of Tish's throat. "Tell me."

"There was blood on the steering wheel and on the driver's seat. What looked like the contents of her purse scattered around. Chapstick, a tin of Altoids, a pair of chopsticks still in the wrapper. Nothing to go on. Finn and one of his guys canvassed Helen's neighborhood, but no one saw a thing."

If anything happened to her mom . . . she'd . . . And her brother, Luke, well she couldn't be sure how he'd react. For that matter, no one could ever be sure how he'd react about anything.

She needed to be proactive. No benefit ever came from sitting and thinking and analyzing.

When they pulled into Philip's driveway, Tish did a double-take. Elyse had told her he'd gone all out on his new house, but she hadn't envisioned this. His damn entryway had more square footage than the space she shared with eight soldiers in Baghdad. The house was all iron and glass and cold-looking. Contemporary? Modern? Space age? She approached the expansive door that made her feel like she might need security clearance.

Tish hadn't seen Philip in over a year. His intense eyes and flat-line smile never seemed to change, but he'd lost the beard and his hair was now sun-bleached. He angled his head and openly admired her, directing his pleasure at her chest. He bludgeoned Dylan with a glance then settled back on Tish. "What a surprise. A nice surprise. I'd hug you, but as you can see, I've been working out." He puffed out his chest encased in a damp Under Armor compression shirt.

Dylan offered his hand. "Dylan Tierny, I'm—"

"Elyse is missing . . ." Tish interrupted. But then she pictured RJ's bloated face, and her mouth went numb.

"And I'm afraid we have more bad news," Dylan continued.

Butter pecan. Mocha nut fudge. Pistachio. Another stress relieving technique. When her heart rate slowed to a trot she whispered, "RJ is dead."

Philip took a step back, stumbled, and placed a steadying hand on the wall. He cranked his head in a circle, like he had a sudden kink, let it drop, bowed, chin to chest. Then, as if realizing he wasn't the only person affected, he moved to Tish, cupped her shoulder. "I'm sorry." A thick pause. "And Elyse? What do you mean missing?" In some strange way, he seemed to take this the hardest, like it was the worst of the two bombshells just dropped.

"We'd planned to meet in Riley's Peak this morning, but she's not answering her phones." She cleared her throat. "The local police found her car . . . and there was blood."

"Wow, I'm having a hard time wrapping my mind around this . . . um . . . let me think." He eased onto a chair in the over-sized foyer and ran his fingers over the white leather as if reading something there in Braille. "She left the office early yesterday, and I haven't heard from her since." Bringing a fist to his mouth, he pressed his eyes shut against tears. "And RJ? When did this happen? How?"

"We found him in the hot tub." Tish tried not to envision the man she'd only recently warmed to. RJ never gave up trying to get close to her, but she'd always held him at arm's length. A decision she now regretted. Another to add to the list.

"When did you see him last?" Dylan asked Philip.

Philip's eyes stalled on him for a long moment before he turned to Tish. "I saw RJ last night."

"What time? Where?" Dylan asked.

Philip massaged his forehead, ran his hands down his face and throat. "Your . . . friend has a lot of questions."

"I'm not a cop if that's what you think."

"I didn't think you were." His lip twitched in protest as if the idea was the craziest thing he'd ever heard. "We had a drink at his place."

"Did he have a habit of drinking in the hot tub?" Dylan pressed on.

"RJ doesn't hot tub without a beverage in hand." He shook his head in disbelief. "Didn't."

"Can you think of anything he might have been upset about?" Tish asked. She couldn't swing her mind away from the fresh imagery, and the thought that RJ might have self-destructed gave her equilibrium a shove. She didn't think she could survive that again.

"He had a great life. Career, money, a beautiful woman. If there's more to life than that, clue me in."

"What condition was he in when you left?" Dylan asked.

"Condition?"

"How was he acting, was he—"

"Drunk? Do you think I would have left if he was so drunk he might drown?"

Philip's phone buzzed. He pulled it from his pocket, glanced at the screen, shoved it back.

"What time did you leave?" Tish asked.

"Around 8:30. I had a meeting."

"On a Friday night?"

Philip's smile was slow to make an appearance, spreading like a lazy fog. "No rest for the wicked."

"Work related?" Dylan asked.

"And you're asking because . . ."

"It would help to know where you were at the time of death and who you were with."

"Interesting question for someone who's not a cop." Philip's eyes locked on Dylan's.

"Can you think of anyone who might have had a grudge against either one of them?" Tish redirected.

"This is a competitive business."

Dylan forged ahead. "Were RJ and Elyse having problems?"

Philip raised a shoulder. "Show me a couple who doesn't have the occasional problem."

"I don't think this has anything to do with their relationship," Tish said. "But it would help to know if you noticed anything out of the ordinary."

"Nothing off the top of my head." Philip granted them a sad, mysterious nod. "But if anything comes to me, I'll be sure to call."

Tish recited her phone number, and Philip nodded as if he'd stored it away. Doubtful, she thought. The first time she met him, she knew this guy was about as trustworthy as a rabid raccoon in a petting zoo. But Elyse seemed to trust him, respect him too, so she'd try to give him the benefit of the doubt. "That'd be great, Philip."

He swung the door wide, waved them toward it. "I hope Elyse turns up soon." He looked beyond them, out into the circular driveway as if expecting someone. "Especially because of RJ." Once they stepped outside, the door snapped shut with a note of finality.

Nutmeg's nose was pushed through the half-open car window, sniffing the cool air, tail tucked between her legs. Tish stopped on the lawn and eyed Dylan. "Take off your belt."

"But we just met." His dimple twitched, eyes danced.

Why did he have to be so appealing while he was being so aggravating? "I need it."

"Since you asked so nicely." He undid his belt, pulled it through the loops, and handed it to her.

She opened the car door and wound it through Nutmeg's collar. The dog leaped out and sniffed around in the grass and along a hedge of forsythia.

"McMuscles is gonna turn us in for property damage." Something in Dylan's expression said he'd welcome any excuse to upset Philip's pristine world.

"Either that or the rental car company will."

Nutmeg finally squatted, looking relieved and embarrassed at the same time.

"Poor thing. Wish we had a Milk Bone or something," Dylan said.

"There's always the tofu."

"You don't like animals very much, do you?" He ran his hand over Nutmeg's head.

"It's not that I dislike them. But they're so needy. I just don't have room in my life for that."

They piled back into the car and Dylan said, "He's lying you know."

Tish exited the driveway. "How could you tell?"

"Didn't you see his flaming pants and growing nose? And judging by the way we were barely out the door before he slammed it, he's already busy working out an alibi."

"Lying about what though?" Even as she said it, she realized, people didn't need a reason to lie. They just did.

"Greed, lust, hate, love, revenge, obsession, sex . . . should I go on?"

She paused, cycled through the options. "But Philip and RJ

have been friends since high school. My mom has worked with them for over ten years now."

"Envy, psychosis, habit . . ."

"Point taken. Should we question Elyse and RJ's neighbors?" Tish asked. "Someone may have seen something."

"Doubt it would do any good. His nearest neighbor is probably a mile away. Our man Philip likely knows more than anyone." Accusation striated his words. "But let the local uniforms sort it out. We need to find your mother."

Dylan's phone sounded. He checked the display and thumbed the screen to accept the call. "Listen, I might not be able to make it on Monday, and I don't want to leave you hangin', so you'll have to get someone else." He disconnected, turned to Tish. "Side gig. House rehabs."

Construction. That accounted for his build. A blip of him working, firing a sledgehammer through a wall, momentarily blurred her thoughts.

"Don't cancel any jobs because of me."

"I made a commitment to Helen."

After winding through the neighborhood, Tish stopped near an empty lot. She got out and pulled a lighter from her pocket. The scritch of her Zippo a welcome sound, the plume of smoke a welcome sight.

Dylan exited the car with Nutmeg in tow and stood downwind. "Those things'll kill ya, you know."

Gee, she'd never heard that. As if Elyse wasn't all over her case every time she lit up. Last Christmas, she'd even grabbed one from her lips and stubbed it out like she'd caught her ten-year-old smoking.

Feeling a burst of defiance, Tish took an extra-long drag, exhaled through her nose. "Only one a day."

"I think that works best with vitamins."

Her phone buzzed. She checked the screen, pushed a button to accept the call. "Mom?"

∽ SIX ∾

Earlier That Day

ELYSE opened her eyes and struggled to a sitting position. Her temples were screaming and her throat felt like someone had scrubbed it with a bottlebrush.

She pulled herself up to the sink with a white-knuckled grip, washed her hands until they were raw. Black mold snaked its way through the chipped tiles. Bile rose at the scent of Clorox barely masking piss and other bodily fluids. Who had last used this nasty bathroom. And for what? She flipped the faucet to cold and cupped her hands under the flow. The water tasted like the rust stains on the cracked porcelain.

A glance in the mirror confirmed that she looked as crappy as she felt. Her hair was a tangled mess, and the split above her left eye throbbed an angry red. Though the room was chilly and damp, beads of sweat were now trickling a very personal path.

As she wiped the dried blood from her forehead with the dampened pads of her fingers, she unspooled to her last moments of consciousness. Last night at Helen's, she'd felt a chill and went to shut the window. Two men, a noir looking Laurel and Hardy, were exiting a black sedan, barreling toward the house. When she heard one announce, "A chick with a name like Leese is probably one a them fancy types," she knew she couldn't stick around. Grabbing her purse, she snuck out the back, worked her way around the property. As she reached for her car door, the fat one appeared out of nowhere, grabbed her wrist, and forced her behind the wheel.

"Drive." He wheezed, a wet gravely sound, as if he'd been smoking a pack a day since he could walk. Elyse trained her eyes on the rearview mirror and saw that the other man was following close behind in the sedan. It was too dark to make out the license plate. The Smoker reached up and twisted the rearview mirror, gave it a yank, and proceeded to throw it out the window. Satisfaction clouded his face. She shuddered to think what else might give him a sense of gratification. She drove and drove until he commanded her to pull off the road. Then came the questioning. And when she supplied no answers, her face got very intimate with the steering wheel.

Elyse was generally five steps ahead of everyone else. Leader of the pack through med school and she could talk her way through almost any sticky situation, yet at that moment, with those two cretins pumping her about the flash drive, her mind had gone blank. Why hadn't she made something clever up? Something that would make them think they'd get what they were after. But it wasn't about what they wanted. This was about whoever had hired them.

Now she touched her wrist. Her watch was gone. A Timex she'd had since her residency at Mercy Hospital. She rubbed her equally blank ring finger, and knife blades sliced through her. A sentimental stone that had been in RJ's family for years. He'd had it reset with a bezel of amber gems to match her eyes. Elyse's heart clutched at the thought of this man she didn't deserve. A man who celebrated her at every turn. A man she might never see again.

Outside the bathroom, she could hear the big one reciting a list. "Mandy's Nails. Dennis Thorpe, Attorney. K9 some-shit." He was going through her business cards.

"Put that away." A thick British accent, strangled with annoyance, pitch ratcheting. "We've been through the bloody lot."

"Well, Sir Scotlin' Yard, doesn't hurt to check again, does it? Besides, it's interestin'. Kinda like lookin' through a chick's panty drawer."

Ugh. She had no doubt Smoker had done that, maybe countless times, and now he was pawing through *her* things.

There was some scuffling, an audible grunt, the sound of something hitting the wall. Likely her purse. Then footsteps. She slammed to the floor, and tried to reclaim the position she'd been in when she came to. The lock clicked, and the door screeched open.

"Looks dead." She felt him draw closer, heard his breath huff in and out above her. Then two fingers, thick as sausages, were groping her neck. "That's right, bitch. Sleep it off."

"She shouldn't be knackered this long." Though obviously upset, the Brit spoke pianissimo, controlled, leaning toward civilized.

"It happens to my momma when she mixes her meds with hooch."

The Brit grumbled something under his breath, then, "She's no use to us like this. Let's see if we can find a decent dinner in this sorry excuse for a town and maybe she'll be awake when we come back."

"'Bout time you learnt American. Say squeet."

"Squeet?"

The big one horse-sputtered his exasperation. "Let's go eat." Said with surprising enunciation and precision. "And it's called lunch. Just lemme tie 'er up first."

"And what would be the point?" The Brit was clearly in charge. She could picture his close-set eyes flashing with authority, bug-eyes that made her think of a cross between a gecko and a baboon. Eyes she'd remember if she got a chance to pick him out of a line up.

"Maybe fer the helluvit."

The bickering continued, their dazzling personalities shining through.

The door closed, followed by the deafening sound of the lock. Elyse jumped up. She didn't want to spend another millisecond on the floor that hadn't seen the business end of a mop in a very long time, if ever. She slid the tiniest cell phone money could buy from her bra. RJ had given it to her so she could stay connected without carrying a purse. She supposed they thought the cell in her purse was all she had. Thankfully, Smoker's frisking was as sloppy as everything else about him.

She glanced at the screen. 1:30 p.m. She'd been passed out in this cave posing as a bathroom for more than fourteen hours. What the hell had they given her? Something that left her with a killer headache or was that courtesy of the big one smashing her head against the steering wheel? She needed to get in touch with someone. She didn't have texting on the phone and would have to wait until she was certain those thugs were gone to risk placing a call.

Because the last thing she remembered before everything went black was the Brit's bulging dark eyes that said he'd slash her throat in a second if the wind blew the wrong way.

Her kids. She had to keep Luke safe and Tish far away. Luke, though brighter than bioluminescence in Maltese waters, was so vulnerable. But he'd never go looking for trouble. Then there was Tish. That girl had always blazed her own trail, and she'd blaze it straight to Elyse if she found even a single bread crumb.

From the age of three, Tish had dressed herself, braided her own hair—okay she twisted it and called it a braid—and made her own lunch. A slice of pickle wedged into a peanut butter sandwich or row of grapes smothered in catsup, nesting alongside a hotdog. An indelible independent streak ran through the Duchene women as sure as their left-handedness and bad sense of direction.

Tish and Helen must be frantic by now. Had they contacted RJ? If only Elyse hadn't fought with him. If only she didn't always need the upper hand, if only she could let someone else call the shots once in a while. They'd argued about whether to give RJ's sister, Annabeth, another loan. As if she ever paid them back. But it wasn't even about the money. They had more than enough to share with his entitled sister. It was the principle. Annabeth was able-bodied. Why couldn't she earn her own money? Elyse had been so pissed at RJ about the way he continued to enable his sister, she didn't even bother to go home to pack her things. Not that she was in a big hurry to get the weekend started. She loved Helen like a mother, but sometimes . . . well, sometimes there was pepper coming out of that woman's saltshaker.

It all seemed so trivial now. Elyse needed to find a way to get back to RJ and apologize.

But as devastating as it was to think about the possibility of not seeing him again, the thought of not seeing Tish and Luke was pure torture. Since her husband died twenty-one years ago, it had been just the three of them. The three bears. The three musketeers. Harry, Ron and Hermione.

RJ knew that nothing would come between her and her kids, and she loved him all the more for understanding. Somehow, he also understood why she could never marry him. Losing her husband so young had nearly broken her. Frank had beaten cancer at twenty-two, slithered from its snare long enough to father two children, before his illness came slinking back like some absentminded grim reaper.

Elyse tiptoed to the bathroom door and pressed her ear to it. Those cretins were out to lunch all right. She almost chuckled at the double meaning. It was now or never. She punched in RJ's number and the call rolled straight to voice mail. RJ always took her calls, even after they fought, especially after they fought. A remnant of anger surfaced, and she considered leaving a message, "I've been kidnapped. But hey, I don't want to interrupt your quality time with your sister." The pendulum of her emotions swung back to remorse. The only message she had any business leaving was: "I screwed up. Royally."

She didn't want to call Tish, but she didn't have many options. And even though this was an emergency, did she really want to explain to the cops why she was in this predicament? Not yet, anyway. She dialed her daughter and Tish picked up on the first ring.

"Mom! Where—"

"Don't talk. Listen. I'm in trouble . . ." Elyse rattled as much information as she could, then ended the call, her insides wrenching as she cut off her daughter's pleading voice.

✥ SEVEN ✥

TISH clamped the phone to her ear. Her mom's words bumped and swerved in her head, not one answer among them. "What're you talking about? . . . Mom? Mom!"

The line went dead.

She punched in Elyse's number. Voice mail again. Folding forward, she grasped her knees with her hands as if Atlas himself had decided to take a break, dropping the earth on her shoulders.

"What did she say?" Dylan asked.

"She's on the run or something. Told me to sit tight and wait for her to call again." Tish hurried to the car.

"Then where're you going?"

"I don't know, but I'm not wired for wait and see." They were prepping for a disaster, and inactivity was the missing ingredient to complete the recipe.

"Give me the keys."

She shot him her best you've-got-to-be-kidding look.

Dylan stood stock-still, that one eyebrow inching up. "I gave you my belt; you give me your keys."

This man was as smooth as a riverboat gambler. A rebuttal that might have come easily on any other day eluded her. This wasn't any other day. She tossed the keys, and he reached long to snatch them before they hit the ground.

He opened the door for Nutmeg, and she hopped in the driver's seat and just stood there. Tish sighed and settled in the passenger seat.

When Dylan got behind the wheel, the dog rested her chin on his arm. "They say animals and kids are the best judge of character." A wink. Punctuated by his slanted smile.

"Whatever." Tish claimed the dog, buckled the seatbelt around them both. Closing her eyes, she dropped her head against the headrest. The next sound she heard was the convertible top unscrolling overhead, and she opened her eyes to an expanse of sky. The waxing gibbous moon in the late afternoon sky evoked a tranquil moment, or maybe that was the nicotine. Nutmeg overdosed on the fresh air, and Tish tried to muddle through the recent exchange with her mother.

Elyse had rattled off directions as if ordering a lab test, her logical mind refusing to succumb to crisis-mode. But what crisis? She was the chief medical officer for a pharmaceutical company not a secret agent. An image hijacked Tish's thoughts: RJ face down in the hot tub. Elyse already lost one man she loved, how would she survive losing another? And Luke, in his own strange way, had formed a special attachment to RJ.

She needed to check on her brother. But going to Turtle House wasn't an option. Her mom specifically told her to stay away in case she was being followed. And besides, she couldn't face Luke until she knew more. Grabbing her phone, she dialed Robert. Damn. He was probably 30,000 feet over an ocean somewhere. She left a message and hoped he'd get back to her soon.

Robert Chase was the only person, outside of family, who understood Luke, who was allowed to call Luke any time. Maybe Robert had more clout because he could describe what it was like to pilot a 747 through the Aurora Borealis. She, on the other hand, was only permitted to call after Luke's nightly shows. Even Skype sessions from Iraq had to be scheduled in advance. Calling him now would only raise suspicion in her slave-to-routine brother.

Feeling like she had been flung off a ship with an anchor around her waist, she crammed the phone back in her pocket.

As they pulled onto the highway, adrenaline continued to surge. She'd seen enough police dramas to envision a gun to her mom's head while she was forced to read scripted lines.

"She said no cops, but I'm not sure that's the right thing."

"What would we tell them? That she's AWOL on the heels of her boyfriend's suspicious death? Do you really want to draw attention to that little tidbit?"

Tish's hands fisted, nails slicing into her palms, until it felt like she might draw blood. "My mom had nothing to do with RJ's death," she ground out, "and if you ever so much as imply anything like that again, you'll be sucking your meals through a straw."

Dylan drummed his fingers on the steering wheel. "Okay, that came out wrong, but I know how cops think. All they need is a whisper of a maybe and they're off and running. And even though they look like they're running, they only slow things down. Let's give it another few hours, see if we find anything out."

This wasn't pure observation. The bitterness in Dylan's voice underscored his experience as an insider.

"You were a cop, weren't you?"

"And I'm not even wearing my 'Washed-up Cop' T-shirt today." He snorted a laugh, but his expression remained humorless.

"What happened?"

"A long story for another time." He massaged the back of his neck. "Give me the goods on Philip Kelrich."

"I don't know much. Mom seems to respect him, and he and RJ go way back. He's one of those guys who could talk his way out of a traffic violation even if he was clocked doing a hundred in a thirty. But then I've seen a decent side of him too. Once when Luke was sick and Elyse didn't want him staying alone at the lake, Philip set her up with everything she'd need so she could work from Turtle House."

"Sounds controlling to me."

"He's every bit of that, but I'm just not sure I have a clear read on the guy."

"Any chance he and Elyse are, you know, taking advantage of RJ's travel schedule?"

Tish gritted her teeth. "Seriously?"

Dylan took a sharp breath and pulled back onto the road. "Okay, okay. I'm just trying to look at every angle, not trying to turn this into a trending hash tag. Can we regroup?" His tone was surprisingly tender, and she was grateful, if not melting. A part of her wanted to fall into his arms, arms that looked like they could hurl a semi across the highway, but instead she leaned her head against the window and stared at the mesmerizing strips of yellow dividing the road. Twenty minutes passed before she realized she didn't know where they were.

"You have a destination in mind?" she asked.

"Back to the Peak."

Riley's Peak meant Helen, and she didn't think she could handle her eccentricities right now.

"It's been a long, weird day," Dylan continued. "I'd like to go home and recharge. It's your car, so you can certainly go ghost after we get to my place, but you'll get closer to finding out what's going on with me than without me."

He was right. In this case, two heads were better than one. He knew the area, had a brother on the force, and for what it was worth, he'd been a cop.

They drove past a shopping center with a Dunkin Donuts, an H&R Block, a Taco Pronto and a La Quinta. She could always stay in a hotel. But she hadn't budgeted for that. She was down to her last dime. Leaving the army without another job hadn't exactly padded her bank account.

"Relax," Dylan said, as if stalking her thoughts. "No ulterior motive here, besides . . . you're not even my type." The last part spoken with flirtatious ribbing.

She was trying to imagine his "type" when she noticed his eyes fixed on the rearview mirror.

"What's wrong?"

"These guys have been riding my ass for miles."

She turned and saw two men in dark glasses in a black sedan. The car zipped along the passenger side and veered toward them.

Dylan swerved, gunned the engine. The other vehicle did the same.

"What the—"

"Watch out," Tish screamed and grabbed Nutmeg. The sedan closed in again, scraping the side of the Sebring. Metal sparked against metal. The landscape outside her window spun into a blur, as her body went completely rigid. Images of the convertible rolling flashed. Fear pounded in her chest.

"Hold on!" Dylan whipped a U-turn. He blazed along a ditch before soaring over the embankment and rocketing in the opposite direction. "Remember this, New York TBR 4392."

She committed the plate to memory as her pulse shimmied out of the danger zone.

They continued west, Dylan's hand gripping the gearshift. "Either that was a serious case of road rage or—"

"This wasn't random."

"Could be one of my collars out on parole. But then again, it could be anyone. There are plenty of nutjobs out there, Tish. I'm going to have my brother run the plate. Then I'm going to stop and get dog food and toothpaste. At my place you can tell me everything you can about Elyse and RJ, from where they vacation to what they eat for breakfast. And speaking of food, I'm going to need something to eat while you give me the four-one-one. My brain is crap on an empty stomach."

By the time they pulled into Dylan's driveway it was seven o'clock, and Tish's stomach was eating itself. It seemed like days since that burger. She grabbed her purse and followed him up the sidewalk, second in line after Nutmeg, who seemed to be pledging an undying devotion.

The dog may be falling for his undeniable charm, but she wasn't. This togetherness was nothing but a necessary evil.

The house was a modest brick ranch with a freshly-painted white rocker on the porch. Minimal landscaping, neat. Dylan opened the door and waved her in, and a faint scent of lemon wafted around her. He cared about this place.

She imagined what it would be like to truly have a home of her own. Not her mom's or Turtle House on Lake Anaba. Not an efficiency in Savannah filled with someone else's furniture. Certainly not military housing. She wanted a place where she could kick off her shoes, plant a few flowers in the yard, paint the walls lime green on a whim. But then, there were the headaches of home ownership: replacing appliances and furnace filters, buying flood insurance, a mortgage, taxes.

She dropped her purse on the coffee table next to a large book,

The Origin of Cinematography. "You're into the old stuff, huh?"

"What?"

"The book, on your table."

Dylan lifted a shoulder, let it ease down. "It's interesting to me." He toed off his boots, put them in a hall closet. "Probably nothing you've seen. Obscure stuff and before your time."

"Right. Because you're so much older than me. What are you, thirty-five?"

"Did Helen's psychic powers rub off on you, or are you undercover OPS?"

"Just a good guesser."

"I know better than to try to guess a woman's age."

"It's only a number. Thirty-two." Tish opened the book to a diagram of the inner workings of an early movie projector next to a picture of a clock. "What got you interested in old movies?"

"Just a hobby I shared with my mom."

Tish noticed how the mention of his mother and "shared," past tense, was weighed down by regret.

"Make yourself at home," he said. "Nickel tour. Bathroom, T.V., remote." He pointed to each in turn.

"Thanks."

"I'm hitting the shower, and then I'll make us something to eat." Dylan started down the hallway, stopped, and pivoted back to her. "Do you want to . . . ?"

Something about his expression looked hopeful, and the innuendo registered.

He threw his head back as he noted the look in her eyes. "I meant before me."

Tish laughed in turn. "It's all yours. I really just want to decompress."

But a hot and steamy shower with this guy who looked disarmingly like Colin Farrell would definitely be more effective stress relief than the single Marlboro she allowed herself each day.

Before heading to the bathroom, Dylan detoured to the kitchen. He returned with a bottle of water, a granola bar and a box of Cheez-Its and dropped them onto the coffee table. "Appetizers." She thought about the way he'd put the top down on the convertible earlier. As if he knew what she needed at that very moment.

Maybe he wasn't a Neanderthal after all.

Tish fell onto the couch and dug into the crackers, surveying the room as she shoved a handful into her mouth. The furnishings were an eclectic mélange of old and new, one foot in the present, one in the past. Two chairs flanked a side table. A newer looking suede one and a time-worn leather recliner. A photo on the wall captured Dylan, his brother, and decidedly their father in front of a small cabin. All handsome, rugged mischief in their eyes. Dylan's young face indicated he'd already trudged through some serious trenches, stomping his own feelings underfoot, strapping on a hardcore demeanor along the way.

As she looked through several other framed photos, she wondered about the absence of Dylan's mother. But then, hadn't her own mother become a figment as work absorbed her life? A family without secrets, without some element of dysfunction, was a myth.

Another photo, Dylan and his brother, side by side in soccer uniforms. Dylan maybe ten and his brother . . . She needed to check on Luke. She couldn't put if off any longer. She dialed, got his voice mail, and left a message, "Hey guy, call me back."

Had her mom already called him? Tish could almost hear the cacophony of the radios he kept in his room broadcasting their different stations at the same time. He rarely listened to more than two at a time, but this situation might call for three, maybe four. No, Elyse would never give him a reason to go off the deep end.

Worry about her mother had stolen her entire day, and now concern for her brother would steal her night. She dropped her head onto a throw pillow and screwed her eyes shut, pretending none of it was happening. Her mom wasn't missing. Or spouting orders shrouded in mystery. RJ wasn't dead. But while deep in the throes of denial, she refused to let her mind drag her back to Iraq. Not even to try to erase what had happened there.

She wasn't sure how long she lay on Dylan's couch that way, drifting, but soon she was aware of a clattering in the kitchen. Propping herself up on one elbow, she saw Nutmeg sitting patiently, her tail swishing across the floor while Dylan poured dog food into one bowl and water into another.

No, not a Neanderthal at all.

⋄ EIGHT ⋄

DYLAN wiped his hands on a dishtowel, noticed a stain from yesterday's pizza. He hadn't expected company. At least he hadn't left a path of dirty socks or boxer briefs strung through the house. "Hope grilled cheese is okay." He flipped one sandwich in a frying pan and then another. "Sorry, I'm fresh out of onions."

Tish made her way to the kitchen, sat at the table like she'd been doing it all her life. "I'll forgive you this once. And anything with cheese is okay by me."

A light tapping started on the kitchen windowpane as rain spilled in rivulets down the glass and beat a steady rhythm on the roof. For a moment, it took him back, cooking for a woman to the music of rainwater.

But this was business, nothing more.

He brought two plates to the table, claimed the seat across from Tish. Nutmeg, who'd been sitting near the stove, moved to the rug by the backdoor, circled three times and dropped with a huff, thumping her tail solidly on the floor.

"Want a soda or milk?"

A note of surprise registered on her face. "Water is fine."

"I don't keep much here. I should have asked you what you wanted when we were at the Stop 'N Rob."

"The what?"

"Stop 'N Rob. The convenience store."

Tish brought the sandwich to her mouth and took a generous

bite. No girly bird bites with this one. He liked that.

"This might be the best grilled cheese I've ever had." She opened the sandwich like the pages of a book. "Sliced tomato."

"Yeah, but that's not my secret."

"Do tell."

"Butter all four sides of the bread then season with Old Bay. Grill lightly before adding plenty of cheese. Cook it low and slow for gooey perfection."

Low, slow and gooey. Did the words affect her the way they did him?

Tish examined her half-eaten sandwich, swallowed hard. "Is butter good or bad for you this month?"

"Let's say good. You must have eaten tubs of it in the army. All those fancy meals slathered in rich sauces."

"Oh yeah, nothing but lobster and coq au vin," she said through a silly grin.

Was this the same person from this morning? Busting out jokes when earlier she'd only wanted to bust his balls?

"What made you decide to join the army?"

"Dad was in the military. Briefly. I guess it's in my blood, and I wanted to make a difference too. I thought about teaching, but kids en mass scare the hell out of me."

He laughed. "So you're on leave?"

"You could say that." She seemed to stumble through her answer. "Your turn. What made you want to be a cop, and what made you not want to be a cop?"

"Guess I wanted to make a difference too. But I doubt I made a dent—"

Lightning flashed followed by a deafening crack of thunder. Tish startled and tucked her feet up under her, nearly curling herself into a ball.

Roused from sleep, Nutmeg rose from her place on the rug and slunk over, nuzzled under Tish's arm, wedging it away from her knees. Reaching for the dog at the same time, their hands grazed and stopped mid-pet. She pulled away but not before sparks shuttled through him. Dylan groped for something to say. Came up short. He went to the fridge, took out the milk, then rummaged through the cupboard. He poured two glasses. Popping an Oreo into his mouth, he washed it down with a gulp, and aimed the package her way.

"There's not enough double stuff in the world for a day like today." Tish set three in front of her, keeping one in hand which she proceeded to unscrew and lick the frosting from the center.

"Oh, you're one of those." The gesture was so innocent it gave him pause. He watched her as she reached for the next and began to twist. She glanced up, caught him looking and blushed. "You're supposed to be telling me about your mom," he said. "About RJ."

Tish pressed her hand under her bangs, sending them into a little spray that reminded him of feathers. "I still can't believe he's gone." Tears welled in her eyes, spilled down her cheeks, and she swiped her arm across her face.

Dylan rounded the table and handed her a napkin. Damn. He didn't want to be that guy. The one who swoops in at the first sign of tears, but here he was reaching for her. He pulled her out of the chair and folded her into a hug. "It's going to be all right." He stroked her hair, trying not to inhale. Because if he caught another whiff of her perfume . . .

He led her to the living room, and she settled on the couch.

She unlaced her boots, drew her feet up under her again, and took some time to fiddle with a thread at the hem of her pants. "I'm drawing a blank here. Like Philip said, it wasn't out of character for RJ to drink in the hot tub."

"But what're the odds that he'd have an accident and Elyse would wind up missing the same night?"

"There has to be a connection."

Dylan grabbed his laptop from the end table and watched the screen chug through its startup routine, a glacially slow process. He needed to replace it. He also needed a new ride. And state-of-the-art lock picks and those camera glasses might be nice. Cha-ching. And if this P.I. thing didn't work out it was back to swinging a hammer full time.

"Any chance you know your mom's phone or credit card logins? We can try to see who she's called recently or trace her last steps by where she might have used her cards."

"Arrive Bank Visa. The only card she uses. *More miles with every swipe,*" she sing-songed as she reached for the laptop. "I can probably guess the login. Let me drive."

"Like I said, I have no problem with a woman taking the wheel."

"Smart ass." This time her tone was airy. Her fingers flew across the keyboard and she shook her head. "Of course. Carina."

"Carina?"

"Mom's password, my favorite constellation."

Favorite constellation? Who has a favorite constellation? This woman had more layers than those onions she was so addicted to, and she was slowly shedding them, revealing facets he found so odd and yet so appealing. He wanted to get to know her in a way he hadn't known someone in ages, but the timing was wrong, wrong, wrong. "Find anything worthwhile?"

Tish hovered over the laptop. "Nothing out of the ordinary. Starbucks on Friday morning at 06 . . . 6:30 and her last phone call was the one to me. The calls before that were to Philip, RJ, and Helen."

"Philip."

"Well, he is her boss."

"I still say something is off about that guy."

"I'm not a huge fan, but he's very protective of RJ and Elyse. They're part of the reason he has all those numbers in his portfolio. Let's keep monitoring this activity. She's bound to burn some plastic sooner or later."

Dylan's "Bad to the Bone" ring tone sounded, and he glanced at the display. "Completely forgot about her." He answered with, "I'm sorry." Scratching a finger at his knee, he filled Helen in about the latest development, the phone call from Elyse; listened for a moment, then, "Let me put you on speaker."

"You must double your efforts to find her." Helen's voice brimmed with authority. "I consulted a spiritualist today, and she confirmed everything I told you: someone wants Elyse dead!"

Dylan leaned forward, rested his arms on his thighs, and laced his hands together. "Oh?"

"Mother Paloma advised that she *is* in insurmountable danger."

"Mom said she'd call back as soon as she could." Tish vaulted from the couch and paced.

"Well we can't wait," Helen insisted.

"It's a good sign that she's made contact," Dylan said. "And as soon as we make progress, we'll let you know."

"We never discussed your fee. If you'll stop by the house, I'll give you an advance."

"That won't be necessary."

"Well, I do intend to pay you."

Tish and Dylan exchanged a glance before Tish said, "There's something else."

"I'm listening."

"We discovered RJ at the Crestwood house . . . " He'd never get used to this part. "He's dead."

A labored silence ensued. "Helen?" Tish said.

"He left this world before his time then." In the background, a teakettle screamed. "I'm making tea," she added matter-of-factly.

"Okay, well, we'll be in touch," Dylan said.

Helen hung up without saying goodbye, and Dylan mulled their exchange. "How did Helen feel about RJ? She seemed . . . unaffected."

"Helen loves anyone my mom loves." Tish snatched her purse, rifled through it, and extracted a charger. "Where can I plug this in?"

The question about RJ must have needled a nerve. "Let me show you the spare bedroom."

At the open door, she stopped. "Do you have a son?"

It would be natural for her to think that. The room screamed boy, from the baseball wedged between two books on the bookshelf to the NASCAR wastebasket. Airplane wallpaper soared around them.

He laughed. "No, I just haven't gotten around to updating."

"Maybe you should keep it this way, then you won't have to redecorate when the time comes." She blushed and turned away. "My bag's still in the trunk."

"I'll get it," he said, catching her arm as she headed for the door.

She surveyed him obliquely, and he let his hand drift away. He'd give her some leeway, but he'd be damned if he was going to let her screw up this already screwed up investigation by running off. Then Helen would have him looking for two Duchenes instead of one.

He pulled on his boots, followed her outside. The rain had stopped, and the air smelled of dampness and worms.

Tish's phone buzzed. She glanced at the screen before answering. "Hey."

In the dark, Dylan thought he saw a smile, elusive, fleeting. Like Sasquatch. Or a big tax refund.

"Oh, good. Thanks for checking ... yeah, me too," Tish continued with no attempt to bottle her southern lilt. "It'll be nice to see you too."

She ended the call, rolled the phone in her hand, and stared past Dylan. And just like that, she was back to being sealed tighter than security at a presidential fundraiser.

Curiosity stabbed. *Who had called?* A not-so-distant car engine back-fired, and Tish seized his arm, then straightened. Jittery. Of course. Tack the events of the day onto a stint in Iraq and it was the only possible sum.

Clicking the key fob to open the trunk, he looked around before pulling out her duffle bag. Light. She probably didn't mess with a bunch of make-up and wardrobe changes. She was no nonsense. In a dazzling sort of way.

He heard the car before it rolled into the driveway. His brother and Bianca. He felt a stirring of annoyance then immediately reprimanded himself. Was he seriously not wanting to share Tish? This attraction was taking on a life of its own.

"Helen gave us the update," Finn said. "And I ran the plate. Belongs to a stolen car."

"Somehow that doesn't surprise me," Dylan said. Finn's tie was askew, shirt half-tucked. "Long day?"

His brother's mouth twisted. "Nesbit's riding me like his new pet pony. Tucker's out with the flu so I caught three extra cases today, and I'm up to my eyebrows in writers. There are days I almost miss Carmichael."

"Bite your tongue."

Finn stuck out his tongue, clamped his teeth into it.

"Uncle Dill!" A high-pitched voice sprang from the backseat. His niece, Kate, was working at opening the door, but the child guard locks were on.

"Kate, honey, Uncle Dill's had a long day, and it's almost bedtime," Bianca said from the passenger seat.

Though it seemed cliché, motherhood had made his sister-in-law even more radiant, from her uncombed hair to the paint splatter across her shirt in the shape of Florida.

"You must be Tish. I'm Bianca."

Tish's gaze stalled on her paint splotched shoulder.

Bianca smiled. "Occupational hazard. I teach art at the college."

"Sorry, I didn't mean to—"

"It's okay. I once had a guy ask me where the 'weenie roast' was."

"Weenie roast?"

"His term, not mine. I had a particularly mustard looking drip down my shirt that day."

Dylan reached for the back-door handle. "Let the kid loose so I can get a closer look at that tooth. And who ever heard of a bedtime on a Saturday night for a sixteen-year-old?"

A riot of giggles as she held up seven fingers. "You know how old I am, silly Uncle Dilly."

Finn and Bianca exchanged a look and turned to Kate who had now clasped her hands together pleading, "Please, please, pul...eeze."

With a click, the door lock released, and Kate bounded from the car and into Dylan's arms. He scooped her up, swung her around, and perched her on his shoulders, bouncing up the sidewalk so she could get the full effect of the ride. "Duck," he said as they approached the doorway.

"Quack," she countered without missing a beat.

Once inside, she let out a sharp yelp of laughter as he emptied her onto the couch.

"Again, Uncle Dill." She fastened her arms around his neck.

He pulled down her bottom lip. "How's that snaggletooth coming along? I could yank it out and give the tooth fairy something to do tonight."

"Noooo." Kate squealed as he tickled her. "She's on vacation. In Bora Bora!"

Bianca held up a foil-covered plate. "Helen made three batches of these and what looked like a lifetime supply of turmeric tea."

Tish peeked under the foil, nibbled the tip off a diamond-shaped cookie, and made a face. "And just when I thought today couldn't get any worse."

"The birds like them," Kate offered.

Finn smiled. "Remember, that's our little secret."

"I know. We wouldn't want to hurt Aunt Helen's feelings," she replied before moving quickly to the next subject. "Uncle Dylan, when will you read the next chapter of *Charlotte's Web?*"

"Soon as I possibly can, Katie-did." He tapped a finger to her nose.

Nutmeg crept forward from the shadows, tail tucked, and gave this new bundle of energy a sniff. "A dog!" Kate scooted from the couch and started fawning over Nutmeg, who kept her eyes locked on Dylan.

"Nutmeg's just visiting," he said.

"That's a funny name," Kate said.

"Want to know how she got it?" Tish asked.

Kate's head bobbed, braids sweeping her shoulders. "Yes, please."

"The day she came home from the shelter, no one could agree on a name. After a while, my mom decided she looked like Aunt Meg—"

"An aunt that looks like a dog?" Kate's nose crinkled.

A dimple flashed in one of Tish's cheeks, and Dylan beat down a desire to skim his fingers down her face.

"Only a teensy bit," Tish said. "Anyway, I'm not sure I should tell you this next part."

Kate leaned forward, rapt.

"All right. But you can't tell Aunt Meg."

Kate moved her hand across her lips in a "they're sealed" gesture.

"Aunt Meg is a bit of a nut. She keeps pens in the freezer and magazines in the fireplace."

"Does she wear gloves when she uses the frozen pens? Don't the magazines burn up?"

"Come to think of it, I only saw her writing with pencils and no, she never has a fire."

"Nutty."

"See? That's how a dog who sort of looks like her ended up with the name Nutmeg."

"And here I thought she was named because of her color," Dylan said.

Tish dipped her chin, and a devilish sparkle lit her eyes. "You know what they say about assuming, don't you?"

Kate gave Nutmeg a long silent appraisal. "Her ears don't match. One is up, and one is down."

"They say God folds one ear down because that dog is special, and He wants to remember it."

"Like a bookmark."

"Exactly."

Tish had let her guard drop, and Dylan admired her softened features, the relaxed posture. She wore dropped guard well.

Nutmeg, possibly uncomfortable with being the topic of conversation, retreated under the kitchen table. But she couldn't shake her new best friend. "I'm going to call you Bookmark," Kate said.

Bianca laughed. "The begging for a dog is going to start all over again."

Finn raised his hands, bowing out. "This is between you two. The cat and I cancel each other's votes." He adjusted to face Tish. "Anyway, what's your next step?"

"It's a waiting game," Tish said. "Wait for Elyse to make contact again. The only thing I know for sure is that she's in trouble. And that's what makes just sitting here twiddling my thumbs so f—" She glanced toward the kitchen. "Oops, sorry, I'm not used to being around little kids."

"Don't worry about it," Bianca said. "She's busy telling Nutmeg a secret."

Kate, nearly hidden by the chairs around the table, cupped her hand next to the dog's upturned ear, and Nutmeg wore a dull expression that said, "Get to the point."

"I have a buddy in Crestwood who can keep me posted," Finn said, "but this is out of my jurisdiction, so the best thing might be for you to chat with them directly."

Tish's panicked expression told Dylan they needed more time. It was certainly possible Elyse was on the wrong side of this, and he wanted Tish to at least have the opportunity to find that out before it was too late. "Give us twenty-four hours and then we'll chat it up with them every which way we can."

"Okay, bro." Finn rose to his feet. "I trust your judgment."

For a brief moment, Dylan's thoughts wandered back to a time when Finn couldn't have said that. He squatted so Kate could climb onto his back and felt Tish's eyes trail them to the driveway where a small struggle ensued over getting Kate into the car.

"Finn and Bianca make a great couple," Tish said when Dylan returned.

An innocent statement, but it pressed a button, a reminder of when he and Bianca held that title. He waited for his stomach to pitch, for the regret to pull him down, but this time it didn't.

"Kate's adorable. A little carbon copy of her mom," she continued.

"Actually, she's adopted. It's a long, long story but I'll give you the abridged version."

"Abridged? Sounds studious."

This morning Helen called him her hope and inspiration, and now Tish was calling him studious. Words for some kind of brooding narcissist, a college professor with patches on his elbows, not him. He shifted his weight from one leg to the other, debating how to describe the situation that had twisted them all in knots for months. "Kate's grandmother died last year and named Bianca and Finn as her guardians. There was no other family to speak of."

"That's huge."

"I'm proud of the way she and my brother have stepped up. And no one could love Kate more."

"She's got a great new family." Tish tilted her head, looking him square in the eye, with something he swore came close to appreciation.

All day long, it felt like she'd been calling him an asshole, now this was something else. She'd caught him all right. Witnessed up close a man who wants to be a better person, hell, who is a better person because of a seven-year-old girl.

∼ NINE ∼

TISH closed the bedroom door. Her mind was a circus of questions and emotions, somersaulting, colliding, and finally falling from the high wire, landing spread eagle at her feet.

She moved to the window, lifted the shade. The rain had stopped and she spotted the Big Dipper looking generous, as though it were about to spill an extra helping of stars from its ladle. How she missed viewing the stars with her dad. Pointing out the constellations. Discussing them by name as if they were old friends. A heated flush crept from her collar bone to her jaw line. The former shredded sorrow over losing her dad was mostly gone, but a leaden ache remained. Perhaps it always would.

She slipped into a pair of cotton pajama bottoms and a tank top. It felt good to be done with scratchy army uniforms and "Be All You Can Be" T-shirts. And she'd be just fine if she never heard another inspirational slogan. As a kid, all she'd wanted was a wall filled with posters of NSYNC and Backstreet Boys. Not the ones her mom plastered all over her room extolling the virtues of "Courage," "Determination," and "Strength."

Forget, "Just Do It." Her motto from now on was, "Just Get Through It."

Pulling back the comforter on the twin bed, her eyes stalled on the sheets, a brown and navy blue plaid, nicely broken in. Dylan grew up in this house. Was he clinging to better days by refusing to part with the remnants of his youth?

For the hundredth time, she willed her phone to ring. Nutmeg was already curled at the foot of the bed, the flaps of her mouth puckering as she slept. Tish spooned in next to her and ran a hand over her soft fur. Maybe there was something to the man's best friend thing.

"What we have here is a classic case of FUBAR, Nutmeg." The dog's ear twitched under her breath. RJ dead, a missing mother, a ... she eyed the door, trying to define the man on the other side. Stubborn. Kind. Indecently Gorgeous. SKIG? She chuckled at her own acronym for Dylan Tierny. She was definitely losing it. Bolting upright, she checked the time. 2300 hours. No, eleven o'clock. She needed to start thinking like a civilian.

Her brother would be placing his ceramic bowl in the dish drainer after an evening of watching *Chuck* reruns at the same time he was listening to John Tesh's radio show on one station and NPR on another while eating three prunes and a bowl of kale chips.

Luke ate all his meals and snacks from the bowl Robert had thrown for him when he was in his pottery phase. Even when they went to restaurants, her brother toted the bowl along and handed it to the server to take to the cook. It was his way of being green. No dirty dishes to go through a dishwasher, no paper products for him. A simple rinse and drip-dry between uses.

Luke answered on the third ring, per usual. Not the first. Not the second. Not the fourth. "Mom didn't call." Tish closed her eyes upon hearing his voice.

"You know she gets busy. Did you have your snack?" She knew the answer.

"Hmm. Mom calls at 11:05."

Their mother had skipped routine, skipped town, and was on the lam. Or kidnapped. "Which episode of *Chuck* did you watch tonight?"

"Season three, 'Chuck versus the Subway'."

"What's that one about again?"

"The intersect is malfunctioning. Chuck should have told his sister earlier. Communication is vital to family harmony."

Of course, Chuck's dilemmas, only reminded Luke of the disruptions to his own routine and the missed call from Elyse.

"What's happening tomorrow?"

"First Sunday of the month. Inventory with Robert."

"Inventory" consisted of an elaborate process of counting all items in the house, declaring their condition, performing maintenance if necessary. WD-40 on doorknobs that might harbor a squeak, baking soda down the drain to make sure a bad odor never wafted up, wind the grandfather clock, and the list went on. It was all about staving off any glitch that might upset Luke's orderly world. Robert was a sport about it, understanding Luke's need for checks and balances, following him with clipboard in hand, pen and highlighter ready to make notations.

His devotion to Luke, and to her, brought on a heavy, claustrophobic pressure in her chest. Robert had always been a breath away, almost magical in his ability to handle her highly eccentric brother, uncanny in his aptitude for knowing what others needed, whether it was guiding them onto the boat or having a towel ready after a swim or fixing a favorite meal. But thoughtfulness and proximity were no guarantee that he'd be around forever. If she'd learned anything so far it was this: don't count on having anyone in your life long term.

"Better get your rest then, Luke."

"Not tonight."

Tish could picture him pacing, reciting prime numbers, pining for his routine; the precisely timed call from Elyse where they said good night to each other in a dozen different languages. They'd started when Luke was in kindergarten. Tish's eyes traveled to the door. Cupping a hand over her mouth, she began. "Bonne nuit."

"Alphabetical order starting with Albanian," Luke interrupted, annoyed.

"Natën e mirë."

Luke said the next one, and they took turns until they made their way to, "Chúc ngủ ngon." Good night, Vietnam.

There was a moment of silence before he said, "That'll have to do."

"She'll call tomorrow." Even as she said this, doubt flooded her mind. But she was talking to air. Luke had clicked off, no need for a boring English goodbye.

Tish collapsed on the bed and tried to let her muscles go slack. One deep breath, and then another, did little to stave off the rising panic. Her insides pulled, a run-away train ramming her stomach lining looking for a way out. The sensations intensified until she sat up. Reaching into her backpack, she found a skein of yarn and started finger knitting. She'd become a cliché. The lonely heart trying to knit the hours away, trying to fool the clock into moving those hands forward and taking her problems with it. Knowing all along, the axe would come crashing down any minute. She needed to stop worrying about her past, obsessing about her present, and stocking up on trouble for the future.

But she couldn't. Sitting in those circles of PTSD sufferers, it hadn't taken long for Tish to decide she didn't deserve to be there. She couldn't help herself to the same label, the same therapy, as these warriors. Some of them were missing limbs, eyes. Those who could still see cast vacant stares, seemingly intent on something, seeing nothing. Still, it wasn't a war wound that kept her awake at night, but her own friend, the one she'd misread, the one she didn't know as well as she thought. The best friend she'd ever had. The one she'd let down. No, Tish's injury was self-inflicted, having to do with being so damn self-absorbed.

Nutmeg stirred, perhaps jolted by Tish's fidgeting. The dog poured herself from the bed, stretched, and headed for the door. Her wagging tail and pleading eyes communicated her need. "Okay, okay. I'll take you out."

She clipped the leash Dylan had bought to Nutmeg's collar. Outside, she waited while the dog sniffed every bush, every blade of grass before deciding on the proper place to let loose. Returning to the house, Tish found Dylan leaning against the doorjamb, hands in his pockets. Shirtless. Well-defined arms tanned and burnished even though it was barely April. Pecs that looked like they were carved and planed by a master carpenter's hand. She fought the heat rising through her like a wild fire and pulled her eyes away.

"I would've taken her out," he said.

Nutmeg yanked on the leash, desperate to get to him.

Tish crossed her arms over her chest, aware of what cold air meant to braless women in thin tank tops. "I'm fully capable."

"Of course you are." Dylan held the door open.

Goose bumps pebbled up and down her arms.

"How about a hot drink?"

"What I'd really like is a cigarette."

"Can't help ya there. Again, those things'll kill you."

Something else might help. Something to make her less than drunk, more than tipsy. She needed to be oblivious, unaware, adrift. "Got any whiskey?"

"Sorry, no, Jack has left the building. Kicked to the curb along with Miller and Mondavi, who I never really liked anyway. But I do have something." He rummaged through the cupboard, then plunked a small glass on the counter and poured a shot of green liquid.

After an internal debate about whether she should drink in front of him that lasted all of a nano-second, she threw the Jager back and closed her eyes as a rope of vertical warmth crawled down her throat. "How do you keep that stuff in the house? Isn't it a temptation?"

"The short answer, no."

"I've got time."

"My best buddy, Tucker, and I polished off a bottle of Jager junior prom night, and I was never sicker. Haven't touched the stuff since, even at the height, or is it the depth, of my raging alcoholic days." He tilted the bottle, set it back down. "Don't let anyone tell you all drunks will drink aftershave or mouthwash. We have our preferences, and of course our cloudy memories. I just keep this around to remind me how much fun drinking is." He drifted for a moment. "As long as we're on the subject, is RJ overindulging a regular thing?"

"I've never seen him drunk." The phantom pain of his death crept back into her consciousness, and she helped herself to another shot. She didn't want to talk anymore. She rose and pointed down the hall. "Think I need to get some sleep."

Dylan nodded. "Good idea. Anything else you need?"

It was all about needs after all, wasn't it? What about what she wanted? She wanted a backrub for starters. "Thank you. No. I appreciate all you've done."

She closed the bedroom door and dropped onto the bed. The double shot swayed her into thinking this was the most comfortable mattress in the world, and the elephant of worry that had been crushing her chest got to its feet, and slowly exited the room. Hoping for the kind of sleep where you hydroplane just above a deep slumber, Tish floated through the hazy Jager buzz but soon jerked to a state of restlessness. She knew what was coming, and she teetered on the edge of it, trying desperately to wake herself up. The scene always played out the same, detail by excruciating detail.

Under an ash-gray sky with a battalion of clouds marching in formation, a panorama of dust and sand whirled into view. The stale rubbery tent smell, a tiny prism of light.

Tish could barely see the faint outline, as if Liv were in a distant fog, or underwater.

Though Tish had always been taught that tears are a sign of weakness, in her dream her own began to flow. Hard. They fell down her cheeks and cemented her lips together. She couldn't speak, she couldn't scream.

Desperation reigned, looming large in the silence. She had to find a way to reach Liv, yet movement eluded her, compounded by a sense of defeat and a bound tongue. *No . . . don't!* She attempted once again to say the words. "No, please, no." But she was a stone, powerless to reach her friend. A tear-dribbling, useless stone. Unable to do anything when it really mattered.

She and Liv had been like sisters, but she had failed her miserably.

It always ended the same, with a "pop." She woke panting and dripping with sweat. Right before Liv's wobbly image came into crisp focus. And as bad as the nightmare was, the following wakefulness was somehow worse as her soul waged an internal battle and guilt and regret took turns pummeling her, over and over again.

∾ TEN ∾

AFTER Tish closed the door to the spare bedroom, Dylan sat on the edge of his bed. She had no interest in him. Too bad. Because despite his earlier teasing, she absolutely was his type. Confident. Smart. Captivating. An understatement. He allowed himself to take it a step further in his mind, envisioned himself peeking into that room across the hall, catching a glimpse of her, motioning for him to come closer.

Cue the brakes. This was a job. Nothing more.

He pulled out his laptop. Philip had seemed genuinely upset about RJ, but even a mediocre actor could manage some waterworks. Plus, the way he looked at Tish, the way he couldn't keep his paws to himself. Add his over-the-top house, the ridiculous gold pinky ring, the villa in Tuscany. This was a guy who was accustomed to owning things, controlling things. Controlling people. From what Dylan could gather, Elyse wasn't someone who could be controlled. Did Philip have a thing for her? Made sense given his primal response to Tish. And based on the picture Helen shared, mother and daughter could be twins. Very hot twins. If Philip offed RJ, he'd have Elyse to himself. It all sounded like one of those soap operas his mom used to watch, but then he'd heard worse, seen worse.

Dylan did a quick Google search, and the first thing to surface was about Saycor's newest drug in Phase III clinical trials, Avimaxx. Touted as a "promising alternative," early reports indicated that if the anxiety drug passed testing, it would blow the competition out of the park. Mainly because it minimized certain side effects common for this type of medication.

Another handful of articles about institutional investors like JP Morgan and Barclays socking hefty chunks of change in Saycor's coffers. The money floating back and forth in this industry was staggering. Saycor's balance sheet was solidly in the black. Cash flow didn't seem to be a problem for the company or the hot shots running it.

Was it a stretch to think Elyse's disappearance and possibly RJ's death were somehow related to the drug? Dylan was grasping at reed-thin straws, he knew that, but most crimes were rooted in love, money, or both.

Clamping his laptop shut, he yawned and crawled into bed. He was about as useless on no sleep as he was on an empty stomach. But it didn't take a minute for him to realize he was too keyed up, too preoccupied. The woman in the next room claimed his thoughts, barreled into every open space. Her sharp, yet tender edges. The way she slurped down onion rings.

Throwing back the covers, he plowed into his jeans, was about to go across the hall when a knock startled him. He swung the door open, and there she stood, hair mussed and nearly hiding a gaze that exposed her intentions. Before he knew what was happening, she reached for him, and he crushed his mouth to hers while gathering fistfuls of soft shirt at the small of her back. Her fingertips dragged at his arms and latched onto the empty belt loops at his sides. Awareness of her gentle tugging frayed his control. He hoisted her up, and she wrapped her legs around him. Prepared to wait her out, he backed her against the wall, still drilling his lips into hers, marveling at her eager response.

Need shimmied through him as a wonderful haze filled his brain. He carried her to bed admiring, exploring, losing himself in the scent that had teased him all day long.

Losing himself in her.

⋄ ELEVEN ⋄

The Previous Day, Saturday, April 4th

ELYSE stared at the grease-stained bag sitting on the broken-down vanity. Was she supposed to be thankful for cold fries and a burger she knew didn't contain an ounce of real meat? When the Brit had casually announced from the other side of the bathroom door that they were leaving, a furious anger unleashed in the form of a scream that had been building. It unraveled from the knot in her chest, a scream that rendered her voice raw while she pounded and kicked the door in a fruitless tirade. "You can't leave me here!"

On the other side of the door, the Brit laughed the laugh of a gracious winner while Smoker sputtered something closer to a cough. Then two pairs of feet thudded across the floor, punctuated by the slam of another door.

She eased herself down on the side of the tub. It was clear what they were after. This could only be about the clinical trial. A total of three people knew they'd moved Clay Jackson into the placebo group, and she was one of them. Who had the most to lose? Was it naïve to think Philip would put their friendship and over a decade of working together above his kingdom? She needed to make sure they didn't get ahold of the flash drive. She didn't graduate Magna Cum Laude to do something as stupid as giving up the proof of their deception, the only thing that might be keeping her alive.

But a father of four was dead, and they'd treated it like a data entry error, a few quick key taps and it would all go away.

Well it didn't, and it wouldn't. Feeling as if a fuse had been lit and all she could do was wait for the explosion, she practiced the only thing she remembered from a string of unsuccessful yoga classes where she couldn't pretzel-twist like the instructor or quiet her mind or body for more than a few seconds at a time. *Right nostril. Left nostril. Right nostril. Left nostril.* Didn't they call it piranha breathing? No, a piranha was a deadly fish with teeth. She closed her eyes, certain she'd never be able to spell either word if her life depended on it. Give her a differential equation any day, but spelling had always eluded her.

As her pulse slowed, her thoughts turned to RJ, landing her in a scene that took place in her own kitchen last weekend after her early morning run. She'd been using the track at the high school for years, every Saturday, 5 a.m., rain or shine. How she loved the luxury to disconnect. No emails, no text messages, no phone calls. Just her playlist and her thoughts. She'd climbed the stadium stairs two at a time, La Roux's "In for the Kill" doing little to distract her, raced to the bottom, stopped. Chest heaving, she rubbed the back of her sleeve across her forehead.

This wasn't the first time someone had died during a clinical trial, and it wouldn't be the last. Was it fair that the company could lose everything they'd invested in the drug, nearly a billion so far, because of unfortunate timing? Many, many people would benefit from Avimaxx. Elyse believed that whole-heartedly. Rules were made to be broken. Especially rules bogged down by bureaucracy that made it nearly impossible to bring a life-changing drug to market. Not to mention the impact on her family. Luke in particular. He may be able to earn money here and there, but he'd never be fully independent. What would happen to him if she lost her income?

She stretched her quads and calves, then ran in a near sprint the four miles home, ready to accept what they'd done, learn from it, and move on.

RJ was in the kitchen, leaning against the island. He set his coffee mug on the counter, glanced at his watch. "Either you broke a record or took a short cut."

"Think I averaged sub-6," Elyse said between huffs of breath.

"Lost count of the stairs."

"Damn, woman, you thinking about dumping me for some Zac Efron type?" He sidled up to her, ran a finger along her collarbone.

"He needs a nanny not a woman. Now that Mark Wahlberg . . ." Elyse nuzzled his ear. "Can't I have you both?"

He pulled her close, kissed her hard. "I don't share."

She wriggled away. "I'm gross. Let me shower."

"Don't you know by now sweat is a turn-on? At least yours is." He slapped her rear squarely, gave it a squeeze. "Hurry, you know how Philip is about his Saturday team building sessions. Not exactly the model of patience."

The name made her blanch. She'd never been as close to Philip as RJ, but she respected him, believed in his business sense. Until she saw this side of him. Maybe once RJ finalized things with Clark Newman she should consider making the leap as well. A fresh start for them both.

Elyse kissed RJ's cheek and headed for the stairs. The trill of her phone on the counter pulled her back.

"Is RJ there with you?" Philip didn't wait for an answer. "Put me on speaker." His voice boomed through the kitchen. "I need you both in the office. Thorpe called."

A Saturday morning call from Saycor's in house attorney, Dennis Thorpe, couldn't be a good thing. "What's going on?" Elyse asked.

"We're being sued."

She fell onto a kitchen stool. A lawsuit. They'd already dodged a barrage of bullets, but the firing squad had just reloaded.

Now, trapped in a nasty bathroom, sweaty, weak from lack of food and the drugs still lingering in her system, the irony welded her in place. She'd worked so hard, sacrificed so much to provide for her children after their father died. What if Avimaxx had left another woman and her children in the same sinking boat? Without a husband. Without a father.

The door burst open. "Lunch break's over." *Lunch?* A raccoon would have left it in the dumpster.

Smoker sank on the vanity, and it buckled under his weight. He started in on her burger, chewing with his mouth open in a disgusting display.

"Put that down," the Brit said. "Were you raised by bloody wolves?"

"Don't start—"

"Shut it," the Brit snapped, then to Elyse, "Now, give it up and this is over."

Over, in the form of a bullet through her skull. "I told you, I don't have a flash drive and never did. I don't even know what you're talking about."

His gaze skittered over her. "What have we here?"

She kept quiet. If she opened her mouth, even a millimeter, her fear would flood the room.

"You said you gave her a proper frisking," the Brit spat at Smoker. "Cocked that one up. Good show. Just like letting her take off while I was staging the flat tire." He looked at Elyse with something that bordered on sympathy, but she knew better. "We wouldn't have had to drug her in the first place if you'd done your job right."

Smoker's lips stitched together in an angry pucker, and Elyse half expected him to charge the Brit. Maybe their bickering was her only advantage, a distraction that would provide a window of escape.

Wishful thinking that ended as the Brit reached out and plucked the phone from her bra. He puzzled over the tiny phone for a minute, scrolled through the call log. It wasn't the flash drive he had been hoping for. He flipped it in the trash. She stared at him, thunderstruck. *Well, at least he didn't aim for the toilet.*

"On second thought," the Brit said, retrieving the phone from the garbage. He dropped it in the bowl with a ceremonious plunk and just like that, a black cloud snuffed out her silver lining.

∾ TWELVE ∾

TISH woke with her head riding the rise and fall of Dylan's bare chest. They hadn't had sex, which by the way, would have been amazing ... but incredibly stupid. The chemistry between them was undeniable. Also insane. She'd just met the guy, and though they'd obviously ended up getting along better than they'd started, there was no way this was more than a few hormones taking leave of their senses. She didn't need unruly hormones calling the shots right now. She had far too many other things to deal with.

After a lingering glance at Dylan, she slipped across the hall to collect her phone. She hadn't planned to be away from it so long. What if Elyse had called? She looked at the screen and was shocked to see ten missed calls from Luke, one every fifteen minutes beginning at midnight. How could she have let herself get so distracted? She punched voice mail and heard her brother's panicked voice, "Something bad happened!"

She grabbed her duffle, flew from the room, and snatched her keys off the coffee table. Backtracking, she thought of something else, and rationalized that it was easier to beg forgiveness later than ask permission now.

On the way to Turtle Cove, Tish called both Luke and Robert. No response. Her fingers numbed as she clutched the steering wheel, and bands of tension crawled up her arms as she flew down I-70, pushing the speed limit, her thoughts racing along with the speedometer.

Time darted back to a spring day at Turtle House. Elyse was packing up to go live with RJ, which meant Luke would be living alone. Even though he was in his mid-twenties, Tish didn't think he was ready. They'd all fought for months. Luke, so determined to prove he could make it on his own. Elyse, arguing that he knew the area as well as Savannah. But there wasn't a loblolly pine in sight in Western Pennsylvania and no one up here said y'all unless in jest. Elyse fired back with more ammunition. He'd summered in Turtle Cove all his life, and Robert was just across the lake. But Luke didn't do well with change. It took him months to adjust. He refused to leave the house, had groceries delivered, and let the mailbox overflow. It was Robert who eventually coaxed him out, and helped him settle into a comfortable routine.

The gray clapboard house had been in the Duchene family since before Tish's dad was born. It towered over an embankment that sloped to the water's edge where a long dock jutted out over Lake Anaba. The deep lot was dotted with a few ornamental trees so as not to block the panoramic view. An array of colors blazed across the sky each evening, the benefit of a house facing west. When the kids were growing up, the family would sit on the screened porch, citronella candles glowing, and watch the sun melt into the horizon while bats skittered under a myriad of stars.

The fluttering dark shadows had always made her wary, the way they appeared from nowhere after the sun went down, cartwheeling across the twilight sky. "It's all right, Featherweight. Bats are our mosquito-patrol." Her father's smooth voice convinced her to unfold the arms crossing her chest. The gentle reminder put her at ease, and the way he called her Featherweight, bolstered her courage. She was small, but fierce.

Now her eyes grew heavy, and she opened the window, but at 4:30 a.m. she needed more than cold air. She needed high-octane coffee on an IV drip. She'd settle for a cup. Besides, the gas gauge was hovering over E. Her headlights lit up a sign. Millburg, PA. Please, let there be a gas station in Millburg, PA.

She propped her elbow on the base of the car window and rested her head in her hand. The episode with Dylan initiated a torrent of self-loathing. But it *had* been a stressful day. She was already trying to rationalize what had happened, compartmentalize it in a way that made it seem normal. It was anything but normal. Or was it? They were two adults who found each other attractive. No. She didn't deserve the intimacy. What right did she have? But denying herself wouldn't change the past.

The phone startled her. Robert. His voice usually had a calming effect, but the thought that it could be bad news about Luke caused her heart to freefall.

"He's fine, Tish," Robert assured her, "but he won't leave the boathouse. He doesn't want me in there with him, but I'll keep an eye out."

"What happened?"

"Someone broke in while he was out on the dock and messed things up pretty bad."

She should have warned him. If she'd been by her phone instead of distracted by. . . "Thank God he's all right. I need to hear his voice."

Silence.

"Robert?"

"Hold on," he said, and seconds later in a near whisper, "You know he'll want to talk to you soon, but right now . . ."

"Thanks for trying." Her lip trembled. Her brother needed her, and she wasn't there. A picture of him cowering in a corner sliced at her. "I'm on my way."

Impending doom washed over her, and she tried to regulate her breathing to keep from hyperventilating. If she felt this way, Luke must be near catatonic. Why would someone do this? Luke's things—his notes from space shuttle launches, spare parts from his first computer, even his Albert Einstein bushy-haired cufflinks—weren't valuable to anyone but him.

Unless . . . From time to time Luke worked freelance gigs from home as a cryptanalyst. His smarts were unparalleled, and he had a certain talent for deciphering coded messages that stumped everyone else. But because of the sensitive information, Luke never worked on his own computer, and he was between jobs.

No. This probably wasn't about Luke. This must be related to Elyse's disappearance. She must have something someone else wanted. And that someone wasn't above harassing her kids and maybe killing RJ.

At the next mile marker, Tish saw a sign for Go Mart and pulled off. She gassed up, used the filthy restroom, then perused the snack options. Powdered donuts and Funyons would have to do. The place had an eerie quality, still and dank. The refrigeration units gasped. Ceiling lights flickered, eeking out their last ounces of fluorescence.

Coffee. She turned to the woman behind the counter. "Any chance this was made recently?"

Her inquiry was met with a bored shrug from a middle-aged clerk, a column of gold studs climbing her ears.

Tish filled a 20 ounce cup with coffee thick as oil. Question answered.

Her phone buzzed again, and she nearly knocked over the coffee reaching for it.

"Where are you?"

Dylan. She'd pushed him to the backburner, behind her mother, brother and everything else. "I'll have to call you later."

"You're kidding, right? You sneak out in the middle of the night and can't even bother to tell me you're leaving?"

She didn't need chastising. Not now. Not ever really. "Listen . . ." She gripped the Styrofoam cup, stopped short of crushing it. A contradictory thought ambushed her. He was her ally, at least until they found Elyse. She bottled her frustration, apologized and told him about what happened at Turtle House. And before she could stop herself, she blabbered on about how guilty she felt for not being there for her brother.

"It's not your fault, Tish."

The old get out of guilt free card. Her face heated, and her pulse raced as her C.O.'s voice superimposed itself over Dylan's. He'd said the same thing. The words reverberated as the gas station door clanged and a man and woman walked in. Both bulky. Him: High school linebacker who'd let things slide. One too many cracks to the head. Her: Bitter. Wronged by life. The type who'd convinced herself men like women with more than a little extra meat on their bones. They stumbled to the shelves, grabbed a handful of snack cakes along with a couple of drinks, and headed toward the counter.

The woman propped a hand at the small of her back, either stretching from a long ride or supporting the weight of her wide-spaced breasts. Her companion turned, ran a heavy-lidded gaze over Tish, then elbowed his sidekick. "Mind if I grab somethin' else for my sweet tooth?"

They exchanged a look as if they'd settled a bet, and the toothpick dangling from the man's mouth shifted to the other side as he licked his lips. "Chocolate milk to wash down these dry-ass Little Debbies."

Tish shot him an acid glare.

"Don't git why that skinny thing's gotcha riled up." The woman's sneer revealed years of neglected oral hygiene. "But whatever floats yer dinghy."

"Did you hear me?" Dylan, still in her ear.

The problem in front of her cracked open a Mountain Dew, took a slug, and wiped his mouth with a filthy paw. He sidled closer. "This ice queen needs thawin' out."

"Tish." Dylan again. More insistent this time. "Are you there?"

"I have to go." She pressed END and paid for her coffee.

The man wedged past her, leaned so far across the counter his toothpick almost touched the clerk's face. "Don't ya got somethin' else ta do?"

The clerk sized-up the situation and retreated to a back room. No help there. The bitter one drained a can of Red Bull, belched like the lady she was, and looked around. "Gotta pee. Try to make yer quickie quick." She laughed at her idea of a joke and headed to the door marked "Popeye," ignoring the one labeled "Olive Oyl" right next to it. An apt decision considering the hint of mustache riding her upper lip.

"Looks like it's just you 'n me." He gave his crotch a squeeze. "How 'bouts I give you a lil' somethin' fer the road."

The only gas station for miles, the perfect place for psycho perverts, and this half-brain had ideas.

Quicker than she expected someone with mammoth proportions could move, he clamped an iron grip on her arm, swung her around, and pinned her across the counter. Spitting his toothpick to the floor, he pressed his lips to her ear and growled through tight teeth. "The tough girl act gets me good 'n hot."

He closed one hand around her breast, cupped her ass with the other as the smell of beer and sweat made her gag. She'd smelled worse in Baghdad, dealt with worse. This guy was just pissing her off. Tish slid her key between her first and second knuckles, clenched her fist, jabbed into his groin, gave it a twist.

"What the . . ." he screamed and doubled over.

She struck him with an upper cut, sending him reeling. Wrenching his arm behind him, she planted her boot in the back of his knee, and he lurched forward. She pushed him to the ground, kneeled on his back. "If you want to keep your precious sweet tooth, or any of your teeth, I suggest you walk away."

Now Popeye returned and angled toward them, mouth agape like a black hole. "Get off him you crazy bitch!"

Her precious mate wriggled out from under Tish and hunched over, wheezing like an old man, even though he was likely still in his twenties. Then, as if he got his second wind, he rushed her again.

"Not another step." Tish aimed Dylan's gun south of the creep's apron of fat.

Stopped in his tracks, eyes wide, both fascinated and horrified. Red patches of color bloomed on his cheeks. "Chocolate milk gives me the—" his throat locked up and the last part came out— "shits-n-way."

Tish never budged from her stance as she watched them back toward the door, hands up. They made a swift exit, and she edged toward the window. Mist was rising from a nearby vacant field, floating about two feet from the ground. They piled into a beat-up Bonneville, and Tish noticed a curly-headed toddler standing in the backseat, grinning and waving a filthy stuffed bunny. God help him. She shook her head. You need a license to drive a car but not to parent a child. With any luck, Social Services would step in before these idiots had time to do any real damage. The engine rattled to life with a gust of blue smoke, and they peeled from the parking lot. When the taillights faded, Tish stashed the .45, bent over and gripped her shins in both hands.

Outside, a bracing wind howled toward her. It would be a couple of hours before the sun even made an appearance. What more would the coming day hold? Bring it. She was too pumped to retreat.

Army strong? You bet your ass.

↜ THIRTEEN ↝

DYLAN had put good judgment, the result of his two years as a sober man, on hold last night when Tish came to his room. Inebriated by her image backlit by the hall light, something passed between them, not quite lust but beyond attraction. Askance then acceptance.

Funny how stressful situations could manifest themselves in unexpected ways. He'd felt himself come unmoored and set adrift in her arms. Floating, floating. Tracing the vine tattoo that crawled from her hipbone up her side to curve under her breast, desire and need transected, but without words it was understood, going further would have only complicated an already complicated situation. The stop was a bookmark, holding an amazing story in place, a story to be savored and finished at a later date.

Before daybreak, he'd reached for her and found a twisted top sheet instead. At first, he felt a burst of panic. Had someone snatched her the way they supposed Elyse had been taken? Anger soon supplanted his alarm. All her things were gone. A note lay on the nightstand: "Had to run. Please take care of the dog. —T."

Like he had a choice. Nutmeg seared him with intelligent eyes that dared him to even think about leaving her behind. He scratched under her muzzle, and she responded by running her tongue over his hand.

"Let's go for a ride."

That one ear perked higher like she was waiting for a detailed itinerary.

Then it hit. Durwood had his truck. Tish took her car. He glanced at the clock. 4:45 a.m. Durwood would be up. He liked to take care of business so he could knock off by noon and spend the rest of the day in a bass boat or a tree stand, depending on the season. The early bird gets the worm, or in his case, the perch, walleye or buck.

Dylan made arrangements with Durwood to bring his truck, then called Tish, but her cavalier attitude only ratcheted his anger. Fifteen minutes later his phone buzzed, and he drew it from his pocket, fully expecting Tish with an apology. Instead, it was Helen, frantic.

"They were here. The men who took Elyse." She spat the words between long swallows of air.

"Call 911. I'm on my way." He raced to his dresser, holstered his Glock, did a double-take. The .45, the one his dad left him, was gone. Shit. Did she really leave a freakin' note about a dog but fail to mention she took his weapon? That strict onion diet must have rewired her brain. She'd better have a damn good reason, or he'd tell Helen to find some other schmuck to take the case.

He scooped up Nutmeg and shot from the house as his truck rounded the corner with Durwood behind the wheel.

Dylan took the seat almost before Durwood vacated it. "Ride with me, and I'll get Finn to drive you home."

"Nah, I need the walk." Durwood patted his ample belly. "Heading over to Tiffany's for a cuppa joe. Diner's quiet till daybreak."

Dylan squealed from the driveway as he yelled out the window, "Tell her to save me a piece of that cherry pie."

In the rearview mirror, he could see Durwood lazily touch one finger to the brim of his cap.

At Helen's, Dylan raced through the open door to find her lying next to her couch, eyes flashing like new quarters behind glasses knocked askew. Nutmeg scrambled from his arms, licked her cheek, then moved across the room to curl up under an end table.

Dylan knelt next to Helen. "Are you hurt? Do you need an ambulance?"

She rearranged her glasses and pulled herself up to sit against the couch. "I don't think so. On both counts."

"What happened?"

"There were two of them. They seemed intent on finding something."

"Did they say what?"

Helen shook her head. Dylan noticed her hands, thumbs folded over the middle joint of each index finger. She followed his gaze and said, "I'm trying to counteract the fear."

"How's that working?"

She shrugged. After a brief pause, her eyes flew wide, looking first at Nutmeg then back at Dylan. "Where's Tish?"

How could he explain that the woman she asked him to shadow ran off with his gun? "She's fine. She went to check on her brother."

"Why didn't you go with her? I prefer you two stay together."

A rap at the door, followed by a familiar voice. Finn's. "Helen! Are you all right?"

"I will be."

"Who did this to you?"

"I'm afraid I did this to myself. When I heard them come in the back door, I hit the deck and rolled under the sofa. Let me tell you it was easier getting under there than getting out."

The antique couch, not unlike the one their grandma used to have, the one they were never allowed to sit on because it was "French," would be a feat for anyone to shimmy under, much less an octogenarian.

"They didn't see you?" Finn asked.

"No, but I got a glimpse of them." She tightened the belt on her bathrobe, a vintage Japanese Geisha number. "One was all pressed and shiny, like someone who had season tickets to the opera. The other like he's never even seen an iron."

"Did you get a look at their faces?" Dylan had asked the same question a zillion times in his career. Investigation was a relentless taskmaster.

"Have to say I didn't get much of a look from where I was, but I heard them plain as day. I have the hearing capabilities of a young child. I suppose that's because I always wore earplugs at rock concerts." She smiled, pleased with herself. "The wrinkled one had a bad cough and the other had a cardigan and tennis shoe voice, you know, like a British Mr. Rogers."

"British, huh?" Finn jotted something on his notepad. "Did they find what they were looking for?"

"Well, no. The cougher was pretty upset, to say the least."

"What exactly did they say?" Dylan asked.

"I'd prefer not to repeat it. Foul language inhabits small minds." A curious mingled look of disgust and resignation claimed her face. "Oh, what the hell. Mostly 'Fucking bitch.' I suspect that meant Elyse."

So much for not repeating it. Dylan looked around. Helen's place was completely ransacked. A large lamp featuring a naked woman in a seductive pose lay on its side on the floor and dizzy-patterned throw pillows were strewn around the room. "What else did they say?"

"The large one tripped, and the skinny one called him 'a clumsy oaf.' Then more name-calling. And ranting about not finding 'shit'—his word not mine. But I'll tell you this, the rage in the British fellow's tone made a black feeling well up in me. I don't know why they didn't check under the couch." She unfolded her fingers and worried something tied to a string around her neck.

"An acorn?" Dylan asked upon closer inspection.

"My good luck charm."

Dylan took a second to regroup. "I know we've been over this," he said. "But can you think of anything else about Elyse's visit? A change at work? Travel plans? Anything?"

Helen pursed her lips, scrunched her eyes shut. "She rushed in here with her hair on fire, dropped her purse by the door, and started in about an argument she'd just had with RJ."

"Did she mention what they were fighting about?" Finn asked.

"No, personal business is personal business."

"Wait a minute," Dylan said. "Did she have an overnight bag?"

For a moment, Helen morphed into a sort of blissed-out oblivion. Was she consulting a memory guru? Then she came barreling back full force. "Why, no. She didn't. I suppose it could have still been in the car . . ."

Silence claimed the room while a new seed of suspicion took

root. Maybe she hadn't even planned to stay. Dylan hoped for Tish's sake that Elyse wasn't involved in anything that had transpired over the past twenty-four hours.

Finn had been taking notes, but he glanced up, his thoughts possibly running along the same wavelength. He took out a separate paper now and placed it on the table, laying the pen on top. "Helen, would you be able to write a statement?"

She sat, flexed her hands against the arms of the chair, looking around as if to digest it all. Her hand crept to the pen. She picked it up, made a single mark, put it down and contemplated some more before picking it up again. Once she got rolling, words spilled across the page in what could have passed for a calligraphy lesson, all loops and sharp angles.

When at last she finished, Dylan said, "You'll want to contact your insurance agent to make a claim."

She pushed her statement across the table and nodded.

"Are you sure you're okay?" Finn asked.

"These are only things." Helen uncoiled her hand from the pen, indicating the debris. "It's Elyse who can't be replaced."

Finn offered to come back and help her clean up after she filed her claim.

"That's very kind," Helen said, "but finding Elyse is our priority." She moved to Nutmeg, coaxing her out from under the table and nudged the dog to Dylan. "I'd keep her here, but RJ was her world. The poor thing needs male energy right now more than anything."

Once outside Dylan asked Finn, "Mind letting her soak up some of your male energy?" His brother puffed out his chest and reached for the leash, but Dylan said, "Maybe I should take her in, get her acclimated."

"I can handle this ferocious beast. You've got a few beasts of your own to conquer. Besides, I'd like to keep things low key. I'm not sure what Picasso will think of this."

"Oh, right, the cat." Dylan laughed. "I've been on the wrong end of those claws."

Finn disappeared inside, and Dylan had one foot in his truck when he remembered what a long haul it was to Lake Anaba.

Better hit the can.

He trudged up the steps to Bianca's, now Finn's house too. Thinking about their joint ownership of this place was becoming automatic. Dylan glanced at the picture windows he'd bought and installed for Bianca. Those two years together seemed like another life, an alternate reality. In some ways, he couldn't imagine his brother with anyone but Bianca. He shook his head. Life was a downright sideshow.

Soft voices were streaming from the kitchen, and the scent of freshly brewed coffee bit into Dylan's senses. A woman was at the table, her back to them, showing something to Kate and Bianca. It looked like a photo album. The woman pivoted, and her face registered a fleeting look of embarrassment before it turned to pure joy. "Dylan!"

In a sort of out of body experience, he saw her rise and fasten expectant eyes on him. All he could do was ride the windblast of shock at seeing the woman who'd abandoned them nearly two decades ago, the mother he'd written off for dead.

❦ FOURTEEN ❦

The Next Day, Sunday, April 5ᵗʰ

WEDGED between Tish and the rising sun, Robert's shadow swallowed hers as they walked the length of the property to Luke's hiding place. Most women would give their eyeteeth and molars too, to have this man by their side. And she knew how lucky she was. They paused just outside the boathouse.

Weathered didn't begin to describe the state of the small building. But it had stood the test of time. Built by her great-grandfather long before it was fashionable to super-size everything, it was barely large enough to store a kayak. She ran a hand across an old paddle hanging outside the door, and a flood of memories briefly sucked her under. Luke had no doubt worked himself into something of a panic, but the question was, had he reached the point of no return?

The smell of two-cycle oil mingled with rotting wood assaulted her. Her brother must have been beyond desperate to hide here, a place he'd avoided since their dad died. It was dark inside the boathouse except for the rectangle of light seeping through the open door. She allowed her eyes to adjust. "Luke?" The place was crowded with empty coffee cans, boxes, and fishing gear. Dull orange life jackets, probably full of nothing but dust by now, hung from rusty nails. Her spirits, already at rock bottom, somehow plummeted even further. Years ago her brother had tried to describe his world to her. "There's an itch on my frontal lobe I can't scratch." At the time, she couldn't relate, but over the last eighteen months she'd begun to understand an itch that morphs to an unrelenting pain.

"Where was he when all this happened?" she asked Robert.

"Down on the dock. It must have been after eleven."

Right after they spoke. She should have warned him, told him to go to Robert's. Here she was again, second-guessing, beating herself up for inaction. When would she stop ripping herself apart? This had nothing to do with what happened to Liv.

A tarpaulin in the corner moved. Her insides pitched. But this wasn't some enemy ambush, this was her brother. She still hadn't decided what to tell him about Elyse or RJ, much less how to get past the idea of an intruder who'd gone through his things, *touched* his things.

"Luke," she said softly, "I know you're under there. Please come out so we can talk."

The tarp went still.

"I know this is upsetting," Tish continued, "but I'm here now."

After a time, Luke threw back his cover. "How can you be certain they won't come back? What kind of guarantee can you offer?"

"There are no guarantees, but I promise I'll do everything in my power to make sure you're safe."

The very words she'd parroted before. Was it just plain stupidity that made her utter them again?

As she crossed to Luke, he pinned her with his gaze, searching eyes slowly filling with trust, pulling away the very layers of her soul. The intensity caught her so off guard that she could only gape. And though he'd sworn off physical contact since he was a small boy, Luke threw himself into her arms and wept.

✧ FIFTEEN ✼

DYLAN shot Finn a look over Rose's shoulder as she crushed him into an awkward hug. He must be in some weird painting, the kind Bianca did with colors flying in every direction that never formed anything in particular.

Eighteen years had passed without a word. Eighteen years. Now his mom was here, drinking coffee, and eating cinnamon buns. He'd never prayed much, never saw the point if God knew everything and had it all planned out anyway, but when she left right before his sixteenth birthday, he prayed every day for her return. Every stinkin' day. When his dad died two years ago, he prayed she'd show up at the funeral. He'd tried to nudge the hand of God, and he was due for an answer.

Of course, he never let on that he gave a rat's ass. For Finn's sake. Show your little brother you don't need her, or anyone. Now, he prayed this was all a dream. A confusing, hellish dream. The bases were loaded, and he was hoping God would hit a home run. If not, well, three strikes.

"What're you doing here, Rose?" His tone anything but congenial. He'd be damned if he was going to call the woman who'd abandoned them, "Mom."

"Getting to know my granddaughter." She stroked Kate's hand tenderly like she'd been doing it since the girl was born. An act. She was always good at reciting her lines, infusing them with the perfect amount of drama. But she'd fled the stage of their lives without a word. He wouldn't let Kate feel the same abandonment. She'd already lost her entire family and was just beginning to feel comfortable with her new one.

"Katie-bear," he said. "Did you make any pictures in that drawing pad I got you?"

Kate beamed and raced from the room, braids flying behind her like a sailboat's tell-tales. She looked so much like Bianca—fair, lean, and blue-eyed—that anyone would smack money down that they came from the same gene pool.

"What's this about?" Dylan asked Finn, but before his brother could respond, Kate burst back into the room flipping through the pages of her sketchbook.

"Here's one I made for Daddy. Lassnite. Look." She threw her shoulders back in pride.

She hadn't been calling them Mommy and Daddy long, but it sounded so natural. Dylan studied the drawing. A family stood in front of what looked like the White House, flag atop blowing in the wind. Two adults, one child, and a tinier version of Kate in the woman's arms.

"Isn't that sweet," Rose said. "She wants a baby sister."

Finn's cheeks colored. Bianca moved beside him, one hand splayed across her stomach, and the other fastened to his waist in a show of solidarity.

His brother and sister-in-law-ex-girlfriend shared a look. "We're pregnant." Said in the harmonized unison that only comes from years of intimacy.

Rose squealed and collected Bianca in her arms, including Finn in her embrace. "A baby. That's amazing! Finny, I'm so happy for all of you. For all of us! Oh, and we'll have to come up with something for them to call me. Grandma sounds like I should be dropping my teeth into a glass every night before bed."

A baby? Grandma? Finny? That old familiar hollow tightening claimed Dylan's insides. He loved Kate so much it hurt, or as he liked to tell her, infinity times infinity, and he could only imagine how much he'd love this new little sprout. But leave it to Rose to zap the joy right out of the moment. Acting like she'd never left. Acting like she deserved to be a part of this new chapter. She'd skipped most of the book and now she wanted to jump in like she knew the story. And Finn. Why didn't he share this earlier, that their sorry excuse for a mother was here? How long had he been keeping her under wraps?

Biting all that back, he hugged his brother, then Bianca.

"Any cravings yet?" Rose asked. "When I was pregnant—"

What a shocker, Rose making it about her. Dylan headed for the back door. "Can we talk outside, Finn?"

"Sure, bro. Lead the way."

Finn followed him to the wooden swing set Dylan had built and started drumming the slide. "Kate's obsessed with this. It was the best thing—"

"We're not out here to shoot the shit." The old Dylan would have landed a fist in his brother's gut by now.

Finn's face flashed with guilt. All at once they were boys again, in the backyard, covered in mud from head to toe. Dylan ten, his brother five. Rose, cross-legged, in the shade of a massive oak, tying knots in dandelion stems. Her hair swept up from her face, woven in haphazard braids. Her cheeks burned pink in the sun. He loved her then. So much that he put an end to the mud wrestling, taking it upon himself to reprimand Finn and hose him down to spare her the trouble.

Dylan gave a letting-go kind of sigh as if he could pull the ripcord on a lifetime of clips and they'd all parachute away like so many dandelion seeds. "A warning might have been nice."

Finn rubbed at his jaw, as if Dylan really had slugged him. The last time that happened was during a period when he was so deep in the bottle he thought he'd never get out. Was the memory still that vivid for Finn?

"Mom and I . . . well, we've been talking lately," Finn said. "On the phone."

Mom. The title should be reserved for women who actually mother, for women who stick around. A mom doesn't vanish without an explanation. A mom doesn't leave you wondering what the hell you did wrong.

"I wanted her to meet Bianca, and Kate and now with the baby—"

"Why didn't you tell me?"

"For years, you wanted nothing to do with her. That was your choice, not mine. I didn't think she'd come. I never invited her. I'm as surprised as you to see her here. I thought we'd send pictures, Christmas cards, maybe Skype. She was here when we got back from your place last night."

Dylan tamped down a divot in the grass with his boot. "It's the last thing I need right now."

"Would it be so bad to talk to her?"

Forgiveness was part of the twelve steps he'd taken to get to today. But the situation with Rose presented a new step that even AA hadn't anticipated.

"Let me know how that works out for ya," Dylan said.

"Listen, I'm sorry. I planned to call you first thing this morning, but then Helen . . ."

"It's . . . never mind. Look, I need to go. Tish took off and I need to track her down."

Finn gave him a questioning look, but before he could voice his concern, Dylan jumped in. "She took Dad's .45."

"How the—"

"Save the lecture." Dylan rapped the slide in frustration. "Between Tish disappearing and you springing our long-lost mother on me, I'm having one helluva day."

Finn's hands flew up. "I get it. You're pissed at me. Hell, you're pissed at the world. But we just told you we're having a *baby*."

Dylan felt like a complete ass. That tidal pulse of his old self pulling, pulling. He reached out and clamped his brother's shoulder, wrapped him in a bear hug. "Congrats, baby bro. I am happy for you." He started for his car.

"What should I tell Mom?"

Dylan turned. "Tell her I'll see her in another eighteen years."

SIXTEEN

The Night Before, Saturday, April 4th

ELYSE watched through a thin slice of window as night engulfed the sky. They had finally released her from that hell hole of a bathroom to let her sit in the living room—or what passed for one in their world—like it was some sort of reward for good behavior.

The house looked exactly as she would have expected. Stained carpet, blinds bent askew at the windows, empty take-out containers covering a crate—a makeshift coffee table—stretching the limits of repurposing. Probably Smoker's place. Of the two, he'd be the one to live in such squalor.

The Brit paced near the front door, speaking into his cell in hushed tones. His gaze swiveled to rest on Elyse before he strolled into the kitchen.

Smoker flopped onto the couch next to her, his knee pressing against hers. Acid swirled in her stomach. "Looks like just you 'n me, baby," he growled, baring corn-yellow teeth, running his knuckles down her hair. "Kinda like a first date." He guffawed, sending a spray of spit across her face.

"Give it a rest ya bloody plonker," the Brit said, coming back into the room. "Time to implement Plan B."

"Wassat?"

The Brit regarded his addled partner skeptically. "You haven't got the sense the good Lord gave a rutabaga."

A zip tie dangled from his closed fist. Elyse's heart knocked at the base of her throat. Faking confidence, she raised her chin a notch and a swell of self-assurance claimed her. She knew something about this.

Last summer RJ had been bunching some cables together with zip ties. She'd made a crack about saving one for the bedroom, and he tackled her to the floor, brought her wrists together with one hand, grinning like a fool. Working her knees up to his chest, she kicked him away. He feigned hurt, presented his hands to her. Playing along, she zipped his wrists. After an earth-quaking kiss, Elyse started to get some scissors, but he said he didn't need them. She watched in awe as he worked and worked to release a thumb and then his entire hand. "Where'd you learn that?" she'd asked. RJ explained the science behind why it worked. He'd crossed and clenched his wrists before they were zipped, giving himself an extra margin of space to free himself. And she was the one with a science degree. He was always amazing her like that.

She had options here, but first she needed to chart these creeps' level of ineptitude.

Smoker's nose wrinkled to a sneer as he sawed between his teeth with a thumbnail. Standing to cross the room, he tripped over the crate.

Pretty inept.

The Brit edged toward her, the zip tie a limp bridge between his hands. "Let's chivy this along now."

Clenching her fists the way RJ had, she crossed one wrist over the other and presented them. The passive victim.

He paused to study her. "Willing subject. I think you fancy the idea."

"If she likes that, she'll love—" Smoker now.

"Do me a favor. Focus that pea brain of yours."

Her hands fused together with a high-pitched z-z-z-t.

"Think I figured out what Plan B is." Smoker belched, his crooked nose now inches from hers. The stench, a mixture of tobacco and decay, nearly brought her to tears. Something akin to excitement flickered in his eyes. "I ain't never been sailin' before."

The pressure in Elyse's chest went from heavy to

claustrophobic as a warning bell clanged inside her head. They were taking her to the lake. Tears blurred her vision.

Luke.

The Brit turned with robotic slowness toward Smoker. "From now on you're on NTKB."

"What the blazes?"

"Try rolling it around a while." He jerked Elyse to her feet as he spoke. She wanted to scream, but couldn't push a peep past what felt like a mouthful of dry lint. Her arms broke out in gooseflesh and her insides entwined as if someone was using her organs as a slide puzzle. Finally, a series of screams burst forth, not unlike the wailing of a humpback, at the same time she began kicking and flailing her zipped wrists. She wasn't about to make this easy.

Smoker hooked his hands under her armpits as the Brit grabbed her peddling feet, and they blundered their way through the room. They wrestled her onto the floor, pressing her down like cowboys branding a squirming calf.

"Get the needle." The Brit, in a that's-that resignation.

Elyse went slack. They were going to drug her again. And if she was drugged she'd be useless to help her son. "No!" she cried. "I'll behave. I swear."

Smoker struggled to his feet and pawed through a duffle bag.

"Don't do this," Elyse pleaded. "Listen, what you want is not at the lake."

"No? Where then, luv?"

This wasn't the way things were supposed to go. Everything in her life these past few years had been pretty much signed, sealed, and delivered. Controlled. Now there was an agonizing crushing sensation, a pestle grinding at the mortar of her core. How long before they gave up and put a bullet in her skull? Or Luke's? She could give up the flash drive, but then what? She'd seen their faces, could describe their car, their house. What would stop them ... from doing away with her? Why had she foolishly hidden the drive at the lake house and put her own son in jeopardy?

From the corner of her eye, she saw Smoker's dirty paw holding a syringe. All kinds of things went through her mind at the sight of the sharp object pointing toward the cobwebbed ceiling. Who else had been poked by it? What was in it and what were the side effects? The irony of her questions hit. If only she'd paid closer attention to the possible side effects with Avimaxx.

"Let's give it in the ass," Smoker said through a shameless grin. The gleam in his eye said he was enjoying this way too much.

"Not sure what I was thinking teaming up with the likes of you," the other one said. With two fingers, he motioned for the needle.

"I have money," Elyse said. "I'll transfer some to your accounts right now."

The skinny one hesitated before his eyes narrowed on the tip of the needle. Then to her surprise, he put it away. "You're in luck, luv. I'm a busy man and can't afford to have you sleep another day away."

Smoker squinted as something snailed across his mind. "Need to know basis."

The Brit cracked a rusty smile. "Crikey Moses, you're not the dim I thought you were!" He reached into a doughboy end table. Sweet memories of her mom's maple Heywood Wakefield surfaced, the coffee ring they'd tried desperately to remove with mayonnaise, and then ultimately covered with a large Bible. The sea of family photos beneath the hinged top. She'd been meaning to have them digitized for years. He fished around, found what he was looking for.

And the stakes leapfrogged over dangerous, landing on deadly.

⚡ SEVENTEEN ⚡

The Next Day, Sunday, April 5th

WHEN Robert and Tish had finally convinced Luke to go back to the house, he headed straight for the bay window, his "thinking spot." He'd spent countless hours there, knees curled to chest, staring out at Lake Anaba, that familiar, moving mass supporting a vacant sky. Tish often wondered what went through his head as he concentrated on the rolling whitecaps. They reminded her of sailing with her father. Did Luke think of him too? Of what life might be like with him still around? But, maybe she was projecting. Those were her thoughts. For all she knew Luke was counting the waves or assigning them to categories. *Longitudinal. Transverse. Surface.*

For once she was thankful for his quirks. A nightly date with the stars had placed him out on the dock as the house was being ransacked. Her eyes skipped from a wooden statue of an angler to an end table stacked with National Geographics.

Robert started to right a chair.

"Stop." Even as Tish said it, she regretted it. There was no reason to voice her disapproval. He was only tidying up to minimize Luke's stress.

Robert blinked, taken aback.

His nurturing had a cumulative effect. The way he cared for her, and everyone who touched her life made her feel more and more indebted to him. But there was also a tinge of overprotectiveness, even judgment, as he took matters into his own hands.

The police had come and gone, reports were filed. Nothing of value broken. Nothing of value was here anyway. Unless the insurance adjusters could assign a dollar figure to the Faux-nopoly set she and her dad had made. She picked up the little top hat, rubbed at a blob of thick paint. He had let her paint the pieces, ignoring the impetuous handiwork of a six-year-old. The old coke bottles smashed to pieces on the floor. How much were they worth? She and Luke had collected them and refilled them with Kool-Aid all summer long. Or the threadbare sail from her first Sunfish that had been torn from the wall. The house was nothing but memories. Pieces of her life. And maybe that's why she couldn't bear to see Robert taking out a big black garbage bag.

She tented a hand across her eyes, hoping for a new perspective. What could anyone be looking for? "Luke, have you taken any new jobs lately?"

Her brother maintained his resolute pose.

"I need to know if you have anything in the house, computers or anything from one of the companies you've worked for."

"Need or want? There's a difference."

Tish tried to summon techniques that had worked marginally in the past, visualizing a peaceful scene, focusing on her breathing. But no amount of visualization, counting, knitting or even smoking was going to calm her frayed nerves. "Do you have to pick everything apart?"

"Give him a break, Tish," Robert interjected. "He'll answer you in his own time. Just like you do things."

She snatched the garbage bag from Robert, tossed it aside. "What's that supposed to mean? I got here as soon as I could."

"Did you?"

"I haven't had any jobs since January," Luke said without looking her way. "Happy?"

A violent rapping at the door sent her pulse racing, and Luke flew from the window seat and clamored under the table.

"Tish." Now a voice to match the knocking, urgent and familiar.

Something inside her sparked with excitement. The kind of excitement she hadn't felt in years, and yet, she was exasperated beyond belief.

She opened the door. Every line of Dylan's body broadcast his anger, and his brow pleated in a piercing, wild-eyed glare. "Do you have my gun?"

"I—"

"You gonna let me in?" He barged past her.

Robert stepped forward, extended his hand. "Robert Chase."

A look passed between the two men.

"Dylan Tierny."

Luke's voice sprang from under the table. "A well-regulated militia, being necessary to—"

"You can come out. It's a friend of mine," Tish said. Webster would need to add another definition to the dictionary under "friend."

Luke scrambled to his feet, still jabbering, "The security of a free state—"

Dylan's eyes narrowed to green slashes. "Is he—"

"The second amendment. The right to bear arms," Tish said. "Luke believes in it wholeheartedly."

"I know what the second amendment is. I just never heard anyone recite it like that. And bearing arms is one thing . . . stealing them is another." Dylan slid an eye over Robert. "I didn't mean to interrupt."

"It sounds like you have some things to sort out." Robert hitched a thumb toward the door. "How about I go get sandwiches? Would you like one?"

"Thanks, no. I'm here for one thing." Dylan's mouth was set.

He meant the gun, right? If he meant more, it was her own fault. She'd opened the gates to this beast in more ways than one.

"Thanks, Robert," Tish said. "I'd love a sandwich."

He took measured steps to the door. Meddling aside, he was a godsend, albeit a slightly controlling godsend, in contrast to the jean-clad apocalypse that had just descended on them.

"Want to ride along, Luke?" Robert asked.

Her brother, who had resumed his perch, broke from his fixation on the lake and drilled eyes into Dylan. "A special kind of stupid."

Dylan broke into a grin. "People usually save that for after they've gotten to know me a little bit better."

"He's still talking about guns," Tish said. "Criminals aren't going to obey gun laws anyway so why take the right to own them away from everyone else?"

Luke grabbed his backpack as he moved toward Robert's jangling keys, and Tish couldn't help but think of Nutmeg, eagerly riding along with RJ every chance she got. A wave of sadness crept through her as well as gratitude that Dylan hadn't brought the dog with him. How would she explain that to Luke? There was already too much to explain.

After the door closed, Tish pressed the .45 in Dylan's hand. "Where's Nutmeg?"

"Thanks for asking about that, too."

"I didn't have time—"

"She's with Finn. Who's the dude?" Snapped like dried twigs under shit-stomping boots.

"Dude? He's a friend of mine."

"I've never heard the word *friend* thrown around so friggin' much. And I've got news for you, that guy wants to be more than your friend."

Tish felt her cheeks burn while she scrambled for a comeback, but Dylan switched gears. "Tell me what happened here."

"The police are on it." She could hear her voice climbing, and after all, didn't this situation require a good old-fashioned shouting match? "Everything's under control."

"Guess it was too much to hope that you'd keep me in the loop like we agreed." Dylan stuffed the gun behind him. "Helen had a couple of visitors last night too," he said, with an emphasis on visitors.

"Is she okay?"

"She's doing fine. That's one tough lady."

Tish adjusted a cockeyed picture on the wall, a lone kayak parting serene waters. "Has to be the same guys."

"Hell of a coincidence if not. Those are piling up, aren't they?" He took a step closer and the scent of cinnamon and sandalwood teased. "Are we still in this together, or what?"

"Elyse is still missing."

"I'll take that as a yes." Dylan pivoted to look out at the lake, which gave Tish an opportunity to study him. He was so ruggedly handsome that it made her forget to breathe. And she liked the way his shirt seemed to struggle to rein him in. He was positively edible, so yeah, she'd work with him instead of against him.

"Wouldn't hurt to talk about what we've got so far," he said.

She picked up a roll of duct tape, started to seal the busted out sidelight by the front door. "I'm listening."

"It's the timing that baffles me. Your mom leaves. RJ ends up dead."

Her frustration returned. "So you're insinuating—"

"Okay, let's back up." Dylan's hands pushed air toward her. "We're on the same side, remember?"

She could feel her heart rate pick up, said nothing.

"For starters," Dylan went on, "is there anything you can think of that your mom would keep here that someone else might want? Cash? Sensitive work information?"

"She could possibly have some work stuff here, maybe even some cash. It's not like she tells me every—"

A series of thunks then a whomp, not unlike the sound of unbalanced laundry. As they turned in tandem toward the sound, a full-out explosion rocked the house. Suddenly Tish was back in Iraq, trying desperately to absorb Liv's fear as bomb blasts shook the camp.

Dylan pulled his gun. Hooking an arm around her waist, he moved her toward the door. He peered through the blinds and then ushered her outside. Tish looped her bag over her shoulder and fell into step like the well-trained soldier she was. But she couldn't quite make herself get into the car.

"Someone wants something and will stop at nothing, not trashing Helen's house or this house, to find it. Maybe even killing RJ," Dylan said, and his tone pulled her from her fugue. "What if Luke had been inside when they were here? What if they'd seen Helen when they ripped through her house? I'm not prepared to pay the consequences, and if we're here we're not out finding your mom."

Another image. A body face down in the water ... this time

Luke. Tish scrambled for the Sebring. "Shit. The keys are—"

They raced for Dylan's truck. Climbed in. A resistant grinding noise belched from the engine before it jolted into action. Another blast pierced the air, and Tish turned to see the house at Turtle Cove explode in a riot of flames. Her mouth fell open, not a word or sound escaped as fire licked the sky and devoured some of her best childhood memories. Her mind scrolled through a multitude of emotions—sorrow, fear, anger—then plucked out one she'd come to know well—determination. Whoever did this would pay.

As they made a quick surveillance circle around the property, she reached for her phone, but Dylan was already calling 911. She called Robert. "Where are you?"

"The sandwich guy is reslicing tomatoes to Luke's specifications and—"

"Stay put. Don't let him out of your sight. I'll explain when we get there."

As she disconnected, the distant whir of a fire engine made her think of God's voice blazing from the burning bush. A sliver of hope returned as she envisioned it playing out on the Bible story flannel board. The bush was on fire, but did not burn. A quick application to her own predicament told her this was not the end.

This was not over.

Dylan called Finn and explained what had happened, telling him to keep an eye on Helen in case the trash and burn was a repeating MO.

Minutes later, Tish was pulling Robert outside the sandwich shop. Dylan stayed with Luke as he finalized his order. Tish would have to apologize to him later for the tedium that was about to follow. Her brother would ensure that the gloved sandwich-maker measured a quarter teaspoon of vinegar and a half-teaspoon of oil, not a drop more. The girl behind the counter would stare at Luke open-mouthed as he explained each step and watched her carry out his directives, oblivious to the line forming behind him.

Luke's wedge of the world was an equilateral triangle—three equal sides and three identical angles, each sixty degrees, no more, no less. How was she going to tell him his home was gone? His mother missing? RJ dead?

It dawned on her how dramatic events parted everything down

the middle of a timeline. Before her mom went missing. After her mom went missing. Before RJ died. After RJ died. Before the fire. After the fire. Before and After. Before and After. How she longed for the Before. She tried another one on for size. Before she went into Dylan's room. After. They'd come close to sleeping together, and she knew, once she crossed that line, there would be no returning to Before.

Switching off emotion, forcing the synapses of her brain to fire on only logic and reason, just as she'd trained to do in the military, she filled Robert in about Turtle House.

He pulled her close and her head fell on his shoulder. At that moment, she noticed Dylan capturing the gesture through the window, arms folded across his chest, his mouth a slit. Irritated about Luke's excruciating ordering process or something else? That she might like Robert? Like Robert? Maybe he'd pass her a note in study hall. *Do you like Robert? Check yes or no.* Add a healthy case of acne and she was back in middle school.

"I think you should lay low," Robert said. "Let the police take care of this. I'll fly you and Luke somewhere safe and—"

"I just need you to take care of Luke so I can find Elyse."

Doubt snaked through her once again. Could she handle this? All the training in the world, following orders to the letter, even proudly wearing a starched uniform didn't mean she could. And, if she had learned anything from the army, it was that earth-shattering sorrow is always a glance away. She pictured her best friend, Liv, slumping forward in slow motion, a mishandled moment she'd play and replay until she took her last breath.

Dylan appeared by her side.

"Where's Luke?" she asked.

"Filling out a comment card."

"We have a few minutes, then. His suggestions could fill an empty warehouse." She attempted a laugh, but it came out hollow and sad.

Dylan pulled keys from his pocket, his impatience mounting.

When the door finally opened, Luke moved toward them carrying his sandwich, cut into quarters, in his ceramic bowl. Now more than ever she saw their dad. Sharp jaw line, strong slashes of eyebrow above almond-shaped eyes. Her heart clenched at the loss of the house her father had cherished.

"Let's go," her brother said. "I'd like to eat outside on the picnic table. There's zero percent chance of rain."

"Listen, Luke, Dylan and I have to go. I'm driving him to work. You're going to stay with Robert."

It seemed surreal that they were talking about picnics when their entire world had literally exploded. Tish struggled to keep panic from her expression.

Luke seemed to analyze the sandwich in his bowl for a moment, then, "Dylan can drive himself."

"He could, but—" Robert started.

"I . . . sprained my wrist playing basketball yesterday," Dylan cut in, cradling it now. "And it's starting to hurt again. Too dangerous to drive a stick shift with a bum hand."

"How come it's not wrapped?" Luke asked.

"It should be, buddy. I plan to do that as soon as I can get to a store."

"Hmm. I'm hardly your buddy, but you're Tish's friend so I can help. We have compression bandages at the house."

"Thanks, but, I'm kinda in a hurry, the boss is breathing down my neck."

"Who's your boss?"

Dylan hesitated. "Helen Gavin."

Luke made a face. "You better get going, then. She knows Voodoo." He turned to Tish. "Safety first. Remember, hands at ten and two is obsolete. It's nine and three now."

Luke had always been leery of Helen's extraterrestrial ways. Did Dylan have a hunch about that? "Robert is going to take you to his house, and I'll check on you later, okay?"

"Turtle House," Luke said. "I need my toothbrush."

"You can't go there, because . . ." *Think, damn it.* "After you left we saw . . . ants. We need to call an exterminator."

Luke turned to Robert. "I prefer Sanderson Drug. They have the best selection of toothbrushes."

After watching them drive away, Tish and Dylan climbed into his truck and pulled from the parking lot.

"You're an excellent liar," Tish said.

"You lied about the ants."

"Only half a lie. Saw two scoping out the kitchen, and where there's two, there's a troop. Good call mentioning Helen, by the way. Luke loves the stars, but he doesn't like anyone predicting his future by them."

"Can't say I blame him." Dylan reached out, stopped short of touching her, and settled his hand on his leg.

Tish peered out the window. Clouds descended from the sky, propped up by the horizon. A light mist dotted the windshield and built to a heavy rain as they rode on in silence. The pouring buckets might have saved Turtle House a half hour ago. It was almost comical, the futility of the battles she was fighting on every front.

Her last pack of Marlboros lay empty, crumpled and useless in the bottom of her bag. If she ever needed to slide one of those perfect cylinders out and strike a match, it was now.

In five minutes, they stood in front of the once picturesque house—now a charred shell. The rain stopped, and the sun broke through that ceiling of clouds, bringing with it the audacity of a partial rainbow.

Tish struggled to channel Luke's ability to view things as if through slatted blinds, parsing out what his mind couldn't handle in favor of what it could. She warmed to a memory of him fishing off the dock when they were kids. He was a magician when it came to casting, landing his lure with calculated precision. They'd raced kayaks, weaving in and out of the sailboats at the marina, admiring the names and inventing new ones: My Other Car, Lay-a-Wake, Did Knot Did II. And then years later after a big party for Tish. She'd graduated high school, with honors, and Elyse spent the day preparing all her favorites foods. Shrimp and grits, corn bread slathered with warm butter, and enough pecan pie for the whole neighborhood. That night she'd talked everyone's ears off about how her daughter was 'going places.'

A firefighter approached. "You the owners?"

"What happened?" Tish ground-out, anger rising, needing someone to blame.

"Anything you could tell us would help," Dylan said.

The firefighter glanced over his shoulder at the two other men in turnout gear securing the hose back onto the truck. "The release jammed. Probably wunta made much difference though. Explosion like 'at does some serious damage from the git go. The fire examiner will make the official report. But between you and me, it was the water heater." He pulled off his hat, wiped a brow too large for his face. "Install a new one lately? All it takes is a faulty connection and, well, as you can see, it ain't pretty."

Tish shook her head. "It's not new. Someone did this on purpose."

"Like I said, ain't up to me." He plopped his hat back on his head, then pointed to a small fire safe on the curb. "Oh and that there was inside."

She nodded, unable to muster even a thank you.

He started to walk away, reaching into an inside shirt pocket as he went. Tish knew that reach. She followed him to the other side of the truck where she found him, cigarette low in the webbing of his fingers, other hand poised on a lighter.

"Mind if I bum one?" she asked.

He humphed a one-syllable laugh and studied her with a look so direct she averted her gaze. "I can usually spot a smoker a mile away. Didn't see this one comin' though."

He handed her a smoke, lit it.

"Learned the necessity of nicotine in Iraq." After a long, slow drag.

"'Nuf said."

A shadow of dread clouded the corner of Tish's eye—it ebbed and flowed, intensified and eased, but it was always there. As she stared at the smoldering rubble, she swallowed against the memories, and the burnt wood smell that now defined sadness and loss, the place where Turtle House had been.

Where *was* Elyse? Now dread scrambled forward, reporting front and center, blacking out the vision of the life she once knew.

After a few more puffs, she circled back around the truck, regretfully dropped the half-finished cigarette onto the gravel and ground it with her boot.

She expected another lecture about the dangers of smoking and was thankful when Dylan merely touched her arm, said nothing.

Sheer exhaustion claimed her. She'd run twenty miles with a thirty-pound pack, scaled walls and slogged through muck as thick as cement in basic training. But this—the biting smell of her past in ruins—had turned her to jelly.

"So far these jagoffs have been one step ahead of us," he said, hand still on her arm. "Why don't we try and take the lead by getting into your mom's head?"

"I wouldn't even know where to start." Oddly, the only two things that came to mind about her mom were her impressive upper body strength and weird habit of squirting spray cheese into her mouth when she was stressed. Mother-daughter chit-chats about boys and clothes weren't exactly par for the course in the Duchene household. She'd had more of a bond with her Dad. Though he died when she was only thirteen, he had always been the first person she wanted to share news with, good or bad. But there had been a barrier between her and her mother as long as Tish could remember, built on a foundation of Elyse's need for perfection and fortified by Tish's need to breathe.

During her mental tantrum, Dylan remained stock-still.

"I think we should go back to Crestwood and see if we can dig up a combination to this fire safe. What's inside probably has nothing to do with my mom's disappearance, but it's all we have right now."

"You're right," Dylan said. "We don't have many other options. Let's just keep an eye out for Crestwood's finest. I still have no desire to get dragged into their investigation."

"Agreed."

She surveyed the lake. Clouds hung low and full over the water, like whipped topping. A sweet contrast to the bitter taste in her mouth.

Neighbors had been driving and walking by, gawking, snapping photos on their phones. A few stopped to ask questions, eying her with pity. Now, a man in a blue Chevy pulled up and got out.

"Leticia Duchene?"

He was in his mid-forties, gray at the temples, a diplomat. Tish wasn't sure why that popped into her head, but it did. At first, she thought he was someone she knew from the army. An officer? A trainer? But he called her Leticia.

She forced a half-smile. "Yes?"

"I haven't seen you in years. The last time was before you graduated. You were seventeen or eighteen, maybe?"

She squinted and scrolled back the clock. The little white church on Champagne Avenue. They attended every week during the summer when she was a kid. Elyse and Luke stopped going, but Tish continued with Liv's family long afterwards. This man was the one who organized a fundraiser for Liv's mom after heart surgery kept her out of work for months. Ethan Aiello.

Dylan extended his hand, introduced himself.

"I know how much the house meant to your family." Ethan looked over his shoulder at the lake spread out like a blue porcelain tray. "Surprised I've never seen you in the Olympics the way you swam from one end to the other." His face paled. "And Liv . . ."

There was something about the way he spoke her friend's name, with an extra note of affection.

A knot swelled in Tish's stomach.

"I uh . . ." Ethan cleared his throat. "I heard what happened in Iraq. And it . . ."

He didn't need to finish for Tish to know what came next . . . *was her fault.* After high school, Liv had wanted to be a teacher, and Tish convinced her that a stint in the army was her ticket to college. In Iraq, Tish had done her best to keep Liv out of harm's way, giving pep talks when the heat and dust and death nearly suffocated them both. She saw the glint of the gun now as she did that night and the memory blinded her.

Dylan, cupping her shoulder, brought her back. Ethan handed her a business card. "Will you call me some time? About Liv."

She glanced at the card, Ethan Aiello, Aiello Graphic Design. He'd always been kind to them, praying Liv through those awkward, confusing teen years. Making time for her. She shoved the card in her pocket. "I will."

He walked away, head bowed, without a backward glance.

"What was that all about?" Dylan asked.

She started for the car, steeling herself against the past and donning her armor to battle the present. "Nothing I'm prepared to deal with right now."

⚜ EIGHTEEN ⚜

The Night Before, Saturday, April 5th

ELYSE propped her head against the cool glass and watched cumulous clouds fade into a dark sky. The Brit aimed the gun her way, resting it on his knee as he sat in the back seat next to her. He scooted over and pulled at her sleeve, indicating he wanted her to lie down. She complied. What else could she do?

They were listening to a radio show where the FCC bleeped out every third or fourth word between eruptions of canned laughter. Smoker was driving, tapping ashes out his window, interjecting constricted chuckles that ended in congested coughs. The Brit leaned forward. "This banger has satellite. Perhaps we could find something that won't make Darwin cringe."

"Got no idea who's Darwin or why he'd give a shit, but whatever blows yer skirt up."

The Brit supplied the channel number and Smoker scrolled to a talk show Elyse had listened to from time to time. They were discussing the importance of reducing one's carbon footprint, and she could only imagine how this highbrow banter must soar high over Smoker's head.

As they exited the highway, her thoughts began to circle and she grew short of breath. Her insides quaked at what these goons might do to her son. She wished she'd been able to call RJ. He could have picked up Luke and ferreted him away.

Of course, RJ would have had to use some acrobatic sales tactics to convince Luke to leave the house, but he had a whole warehouse of persuasive techniques. Tires crackled over a stone driveway. The car rolled to a stop. They ushered her out, doors slamming in rapid succession.

Elyse inhaled a deep lungful of air. The familiar scent of pitch pine mixed with a fresh water fishy smell that wafted up from the shoreline induced a flood of memories. Good memories. Memories she clung to now.

Waves lapped quietly at the shore, at odds with the thundering in her head. From the corner of her eye, she spotted something down on the dock. There, at the end of the pier, was the silhouette of a figure lying on his back gazing at the sky heavy with stars. He raised his arms, thumbs together, index fingers pointing, creating a frame. It was how Luke took mental snapshots of constellations. A chill filtered through Elyse as her chin began to wobble and fresh tears burned her eyes. She didn't want him to see her like this, with her hands zip-tied and a gun pointed at her. "Stay put," she murmured inside her head, trying desperately to teleport the message to her son. Her murmurs turned into prayers and she prayed like she'd never prayed before, bargaining, making promises, if only God would spare him.

She could give them what they wanted now, but then she'd have no way of stopping the clinical trial if Avimaxx really was flawed. She couldn't have that on her head. And worse, once she gave up the flash drive what was to keep them from killing her and her kids? All she could do was stall.

The Brit yanked her toward him. "Let's get this over with." He pulled a set of keys from his pocket, her keys. "Which one?"

Elyse pursed her lips, narrowed her eyes.

"Gotta key right here." Smoker retrieved a sledgehammer from the trunk and moved toward the front deck.

"Wait," she said. "You don't need that." She notched her chin toward the keypad. "If you let me go, I'll open the front door."

"Lady, you're all kinds a crazy. That there's the back door." Smoker swung the sledgehammer like a pendulum.

"No, the front door on a lake house is the one on the lake side."

Elyse schooled him as gently as she could, resisting the urge to tell him exactly where he fit on the bell curve.

Smoker scrutinized her. "You think you're better than us, don't ya?"

"We don't have time to measure who's higher on the social ladder. Put in the code." The Brit.

Elyse raised her zipped hands and awkwardly punched in the last four-digit code she could remember. Nothing. What was that update Luke had sent her? She tried another option. Smoker was still swinging the sledgehammer low, growing impatient. As her fingers fumbled over the pad again, Smoker pushed her aside and let loose on the sidelight. He reached through the gaping hole and unlocked the door.

They stormed through the house, hollering as they upended furniture, leveled a chess board, and scattered knickknacks from a shelf. When the Brit pulled the monopoly set from the bookcase, scattering the pieces to the floor, a ring of grief encircled Elyse and held tight. She imagined Tish and her dad huddled over the handmade pieces, laughter floating through the air. Frank's time with Tish seemed absolutely effortless, while Elyse struggled for even the smallest victory with her.

"Now you wanna tell us what you did wit the flash drive?" Smoker spat out as the Brit held the gun to her temple. He pocketed the firearm and began thumbing through a copy of "Architectural Digest" pausing on a two-page spread of a Malibu beach home Elyse had always admired. "You're a smart lady." He slapped the pages shut. "So give us what we've asked for, or we'll have to go to Plan C."

Smoker raised his hand, obviously intending to backhand her, but the Brit caught his wrist. She felt a modicum of relief but wondered how long these two prey-stalking animals could beat down what came naturally to them.

Smoker wrenched his arm away, turned his attention to a small pine desk, and started raking through it. "Where's yer kid? Isn't he a retard or something?"

Heat flashed through her. She wanted to stab his tongue with something sharp and rip it right out of his mouth. "What kind of mother would I be to let my retarded son live alone?" Saying the word made her throat burn. Through the bay window, she willed the multitude of stars to keep her son busy while these cretins pawed through their things.

And she prayed for a chance to tell Luke, to tell them all, she was sorry.

~ NINETEEN ~

Sunday Night, April 5th

DRIVING under a bruise-colored sky with this woman, a woman who had every right to be broken and battered, Dylan had never felt more inadequate. One man dead. Elyse missing, and someone torched her house. Two of Saycor's head honchos were targets. Two of the three amigos. *So that means either amigo tres is soon to be adios or he's enemigo: the enemy.* At least Dylan hadn't said this last part out loud. Tish would think she'd hitched her wagon to a lunatic.

His truck rattled beneath them. Another sharp-toothed reminder of the state of things. "We won't make it to Crestwood in this."

"You need a new truck."

Tell me something I don't know. "We're gonna have to stop and borrow Finn's car."

Tish slumped, resigned, zombie-like against the window. Dylan longed for something to say to bring her back to the land of the undead, but anything that came to mind sounded clichéd and trivial.

An hour later, they pulled into Finn's driveway. A beater was parked at the curb, even more pathetic looking than his, if that was possible. Body covered with Bondo, passenger door held shut with a coat hanger.

Rose had a truck? He'd almost forgotten his long-lost *mother* had returned.

The cherry on his freakin' sundae.

They were all in the living room. Finn, Bianca, Rose, and Kate. And this guy, standing too close to Kate, with a hand planted on her shoulder like it belonged there. Scrawny, with a goatee that looked more like a dirt smudge, his hound dog eyes and skin spackled with acne elicited a moment of pity. But something else bracketed that pity, something Dylan couldn't quite define.

"This is Kate's ... Rusty," Bianca said, and Dylan felt his insides quake and then fall. Kate's biological father. The fangs on this situation bit him squarely in the ass.

Finn was Kate's dad.

Dylan coaxed Kate from Rusty's grasp. "Uncle Dill sure could use a Katie-bug hug." Spoken too loud with too much emphasis on "Uncle." Forget the "blood is thicker than water" bullshit. He'd lay down his life for this little girl. That's what mattered.

"Like I wuz sayin'." Rusty now. "Been clean for six months, outta da joint and ain't never goin' back 'ere again. My P.O. says—"

"Katie," Finn interrupted. "Why don't you take Grandma Rose to see your five-leaf clover?"

"That's all right, Finn. We can always look at it later," Rose said.

Was she actually that dense? Or simply that nosey and selfish? "Nope. *Now* is the right time."

Kate latched onto Rose's hand as if she'd been hoping for any excuse to leave the room. "And Kate," Finn hollered after them, "make sure she reads the newspaper article too."

"Think I'll join them," Tish said.

As he watched them go, Dylan's mind spiraled back to the first time he'd heard of Rusty Doyle ... as a suspect in the murder of Kate's mom, Lisette. This miscreant wasn't getting anywhere near Kate.

Rusty rolled his eyes. "Ain't no such thing as a five-leaf clover."

"They're almost impossible to find," Dylan said, adding, "but you'll have a better chance of finding one than—"

Finn interposed himself between them. "I think it would be very confusing for her, to have you pop in and out of her life."

"Ain't said nothing 'bout that," Rusty said. "I wanna be ... I am

"... her daddy."

"We all want what's best for Kate. She's been through so much," Bianca said.

"We adopted her," Finn ground out. "You signed the paperwork."

"Signed 'at paper under dew-rust."

It's *duress*, genius. This guy was either getting advice from some washed-up lawyer, or they showed reruns of "Law and Order" in the joint.

Rusty shifted from one foot to the other. A boyish move at odds with hands clenched into fists, hands that had thrown a few punches in the prison yard. "Fer cryin' in da sink. Her momma was kilt. She needs her daddy furill."

Bianca released an audible sigh at the reminder of the nightmare they'd all miraculously survived. "You should leave, and I think we should have a conversation with Kate before you visit again. Next time, call first."

"Daddies don't hafta call." As he said the words, Kate returned, sandwiched between Rose and Tish. She went straight to Finn, slid her hand in his.

Good girl, Katie-bug, Dylan thought.

Rusty stretched out his arms. "Junna give yer daddy some sugar? Kimm'awn." Kate shied away, but he pulled her into an awkward embrace. "Shy. Likya mamma was."

Kate was anything but shy. She was more than likely scared of being swept away by this persona non-grata whose only achievement in life was standing rigidly in his arms.

Rusty sauntered out and a pained silence suffocated the room.

The fact that he was gone and Kate was still here should have been reassuring, but somehow it wasn't. Dylan knew what he needed to do: broadcast support, even though his gut was churning. Infecting everyone with his own paranoia would serve no purpose. He stared at the wall, trying to figure out what to say before making eye contact with Finn and Bianca. "Let's all take a deep breath here. We'll talk later, but unfortunately, we have to go." He glanced at Tish who nodded her agreement.

Bianca was chewing the inside of her cheek, looking as if she would shred to confetti if she allowed herself to relax. Finn braced her from behind as they exchanged good-byes.

Dylan and Tish were almost out the door when he remembered. "Mind if I borrow the 300? Truck's out of commission."

"When is that dumpster you call a ride in commission?"

"The keys?"

Finn slid them from his pocket, tossed them to Dylan. "Needs gas."

"Thanks man, I owe ya."

Finn walked him to the door. "Let me get my stuff out of it."

Outside, Finn slapped his hand on the Chrysler's hood, blew out a breath. "He can't get her back, can he?"

"He'll have to get through the Tierny boys first." Their Dad, Mack, materialized, fighting his way through Dylan's repressed feelings. Mack, who they'd joined in his steadfast belief that Tierny men were ramparts against the rest of the world. Together they were impenetrable.

"No small feat."

"Besides, that low life will get caught up in something else, and you won't hear from him again."

"Hope so, man."

Tish's hand was splayed across her chest in a gesture so gentle it made Dylan's throat hurt. When she saw him looking, she slid her hand to her hip and said, "We better go."

Helen's voice drifted over the hedge of boxwoods dividing the properties. "Hey you two. Don't leave. I'll be right there."

Great.

On the surface, Dylan was all "glad to see you, Helen, we should talk," but deep down he was already walking away. There was no time to fill her in on all the particulars and then wait for her to add her latest consultation with her cards, a high priestess, or whatever.

"Any news on Elyse?"

"Not yet," Tish said.

"I promise we'll call when we have something," Dylan said with more frustration than he intended.

"Since you're here, Helen," Finn said. "We have a favor to ask."

"Anything for my favorite neighbors."

"Mind if Dylan parks his truck in your extra bay for a day or so? Rose is getting a rental car and I'll be issuing myself a ticket if we have to park one of our vehicles in the street after hours."

Helen hesitated as if regretting she'd opened the door to "anything."

"If that's a problem . . ." Finn started.

"We can put it in your garage, out of sight," Dylan finished. "You wouldn't want the neighbors to think you've fallen on hard times."

Helen puckered her lips, blew raspberries. "You know I don't give a flip about what people think. Leave it in the driveway. Let them wonder about who I've taken up with now."

"They probably won't wonder long with Stanley looking out the window in his boxer shorts," Tish said with a laugh. "You might need to go help him find his pants."

"Well, I have had some practice in that department," Helen said as she trotted off.

Finn eyed Dylan suspiciously. "You're not actually going to pour more money into that hunk of junk, are you?"

"That *hunk of junk* has seen me through some rough terrain." He glanced back at Finn's house, imagined their mother, putting on a mothering show to beat all shows. "But it's time to move on. I'll let Durwood drool over the parts."

Finn nodded, clapped him on the back.

Dylan grabbed the fire safe from Turtle House out of the truck, dropped it into the backseat of the 300, and they climbed in.

Thankfully, Tish seemed no more in the mood to chat than he was and neither said a word. When they hit the light at Laurel and Maple, Dylan called Durwood. "Know you just got the thing rolling again, but I've been thinking, and I'm finally ready to retire her. Pick 'er up when you can. At Finn's neighbor's. The yellow house."

"Sure thing." Durwood gushed like he'd won the lottery. "But I'm jammed up over here. Can it simmer?"

"It'll be simmering at Helen's."

As he drove through streets he'd known his whole life, watching the setting sun dress the tree line in an amber sheath, Dylan kept returning to Rusty, his mind stumbling over the implications. After a stretch of silence, Tish voiced thoughts in the same vein. "What do you make of all that business back at the house?"

He thought for a moment, echoed the words he'd heard her speak only a day ago, "Nothing I'm prepared to deal with right now."

≪ TWENTY ≫

TISH could see Dylan puzzling through things, thumb almost rubbing his forehead raw. He hadn't said a word since they left Finn's house after the encounter with Kate's biological father.

As the stillness hung like a thick, wet blanket, she pitched a few innocuous questions. "You've lived in Riley's Peak your whole life?" "Yeah." "Small town. I bet you know everyone." "Not really." The back and forth reminded her of some tune she could almost name, but not quite, and they rode on in silence.

They neared RJ and Elyse's house, and Tish prepared to watch Dylan in an encore performance, unceremoniously breaking in the back door like the night they'd found RJ, but when they arrived, a red Scion FR-S in the driveway sidetracked her attention.

The history with the owner of this car started an internal time bomb ticking. Her stomach curled.

"Who's here?" Dylan asked.

Tish felt herself balk at the question, or maybe the answer she'd need to supply. "Annabeth. RJ's sister."

Time unraveled to a Fourth of July party before RJ and Elyse had even started dating. Annabeth was there, complaining about being passed over once again for a promotion at the marketing firm she'd been at for less than a year. "That girl's only talent is knowing when to play the race card," she'd griped as she peeled the label off her hard lemonade, letting the strips float to the grass.

Annabeth was filled to overflowing with bitterness toward

anyone different, anyone who pierced the bubble of her narrow-minded world. And in Annabeth-land everyone owed her.

They piled from the car, and Dylan reached for the fire safe.

"I'd rather bring that in later," Tish said. "Not in the mood to field Annabeth's questions, and if she thinks something in here could benefit her, there will be plenty of questions."

Tish shoved the front door open, steeling herself against the inevitable storm and was met instead with an amber glow cast from the setting sun, lighting the foyer the way RJ had loved. Twilight had been his favorite time, and he often said all he needed to close the day was Elyse, a cocktail, and his hot tub. In that order. The memory evoked a twist of melancholy. Her mom had someone in her life who had put her first, but any joy that brought spiraled away at the sight of Annabeth making her way down the winding staircase. A black suit was draped over one arm, and her blonde hair was cut in a fashionable bob. A split second of mutual recognition followed by seismic aftershocks of hatred. Previous encounters flashed, and a heaviness weighed on Tish. Was that Elyse's scarf slung around Annabeth's self-righteous neck? The sun mellowed and retreated from its slant through the windows as if a ravenous cloud had swallowed it whole.

Tish steadied herself. "I'm sorry about your brother. He—"

"RJ should have never gotten involved with your mother. There's something very suspicious about all of this. She hasn't even called."

Suspicious didn't even begin to describe it. The open questions about RJ's death could fill the pages of *Crime and Punishment* and the lack of a follow-up phone call from Elyse would barely warrant a footnote. Did Annabeth even give a damn? Did she care about the circumstances that lead to her brother's death? Or was she merely miffed because she was finally going to have to grow up and learn how to manage her own life? Tish wanted to bare her teeth and snarl back. Instead, she took the high road, a road Annabeth would never be able to find, even with the latest GPS. "I'm afraid she can't. And she doesn't know what happened yet. It's complicated."

Annabeth pinned her shoulders back, thrust out her chest. Never self-conscious about her size. In fact, she flaunted her voluminous figure and used it to her advantage, always the dominant personality in the room. A woman who liked to push others aside to be first in line. The same way she had last summer. When they'd upgraded their front door lockset, RJ only had three keys made, and Annabeth swooped in to get hers even before Elyse got one. Me first.

Now Annabeth donned a pair of sunglasses, purely for show given the time of day. A diamond bracelet flashed on her wrist. None of her ex's would have given her such a strand of rocks. It was more like something RJ would have given Elyse.

"I noticed the mutt is gone." Annabeth moved closer in a smug "upper hand" move and the blend of spice and fruit tones in her perfume made Tish's eyes water. "Never understood why RJ complicated his life so much," she continued.

By taking in a stray? "Nutmeg is with a friend."

"We'll do our best not to *complicate* things for you." Dylan chimed in with a thin layer of sarcasm. "We're just here to have a look around."

Annabeth exhaled a sharp, exaggerated breath through her nose. "Not without a warrant."

Dark thoughts moved slothfully through the recesses of Tish's mind. Thoughts about giving this woman a well-deserved push, maybe a punch, and watching her topple to the floor. Instead, Tish lashed out with a simple statement of truth. "I don't need a warrant. This is my mother's house, too."

Annabeth pulled her lips back into a down-turned, mock smile. Her toothy overbite reminded Tish of a neighing mule. She transferred RJ's suit to her other arm and dug a phone from the large bag slung over her shoulder. "Actually, it's not. And with one phone call I can have you banned from the property."

If there was any truth to what Annabeth was saying, maybe Elyse's name wasn't even on the deed. Tish wouldn't be surprised if they'd never gotten around to adding it. Either way, classic Annabeth. Using. Taking. Getting people to side with her as she pointed out, "One of these things is not like the others; one of these things doesn't belong."

From the corner of her eye, Tish could see Dylan leafing through books in the library as Annabeth broached the subject

Tish had been dreading. "I don't suppose you're coming to the funeral?"

Under normal circumstances, nothing could prevent her from being there. But this situation wasn't even in the same zip code as normal. "I'd like to but—"

"Just as well. It's only going to be family." Annabeth's brow pinched. She swung her gaze in Dylan's direction. "Please tell your boyfriend to stop snooping."

"He's not—"

"I'm looking for a good read." He selected a thick red hardback from the shelf, examined the spine. "Here's one. 'How to Unclench Your Ass and Open Your Mind.'" He offered the book to Annabeth, and she huffed and looked away.

Tish almost cheered at the small victory until her eyes fell to the suit in Annabeth's grasp. "Where . . . are his shoes?" Her voice rose a little before it caught.

Annabeth lifted her chin, sniffed. "He really won't need them, will he?" Spoken with chilling indifference.

RJ always wore shoes. They often teased him about wearing them on the beach, flip-flops in the shower, slippers around the house. Always something on his feet. A thought came to her that was so slick it squeaked: The only place he didn't wear shoes was in the hot tub.

Tish opened the coat closet and spotted a pair of Brooks running shoes. They'd have to do. She scooped them up and pressed them into Annabeth. As Annabeth stumbled to keep her balance, the weird vibe in the room spiked. Arguing over whether or not a dead man needs to wear shoes to his own funeral was the epitome of strange. And she couldn't help but feel she knew him better than his own sister did. He'd want something on his feet.

She counted a dozen marble floor tiles before returning her attention to Annabeth. "When was the last time you saw him?"

Annabeth glared. "Are you interrogating me?"

"Do we need to?"

"It's been . . . a while. Happy?"

"Care to elaborate on *a while?*" Dylan asked. "Maybe, I dunno, be ninety percent less vague."

Annabeth's phone rang, and she altered her tone, adding a touch of saccharin. She listened to the response on the other end and the forced sweetness drained from her voice. "Is he okay? . . . Tell him mommy will be right there."

She ended the call, sat down on the steps and punched in another contact. "The school says they think Price broke his arm in the locker room. What's a broken arm worth these days?"

Tish and Dylan stood by, baffled.

"Well, you should. You're my attorney." She clicked off, pulled herself to her feet, and stood there juggling designer suit, phone, purse and sneakers. After lobbing the shoes into a corner, she scurried out the door.

Through the window, they watched her race down the walkway, Elyse's scarf flapping behind her, the bulging bag bouncing against her hip. Packed with more of Elyse's things? Tish kicked herself for not confronting her about what else she might have taken. Annabeth jumped into the car and screeched from the driveway, taking the corner with a squeal.

"What's her deal?" Dylan asked

Tish shook her head. How to explain.

"RJ had been in a long-term relationship with a woman named Carol before he and my mom got together." Tish brushed her bangs aside, moved them back. "It took RJ about two months to ask Elyse out. It took a lot less time for them to become exclusive."

"Some take the scenic route; some go from zero to hero in a blink."

Tish teetered briefly on the underlayment of his words. "Anyway, RJ's family . . . let's just say they didn't hold back their feelings, but the objections with the most teeth came from Annabeth."

"From what little I know about Elyse, I can't imagine her taking them seriously."

"She's been down that road before, my dad was white, so she'd grown accustomed to the stares, the judgment. Once, my mom overheard Annabeth tell RJ that Elyse was a 'downgrade' from Carol. When you compare the two women, it doesn't add up. Elyse was top of her class in med school. Carol dropped out of college. Elyse keeps herself fit. Carol prefers to let gravity take its course. Not that I put much emphasis on looks, but my mother is an exotic beauty, and Carol, well Carol isn't. I met her once. Don't mean to be harsh, but she was a snooze all the way around. None of those comparisons painted Elyse as a downgrade. Far from it. But Annabeth didn't care about those things, she only cared about one thing. Elyse is chocolate, Carol vanilla."

Tish was shocked she'd shared so much. She barely knew the man. What was it about Dylan that made her want to open up?

"A real case of head buried deep."

Tish laughed. "It doesn't get more real. Or more deep."

Dylan slid the back of his hand down her arm. "I feel sorry for her."

His touch told her that Annabeth had it all wrong. His touch relayed his own appreciation for what RJ's sister could never understand. "I don't want to talk about her."

Dylan guided Tish into the kitchen. "Looks like there might be something we could use here."

He pointed to a framed chalkboard with an intricately hand-painted border. Tish had given it to Elyse for Christmas and was surprised to see it. So many gifts went unused.

Tish read through the notes scrawled in various colors of chalk. Dental appointment. Two weeks past. Chiropractor. Dated for tomorrow. Should she call and say her mom wouldn't be coming? Pick up dry cleaning. A note in RJ's scrawl, "Kiss RJ at least once an hour" twisted and wrung her heart out like one of those old-fashioned mops. K9 COUTURE. Annabeth's comment about Nutmeg resurfaced. Why would she be so unfeeling about a pet who'd meant so much to her brother? In the bottom right corner in her mom's precise, squared off print: FS@TC4224.

She stared at the code, trying to make sense of it. She remembered looking at her mom's calendar as a kid. Numbers and letters in a random pattern. Elyse's shorthand. These numbers looked familiar though. FS@TC4224. Of course, the address in Savannah.

TC for Turtle Cove. Tish laughed.

"Inside joke?" Dylan asked.

She was already brushing past him. "Mom finally threw me a bone."

After retrieving the safe from the car, she went back inside, and Dylan moved an oversized flower arrangement from the foyer table to make room for it.

The day her mom had stashed the fire safe in a cut-out section of drywall behind a mirror, she'd said, "In case RJ and I are abducted by aliens." In other words, "So Annabeth can't get her greedy mitts on it."

Annabeth's overblown self-confidence and sense of entitlement stumped Tish. What fed it? Three failed marriages. A handful of dead end jobs. Unemployed more than not. Always depending on the generosity of others. A puffed-up leach.

Tish punched in the code, 4224, and jiggled the handle. Nothing. She tried again. Still no movement. She slapped the top. "Seriously!"

"Maybe she mixed up the numbers."

Tish tried reordering them with the same nails on a chalkboard results. She pressed her eyes shut. Shook her head. Every time she thought she was close to finding an answer, another big ass roadblock rolled into her path.

But Dylan just stood there, shining that high-beam smile, amped, on its way to triumphant; his springboard for launching military cracks, gone. Replaced by this flirtatious grin seasoned with a sprinkling of arousal. A grin that stirred delight in Tish despite the circumstances.

"Point me to the office," he said.

"The office?"

"Trust me."

She'd never been good at that. Trusting someone else to take charge.

"Okay." She gave him a firm, but tender shove. "But only if you wipe that grin off your face."

In the office, her heart constricted as she envisioned Elyse at her desk, RJ in the chair by the window, both buried in their work, but still somehow connected.

Dylan opened the bottom desk drawer, pulled out a hanging file and emptied the contents. They returned to the kitchen, and he stripped off the paper folder leaving the thin metal hanger. He bent it and slid it in the top right corner of the fire safe. As he did, he punched in the numbers 1, 2, 3, 4 and the safe clicked open.

"Unbelievable," Tish said. "Safe cracking?"

"Watched a lot of Youtube between jobs."

Tish's eyes landed on a stack of folded papers in the safe. She carefully opened the first one. Her parents' marriage certificate. The next one was Luke's birth certificate followed by her own. Honor rolls. Savings bonds. The deed to Turtle House. The house that no longer existed.

At the bottom of the safe, a sheath of yellowed tissue paper. Tish found herself in a white-noise vacuum. A golf ball lodged in her throat. She pulled back the tissue and picked through her raw emotions to find words. "Luke knows all the constellations from the Big Dipper to the more obscure ones like Limax. A limax is a slug, by the way. Guess at some point they must have run out of names."

Dylan's expression morphed to a smile, then contemplation, and then eagerness to know more. This man had an arsenal of looks that telegraphed how much he cared. And that's why Tish suspected she found herself wanting to share the long version of this story, not just the cliff notes.

"My dad taught Luke how to make a telescope." Tish glided her fingers over it. "It took them six years to perfect the lens on this."

Dylan reached for the cylinder, the size and shape of a small clarinet, pressed it to his eye. "It must have some powerful magnification."

"It does, but Dad always said its ability to gather light is even more important than that."

Dylan nodded and handed it back to her.

"After my dad passed away, Luke begged mom to put it somewhere for safe keeping. I'd forgotten all about it."

There was something else in the safe. A certificate with NASA sprawled across the top with four stars stamped beneath it. Her hand flew to her mouth, as she pressed her eyes shut, remembering. A single fresh tear scrolled down her cheek, and she passed the paper to Dylan.

"Somewhere in the north sky, billions of light years away, there are four stars named Frank, Elyse, Luke, and Leticia. Dad bought them the year before he died, a gift for all of us, but he gave the certificate to Luke, calling him, 'Keeper of the Stars.'"

A pulsing pain webbed its way from her core to her extremities and back. Dylan wrapped his arms around her as she rested her cheek on his chest. The steady cadence of his heartbeat lulled her, and she lifted her face to his. With a feather touch he ran a finger under her chin, pressed a kiss to her mouth. A kiss filled with equal measures of empathy and healing. A kiss that surpassed any she'd ever experienced. It was like trying to compare a flute solo to a thirty-two piece orchestra. She'd had tender and sweet. A soft cadence. Even rough at times. Now this was different, almost a religious experience, coursing through her entire being, melding body and soul. The kind of kiss that makes a believer out of you. She needed an escape hatch from the intimacy, the . . . she didn't even know how to label it.

All she knew was that as their lips moved in a sweet dance, the shackles of her circumstances untangled and drifted away.

⋦ TWENTY-ONE ⋧

Two Nights Earlier, Friday, April 3rd

RJ'S Friday night alone had become more crowded than a Tokyo subway station. Philip, then Annabeth, then a neighbor asking about a lost cat, then the pizza delivery kid. At last, quiet. He stepped back into the hot tub and stood there for a moment, letting the bubbles caress his calves. He had the perfect buzz going, limbs relaxed, thoughts weightless. Thank you, Macallan. His stomach was full. Thank you, Pizza La Bella. And for once he had nothing pressing to do, nowhere to be. He and Elyse would make up, and making up meant sweaty, sticky sex followed by a snuggling finale and all night spooning session. Yeah, he was man enough to admit he liked to cuddle.

If Philip knew anything about Clark Newman, he didn't let on. RJ and Elyse agreed it was best not to share anything until he'd worked out the final details. Did he feel guilty? Sure as shit, but ultimately he had to do what was best for his future. Their future.

Dropping to the recessed seat, he pressed his lower back against the pulsating jets and recalled the first time he saw her. The determined set of her jaw, the intelligence in her eyes. And of course, that body. Curves for days, legs for miles. Elyse was everything and he thanked God, Buddha, and Allah every day for bringing her into his life.

A hand clamped his shoulder. He glanced up and offered a

slow, inebriated grin. "You're back." He continued to babble, his lips moving but he wasn't even sure what he was saying.

All at once he was shoved underwater. He grabbed for the sides of the tub. But his arms were thick windmills, scissoring through the air, thrashing, flailing. What the . . . Tilting his head back, he rallied to the surface, snatched a breath before he was forced under again. And again. And the weaker he got, the more he questioned why this was happening. He watched his words transform to bubbles. Choking now, panic reigned. Cursing streaked through his head while his lungs filled with water. All he could hear was a muted sputtering noise, and he was hyperaware of the relentless pressure holding him just below the surface, keeping him from the air he craved. If only . . . his palm found the tile bench seat. He thrust himself upward. Gasped for air, but he'd already swallowed too much water. He tried to scream, but was forced below again.

As his chest burned white hot, he realized, this was it. His fantasy future disintegrated, and Elyse filled his mind's eye.

~ TWENTY-TWO ~

Monday, April 6th

DYLAN pushed open the heavy glass door marked Saycor Corporate Headquarters and waved Tish in. She increased her pace to squeeze ahead of him with just enough sway to accentuate that amazing rearview.

He admired for a beat, then caught up in two strides. Last night they'd gone back to his place after leaving Crestwood and barely exchanged a word before disappearing into separate rooms. The kiss at RJ's after their encounter with Annabeth had meant nothing.

And the way she came to him the night before. He was the distraction du jour. No one could relate more. In his lowest moments, diversion had been his middle name.

"Wonder how many heads Philip had to step on to get here," he said, dragging his thoughts back where they belonged.

"You don't like successful people?"

"It's not about success. These drug companies prey on vulnerability. Think about it. When you're sick, it's not like you have a choice. Like, nah, doc, think I'll pass on the meds and hope for the best." He stabbed at the elevator button. "And they're all in bed with each other, too. There's nothing keeping the medical world in check."

"Oh, so the FDA and the World Health Organization are make-believe?"

"You mean government puppets with lobbyist puppet masters?"

The elevator doors slid open on the tenth floor. "This industry has helped far too many people to say it's all bad."

"Guess we're at one of those agree to disagree impasses." The whole system seemed rigged, the eligibility stuff, the insurance stuff, it all rolled together to a big headache for anyone who drew the short straw in the health department.

They entered the executive suite guarded by a receptionist with a blinding smile. In two blinks, Dylan saw through it; behind that eager mug lurked a worker bee, bored beyond belief.

The space was ultra-modern. Sleek fixtures and chairs that offered torture rather than comfort. How did people work in places like this?

"May I help you?" The sweet-tart said, adjusting her headset around hair drawn back into a thick ponytail.

"We're here to see Philip Kelrich," Tish said.

The receptionist glanced at her computer. "He's not in. Do you have an appointment?"

A spray of crumbs decorated her purple blouse, and Dylan imagined her picking at a muffin all morning instead of dealing with the stack of mail on her desk.

"Mind if we wait?" Tish asked.

"Sure, whatever. But I can't promise you when he'll be back, or if."

"I noticed on the way in that the café has bear claws the size of my head," Dylan said. "I could always grab one of those to pass the time."

"They're epic," she said, finding the silver charm around her neck and dragging it up and down its chain. Deep dimples bracketed her mouth like two crescent moons. "I'll let you know if I can find out when Mr. Kelrich is going to be back."

Dylan peered around until his eyes landed on a notepad on her desk. "Thank you . . . Mae."

"How do you know my name?"

He motioned to the pad.

"How do you know it's not the month?"

"Because it's April. And that's not how you spell the month."

"Maybe I'm a creative speller . . . and I plan ahead."

Now she was flirting. She wanted this banal conversation to go on and on.

The office phone jangled and when she answered, Tish and Dylan dropped awkwardly into bowl-shaped chairs circling a black coffee table. He pulled out his phone, scrolled through missed calls and text messages. Helen again, asking for an update. He dashed off a quick, "Still working on some leads."

That was a stretch. They'd come here to sniff things out, see how Philip and others reacted to their presence. Like a hawk who screeches to entice chipmunks to peek out of their holes to see what all the ruckus is about. They'd make just enough noise to see who squirmed. And with any luck a game of whack-a-mole would follow.

After a few moments, Mae took another call, speaking quietly at first before her volume ratcheted.

"Girl! You've missed alla drama up here. This past week has been like some show on Bravo." She paused, adjusted her headset and played with her long, straight hank of ponytail. "Remember the deli guy? The one with the nice . . . eyes?" Giggle. "Anyway, he stomps in here demanding to see the boss." Air quotes. "I know, right? Yelling . . . at *me*! He's on a big rant, maybe high or whatever, and I start to tune him out, but he says something about one of the meds, I think." Her voice dropped to a stage whisper. "I know, right? Then on his way out, he smashes that huge statue in the corner. Glass was *everywhere*. Somebody said it cost over twenty thousand dollars. So security takes him away. Then last Friday, Mr. Kelrich and Ms. Duchene get into this sick shouting match. *Atomic* blowout." The ponytail fiddle again. "Oh, and, Mr. Corman drowned in his pool or hot tub or something!" A pause. "Yeah, he was nice, and I thought it was weird that I didn't hear from you. Didn't you get my texts? I still can't believe it." She noticed the crumbs on her chest, wiped them off in two swishes. "I know, right? Call me when you get back. Think I found the *perfect* wedding dress." She reclined in her swivel chair with a can't-believe-I'm-getting-married grin.

Despite the frivolous way she flitted from talking about a dead man one second to her wedding dress the next, Dylan was thankful for the gabby receptionist whose voice could carry to Guam and back. As he leaned over to say something to Tish, a woman walked in. Six feet tall if she was an inch. A split so big between her two front teeth that another tooth had been added. Three teeth front and center.

Mae pointed to Dylan and Tish. "These people are here to see Mr. Kelrich."

The Amazon woman barely masked her irritation behind her odd, enchanting look.

"I'm Gretchen Nuwenhys, Mr. Kelrich's executive assistant. How may we help you?" Spoken with a wave of the wrist as though flanked by a hologram of the man himself.

"Is there a place we could talk privately?" Dylan asked, glancing at Mae whose ear was cocked in their direction, practically salivating for more water cooler fodder. "It's about RJ Corman."

Gretchen checked the watch on her wrist. Undoubtedly one of those smart ones. "My office would be fine. I have five minutes."

They followed her long-legged stride. It would take some doing to keep up with this one. Type A on steroids. And he'd bet his boots she could do long division in her head.

She closed the door, motioned for them to sit. "RJ was a great guy." She looked away, shook her head. "So . . . specifically, what do you need?"

"I should tell you, Elyse is my mom," Tish said.

"That's where I've seen you! Pictures in her office. How's she coping?"

"She's missing," Dylan said.

Surprise arched Gretchen's eyebrows as if she'd just been told their next staff meeting would be held on the moon. "Missing?"

"She wasn't expected in the office today?" Dylan asked.

Gretchen shook the mouse on her desk, punched a few keys and let her gaze wander over the screen. "I don't always know. I work for the three of them . . . but Elyse prefers to manage her own calendar."

She offered Tish an expression of condolence. "Hold on a

second." She picked up her office phone. "Do you show Elyse checking in and out Friday? ... What time? ... " She eased the handset back on its cradle. "She arrived Friday at 7:00 a.m. and left at 5:00."

Another glance at her watch. "Excuse me. I'll be right back. The break room is across the hall. Help yourself to coffee or anything."

She sprang from her chair and zipped out the door.

Dylan scanned the room for cameras. Force of habit. The air vents in the ceiling would be the perfect hiding spot. The average schmuck had no clue he was being watched. Big Brother and all that. The devices weren't easy to spot, no flashing lights, but sometimes if you caught the angle just right ... bingo, a reflection off the lens. Saycor had eyes, maybe ears too.

He scouted the room to see what the camera might see. A framed diploma. A brass statue of the Eiffel Tower. *The Seven Habits of Highly Effective People, Strengths Based Leadership, Lean In: Women, Work, and the Will to Lead* placed purposefully on bookshelves. Gretchen's wallet and mini tablet open to what looked like Philip's schedule were the only things on her desk. A trusting soul, and based on her reading material, one with ambitions. He decided a peek at the calendar would tell him more than any conversation with Philip, but the electronic eyes were watching.

Time for a diversion.

He maneuvered into position to block Peeping Tom's view from the ceiling vent.

"What're you doing?" Tish asked.

Good question, and one he'd asked himself countless times. Here he was invading someone's privacy, someone who might very well be innocent, wrong place, wrong time. But that was his job. Spying on people for cash. Did the times he busted the legitimately guilty make up for the times he crossed the line into the personal territory of someone whose only offense was marrying the wrong person or having the wrong boss?

He crushed Tish into his arms and drew close to her ear. "We're being watched. Play along." Leaning into the desk, he slid Gretchen's tablet into his palm. Then he laid a kiss on Tish, might as well make it convincing. She played along, and then some, making it next to impossible to concentrate on the computer screen.

◆ TWENTY-THREE ◆

The Day Elyse Went Missing, Friday, April 3rd

AFTER Vanessa left, Elyse took a few minutes back in her office to rein in her scattered thoughts. Things had gone too far and were escalating by the minute. No time to reason this out, no scientific method to garner the best possible outcome. Just act. After copying everything she could about the clinical trial and the audio file from Vanessa's phone onto a flash drive, she stashed it in her pocket. Her eyes made a slow revolution around the room. Was there anything here heavy enough to smash this phone to pieces. A huge brick would do the job. She pictured herself hefting it over her head and coming down hard with everything she had. The feeling of satisfaction that would bring gave her a start. She shoved the phone in her purse. She'd figure out what to do with it later.

She stormed into Philip's office. "This needs to stop."

"What?" He swiveled in his chair, steepled his fingers, and drew them to his mouth.

She wanted to swipe that plastic look of confusion right off his face. "I don't know why I let you talk me into this."

Philip rose and crossed the room to grasp her shoulders. "Let the lawyers do their job."

She threw up her hands, knocking his away. "You don't get it, do you?"

"We both knew there might be fallout. C'mon, Elyse. There's

always fallout."

"Fallout? Someone didn't get a headache or an oily bowel movement, Philip. We may have *killed* a man." The thought made her knees weak. "We should have never moved him into the other group after the fact. We should have immediately stopped the trial. What if there is something wrong with Avimaxx? What if someone *else* dies?"

"You tell me. You're the CMO."

"Did you really just say that?"

"You blow the whistle now and you know what will happen, right?"

A slow burn meandered through her. She knew how the courts loved to make an example of people like them. People like her. She'd become that person in an instant. She'd become that person in a weak moment riddled with poor judgment. And now Vanessa had them by the balls. Elyse could share that tidbit with Philip if he wasn't so busy pointing an accusing finger in her direction. At least the mousy little blackmailer's recording proved his involvement. And if Elyse was going down, he sure as hell was going down with her.

"I need your word, Elyse. I need to know that you're with me on this."

With you? I wish I'd never laid eyes on you. "Fine, Philip. Status quo it is."

She fled Philip's office with him trailing behind her, convinced he would have followed her into the parking garage if the doors to the executive suite hadn't burst open and in stepped the Chairman of the Board, Xavier Dibolt.

He pressed his triple chin to his chest. "Elyse."

"Xavier." Now was her chance. She could blurt everything out in one painful sentence. But she wasn't quite ready to throw her life away, and she wasn't even certain who she could trust anymore. Xavier wrapped an arm around Philip's shoulder and led him down the hallway. "Just the man I need to see."

"We'll finish our meeting as soon as I'm done, Elyse," Philip called out without turning.

She walk-trotted to her car, checking to make sure she wasn't being followed. *Unlock it. Get in. Ignore seat belt sign.* She screeched from the parking garage with no idea where she was headed, but putting a few miles between herself and this brewing catastrophe might help her figure out what to do next.

⚜ TWENTY-FOUR ⚜

Monday, April 6th

TISH had run countless operations in the army, without apprehension, without a moment of hesitation about the potential negative outcome. She'd been conditioned, like one of Pavlov's dogs. So why now, snooping through Gretchen's office, did she feel like she had her finger looped through the grenade pin, ready to lob it, but with nowhere to hide?

She rolled her lips inward, still wet from Dylan's kiss. A kiss that transcended every emotion, made her lose focus. Reasons she should have stopped him lined up like planets on an astronomer's chart. She studied the chiseled angles of his face, the way the mole dotting his lower lip resembled a fleck of chocolate cake batter. Maybe devil's food. Tish liked raw cake batter. Liked to lick it off . . . *Damn girl, keep it G-rated.*

"Get anything?" she mouthed, feeling silly for the cloak and dagger routine. But maybe Philip really wasn't above spying on his employees.

He nodded and slipped the tablet back onto the desk.

"Well?" She looked at him expectantly.

He advanced, drew her close.

"If your brain was half as large as your ego you'd be Einstein reincarnated. There was nothing suggestive about the way I looked at you."

Dylan's lips were so close to hers she could almost taste them. "Anything suggestive about this?"

Tish shook him off—literally. Figuratively was a different animal. But he was merely a P.I. helping her find her mother. So why did she kept picturing their bodies moving together like well-oiled gears? She needed to retreat and fast. After she found Elyse, after she dealt with whatever was going on, she'd fly back to Savannah where she belonged and never see Dylan again.

"Us, together, the other night, was . . . a mistake," she said.

He stared at her for a long moment, shrugged. "It happens."

It happens? Two letters away from shit happens. And this sort of stuff didn't just happen to her. She headed for the door. He followed. The executive suite was quiet and removed from the commoners, and she imagined Philip, RJ, even her mother, in their inner sanctum, fingers perpetually on the pulse of company activity.

Her mom's office was locked.

Dylan tried RJ's, directly across the hall, shook his head.

Back to Gretchen's office.

"What's this all about?" A voice from behind turned Tish's blood to ice as she spun around to face the man who was quite possibly responsible for her mother's disappearance and RJ's death.

"Nice to see you again, Philip." Dylan picked up a pen. "I was leaving Gretchen my number." He eased onto the credenza, grinning like a fool.

While he was clearly loving this, she felt like she'd walked straight into a swarm of bees, holding her breath, waiting for the sting.

"Or, would that be a problem for you?"

"Why would it be?" Philip gave him a once over. "It's none of my business what Gretchen does on her personal time, but I highly doubt she'd be interested."

"We came for something,"—Tish scrambled for an excuse—"for RJ's memorial service. Since mom isn't here, we thought you might be able to help. RJ deserves a proper send off. Don't you think?"

Philip straightened the knot in his tie. "Of course. I'll have Gretchen put together some ideas."

He escorted them to the reception area and promptly disappeared back into the executive catacombs as if he'd risk catching something if he stayed a minute longer.

"Asshole," Dylan said, barely above a whisper.

Mae laughed. Her hearing was good despite her inability to gauge the decibels in her own voice.

Dylan planted a hand on her desk. "I'm still thinking about that bear-claw, but since it's almost noon, how are their sandwiches?"

Mae was staring at him, practically sucking the color off her bottom lip. "They're even better now that Seth—we used to call him the cold cut Nazi, two slices of meat and one cheese on every sandwich, not a smidge more—got fired." She finger-combed her ponytail, flipping it across her shoulder and then back.

"Everyone knows it's all about the meat," Dylan said.

"I thought it was all about the bass," Mae said, snatching the opportunity for repartee before she leaned in conspiratorially. "I think he got fired on account of his big throw down with Mr. Kelrich. But you didn't hear that from me." Her mouth pulled to the side. "Anyway, tell them I sent you."

"Will do," Dylan said, making his way to the elevator.

Tish rerouted him to the stairwell. Hoofing ten flights down might just deliver some much-needed oxygen to her gray matter. Once they'd reached the first landing, she said, "Seth must have a pretty big beef with Saycor to smash a twenty thousand dollar statue."

Dylan angled a grin, a fisherman casting his line. "Makes sense. The beef part, anyway. For a cold cut Nazi."

She couldn't hold back a smile.

"Twenty G's for a statue?" Dylan let out a slow whistle. "Now I know why meds cost an arm and a kidney. Add Sandwich Boy to the list. And Philip's calendar on Gretchen's tablet said IU with TD, Friday night at 9:00 p.m."

"Well, that's helpful."

"Patience, little one. I scrolled through Philip's contacts, and lucky for you, I have a near photographic memory. Write these down."

She pulled up NOTES on her phone. "Shoot."

"Teresa Dorfman. Terrance Dixon. Tom Dalloway."

"Any chance you remembered numbers?"

"I'm good, but not that good."

They stepped into the lobby. "Let's grab something to eat and see if we can find out what the sandwich Nazi and Philip were arguing about."

"Sounds like a plan. Two birds, one stone."

The synchronicity to their partnership was starting to feel comfortable, and half of her was ready to embrace it, but the other half wanted to cut and run. She had to remind herself, yet again, this was business. Maybe she needed a cadence. She'd been practically chanting them in her sleep for the last eight years. "I don't know but I've been told. A guy like this will steal your soul." She chuckled at the thought.

"What?" Dylan asked.

"Nothing."

"You should laugh more often. It suits you."

I don't know but I've been told. A guy like this will steal your soul.

Tish felt the old familiar flush climb from her neck to her cheeks. She hustled past Dylan, nearly knocking over a woman as she powered into Cut Above Sandwiches.

At the counter, she inquired about Seth.

"Lives with his mom over on Hubbard. The white house on the corner," a lanky kid with a helmet of dreadlocks replied. "He's not in trouble, is he? Maybe I shouldn't have told you that."

⚘ TWENTY-FIVE ⚘

DYLAN assured the kid at the sandwich shop that Seth wasn't in trouble. Probing a bit more had revealed that Seth Jackson was two years out of high school and working two jobs. Saving for college. Other than that, all they learned was that he "has a rad music playlist."

Why would a hard-working kid like that throw a temper tantrum that got him canned?

On Seth's porch, a welcome mat sat crumpled at the door, warding, uninviting. Like so many cop calls Dylan had answered where something had gone horribly wrong inside. A crack in the plastic doorbell cover exposed twisted wiring and a small light underneath. He knocked instead.

A middle-aged woman with a tapered knob of a chin opened the door.

"Is this the Jackson residence?" Tish asked.

"Yeah, but whatever you're selling, I'm not buying." She motioned to the NO SOLICITING sign above the doorbell.

Dylan grabbed the door before she could slam it, gave her his most charming smile. "We're not selling anything. Just hoping we could talk to Seth."

On the other side of the room, a young man stretched out on the couch, shirtless, pants barely holding on to his skinny hips, arm thrown over his forehead.

He rolled onto his side to face the wall.

"May we come in?" Tish tried. "It's about Saycor. Don't worry, we don't work there."

A look of disgust crossed the woman's face, but she stepped back, offering just enough room for them to squeeze by. Contrary to the exterior, the inside didn't evoke the same domestic-dispute-in-progress vibe. A desk in the corner was heaped with what looked like pre-school paraphernalia: popsicle stick houses, Lego people, and rainbow pinwheels. A framed cross-stitch overhead announced, "Bless my trucker out on the road, keep him safe with every load" in fancy red script surrounded by hearts. A sad-looking peace lily and two mixed-flower arrangements littered the coffee table, and Dylan wondered briefly who died.

They introduced themselves and Dylan noted the woman's Minnesota Vikings jersey as she supplied her name accompanied by a limp handshake.

Outside the kitchen window, three red-headed girls jumped on a mini trampoline in the backyard.

"Had high hopes for Treadwell. Guess there's always next year," Dylan said.

Her brows scrunched in confusion. He pointed to her shirt.

The dark bags under her eyes seemed to fade as she ran a hand absently down the sleeve of the Vikings' jersey. "My husband was the Minnesota fan. I rooted for the Packers, the Browns and the Chiefs. Guess I got tired of moving. I don't have much hope for the Steelers—"

"They don't need our life story, Mom," Seth said, still facing the wall.

"Is your husband . . ." Tish started.

Sandra rolled her lips inward, closed her eyes. "He passed last week."

"Why say passed. It's not like he took a test," Seth said, and his words carried heat. "He died."

Dylan had been about Seth's age when they almost lost his dad to a heart attack, and he remembered being furious at everything and everyone, from the doctors to Uncle Sam who'd delivered a tax bill the day before.

Tish craned her head around Sandra and spoke through the

dust-moted air to include Seth. "I'm extremely sorry for your loss."

"We've heard all the apologies," he grumbled.

"Clay was always trying to find something better for us, you know?" Sandra dabbed at the corners of her eyes with the ample Vikings sleeve. "He worried most about the triplets. How we'd be able to afford college for three at once. Three cars. Three weddings." She looked out the sliding glass doors, shook her head.

"My father," Tish started, "well he was like a father to me, passed away recently too, and to complicate matters, my mother is missing. They both work for Saycor. We heard you spoke with Philip Kelrich last week, Seth."

He bolted upright and swung his legs to a sitting position. "My dad died because of one of their effin' drugs. They said he took a heart attack, but wasn't nothin' wrong with his heart before they gave him that crap."

Shock registered on Tish's face, and in Dylan's gut. "Do you know which drug?"

"All I know is that they needed people to test it on, so he could get it for free."

"Avimaxx?" Dylan asked.

Seth's eyes burned wild, canine. "Yeah, that's it. Then that drug pusher in a suit thought they could throw money at us." He barked a hollow laugh. "Money's not gonna bring him back. What a bunch of hypocrites. They can all go to hell!"

His mother raised her hands in a placating gesture. "Remember what the lawyer said—"

"I don't give a damn about the lawyer," Seth gritted out.

Sandra grimaced, but seemed to realize Seth might be right. What difference could lawyers make now when they'd lost everything? "That CEO, the one who always looks down his nose, he offered some college money for my girls. Said he did it for lots of *unfortunate* kids." Her anger rose. "We're barely scraping by, but we're no charity cases."

"That Frankenstein treated my dad like some guinea pig."

"Why did Mr. Jackson sign up for the trial?" Tish asked softly.

Sandra wrung her hands, seemed fascinated by them. "He was anxious alla time. He drove a truck and sometimes went weeks between runs. I work when I can, but with the girls . . ." Her eyes glistened as she watched the three bouncing redheads.

Seth shot to his feet and paced now in an exhibition of some of that same anxiety that must have plagued his dad. The anxiety Clay had hoped Avimaxx would alleviate.

"You need to go," Sandra said. "All we want now is to be left alone."

Dylan reached into his wallet, handed her his business card. "If there's anything we can do."

Fresh tears trailed her cheeks, and a deep sadness suffocated the room. They made their way to the door, and Sandra closed and latched it behind them.

"Of course they're angry," Dylan said once they were in the car. "His dad volunteered for a drug trial and wound up dead."

"People have heart attacks every day."

"But given RJ's death and Elyse's disappearance . . ."

Tish was silent, and Dylan wondered what she was thinking. That her mother was more than a pawn in all this? He chose his next words carefully, "Once we know Elyse's side—"

"Not sure when that'll happen, or if." Her face coiled to a knot as she pulled her phone from her purse. "Let's follow up on those names we got from Gretchen's tablet." She tapped at her screen and jotted notes.

Teresa Dorfman turned out to be an investment banker who'd been out of the country for the past three weeks. Tom Dalloway's hatred for Philip was palpable. "I haven't seen that back stabber in two years. But hey, hope he's on my hockey team in hell."

That left Terrance Dixon, architect. "Yes, I know Philip," he said after a thick pause. "Who did you say this was?"

"I'm his cousin. . .on his mother's side, second cousin. I. . . well, the family, is worried about him so we're reaching out to his friends."

"Worried?"

"We think he's working too hard. That's the Kelrich way, but we want to make sure he's not overdoing it. So I guess we're planning kind of an intervention."

"I'm still not clear why you're calling me," Terrance said.

"Have you seen him recently?"

"Friday night, but . . . listen, I think you need to talk to him directly. Please don't call me again."

Tish hung up, shook her head. "Well, that got us a big fat zero."

"Not entirely," Dylan said. "That accent is hot."

"I didn't realize, I mean I didn't mean to . . ."

"As hard as you try, you'll never be able to bury your southern roots." He offered her a smile. "But at any rate, good work. Depending on the time they were together you might have just uncovered Philip's alibi."

Her phone buzzed and she answered, leaving it on speaker.

"Luke saw Turtle House," Robert said, from what sounded like a cave. "I mean what's left of it. He's not good."

The news seemed to hit Tish hard, knocking her off her small perch of stability, but in a matter of seconds she rallied, recovered from the sucker punch, her body poised as if ready for take-off. And Dylan knew what he needed to do.

He had to get her to Lake Anaba.

✦ TWENTY-SIX ✦

A Week Earlier, Monday, March 30th

ELYSE watched as Sandra Jackson pulled at a little string dangling from the button on her blouse. She wanted to grab a pair of scissors and help the poor woman out, but she'd undoubtedly fidget with something else. Philip had invited Sandra and her sullen teenage boy, Seth, to the office in hopes of talking them out of filing a lawsuit. And they were just naïve enough to show up without a lawyer. Saycor's in house pit bull, Dennis Thorpe, would have their heads on a double platter if he knew about the meeting.

Philip leaned toward Seth and Sandra, as if the gesture could infuse a bit of warmth, could traverse his barge-sized desk. Always the biggest and best for Philip Kelrich. "Again, we're sorry for your loss." Spoken like a televangelist, smooth as butter. "Of course, Mr. Jackson was given the placebo."

The blank look in Sandra's eyes, the utter desperation, transported Elyse back to her own dizzying carousel of numbness, fear, anger, and self-pity after her husband, Frank, died.

Elyse stepped from behind the desk, drew close to the Jacksons as if in solidarity. They were in the same club, after all. She settled her hand on Sandra's shoulder.

Sandra shifted away.

"As a company, we pride ourselves on putting people first," Philip continued. "And in that spirit we'd like to help your family out."

"We'd appreciate that, Mr. Kelrich." Seth, pinch-hitting for his silent mother. "The triplets are still runts and I'd—"

"I know it's a long way off." Philip kept his attention trained on Sandra. "But we'd like to offer a scholarship for your daughters to Penn State. Contingent on acceptance of course, but it will ease your burden, not having to stress about paying three tuitions at once. For the first year at least."

Sandra, who'd been worrying the strap of her purse, looked up. "College? They're only four."

"Never too soon to start planning." Philip took an envelope from a drawer and slid it across desk to Seth. "For you."

Seth stared at it for a long moment, slack jawed, but expectant. He glimpsed inside and pulled to his feet in slow motion. "You effin' kidding me? A thousand dollars for community college?" He ceremoniously ripped the envelope into pieces, and flung them at Philip. "Didya think that'd 'bout cover it?" He hoisted Sandra from her chair. "We are so outta here."

Elyse wanted to step in and tell Philip to find a pulse in that shriveled up heart of his, but she kept quiet. Maybe after all this was over she could find a way to really help the Jackson's.

A grudging downward curve bent Philip's lips. "You'd be wise to reconsider, Seth. Our lawyers are talking countersuit." The air around them hummed with tension. "I'm trying to discourage it, but I can't guarantee—"

"What the hell does that mean?"

"Your lawsuit has no merit. When you lose—and you will—we'll make sure you pay for any court costs, which will likely be more than you'd make even after a lifetime working in that little panini dive."

Seth launched toward Philip, but Elyse placed herself between them. "Maybe it's better if we talk another time," she said.

Philip said nothing. Sandra tugged gently on Seth's shirt. His features pinched, making him look like one of those angry troll dolls. "Nothin' else to talk about."

Philip snapped to his feet, rounded his mammoth desk, and followed them into the reception area. Offering a wary incline of his head, he admonished, "You're making a big mistake."

Seth spun around and closed the space between them until they were nose to nose. "No, you are, jagoff. And do not call us again."

On his way out the door, he swiped a hand across a marble pedestal, sending a priceless Chihuly sculpture crashing to the floor.

✧ TWENTY-SEVEN ✧

Monday, April 6th

WHEN Luke was thirteen and his dog, Vector, was hit by a car, his response had been tearless, bordering on callous. Tish remembered his exact words: "Vector's no match for a station wagon. We should get a St. Bernard. A St. Bernard has better odds against a station wagon."

But losing his dad and then his dog in the span of six months had proven to be too much. Once Luke buried Vector in the backyard, he had started acting strange, stranger than usual. He ate copious amounts of spinach, and little else, resulting in a thirty pound weight loss and a ticket to the ER. The diagnosis—hyperoxaluria, oxalate rich foods, kidney stones, renal failure—had made Tish's brain hurt. Their mom explained what it all meant, but matching definitions with those menacing terms made it that much worse. Seeing her brother in the hospital bed, his parchment-like skin barely containing his jutting bones, brought Tish's resentment to a head. How could her mother have been so focused on her work that she let this happen to Luke? Tish had given her the cold shoulder for months and silently vowed to keep her brother from ever doing that to himself again.

Could she keep that promise when he learned his home had been burned to the ground?

Dylan, possibly sensing her unease, placed a bolstering hand on her arm.

Once they reached Lake Anaba, they piled out of the car and Tish savored the crisp air. Her mood softened as she observed the full afternoon sun glistening through a wall of stately pines. Sand, beach grass, and water as far as the eye could see. Turtle Cove always made her feel better.

She reached into the backseat for the fire safe, and they headed up the flagstone walkway.

The door swung open. It shouldn't have been such a shocker to see Robert in his own house, but his sudden presence made her come unhinged, at least on the inside. She was a loose bag of nerves, and she needed to pull it together. They exchanged greetings, and Dylan fell uncharacteristically quiet.

She took in the space. Robert had done well for himself. In the kitchen, top of the line cabinetry, granite countertops, a backsplash of black and gray Italian tiles. Double ovens. Eight-burner Garland stove. A wine cooler. Any man who knew his way around a kitchen like this would make some woman extremely happy.

The kitchen flowed into a cozy dining area, which opened to a massive great room with vaulted ceilings. Part home theater, part library, and a virtual gamer's paradise.

"I tried, Tish," Robert apologized. "I kept putting him off, but he snuck out and went to the house by himself."

"There's nothing anyone can do when Luke gets something in his head." Burdening her friend with this made her feel about an inch tall. "Where is he?"

"He won't leave the guest room. He won't eat. Head on back. He's not real happy with me at the moment." Tish knew exactly how that felt—the daggered stares, or worse yet, no eye contact at all.

"Good luck," Robert said. "I've got a conference call so I'll be in the office if you need me."

He left, looking more than slightly relieved to be off Luke duty, at least for now. Tish and Dylan moved to the back of the house where they found Luke perched on the edge of a perfectly made bed.

The rhythmic thrum of the overhead fan punctuated the silence. Luke didn't move, didn't say a word, as they entered the room.

"I should have told you," Tish said.

Luke narrowed his eyes. "The ants are gone."

"I want you to understand, we can rebuild the house, but we can't rebuild you."

His jaw shifted from side to side. Counting his losses, or engineering his own reconstruction? Tish could never be certain what was in that mind of his.

She needed a way to get through to him. *Please be the right decision.* "I did manage to find something of yours."

He took it, held it for a few seconds, fingering the rumpled paper, possibly analyzing the crackly sound it made. When he got around to opening it, streaks of red spiked above his collar, thunder rolled across his face as he stood and hurled it across the room. It crashed against the wall, barely missing a window.

Wrong decision. She should have known that anything from Turtle House, anything that reminded him of all he'd lost, might elicit this kind of reaction.

Dylan picked up the telescope pieces as Luke fled the room. A broken lens, shards of mirror, a damaged housing. Sieving through the wreckage, he said, "Take a look at this."

Tish, conflicted about whether to run after her brother or give him some time, decided on the latter. Time seemed to be what he needed most right now. Time and space. She looked at Dylan's hand, perplexed, unable to process at first what he was holding.

A flash drive? She snatched it, and they shot through the hall to the kitchen. She woke Robert's laptop from sleep mode, and her fingers stalled on the keyboard. *What are you hiding, mom?* "Mind if I look first?"

Dylan stepped back. "Go ahead."

Scanning the folder names, Tish blew out a sigh of relief. "All work stuff." She didn't know what she'd been thinking, that her mom was caught up in some nefarious dealings—stealing identities or trading body parts on the black market? Elyse's idea of veering from the straight and narrow was sneaking twelve items in a ten items or less lane at the grocery store. But after what had transpired since she arrived at Helen's, Tish wasn't sure if much would surprise her.

She began to open documents and spreadsheets with no clue what she was looking for. Her eyes landed on something called MeetingNotes.m4a. She clicked on it. Nothing.

"It's an audio file," Dylan said. "Try the volume."

She did. Still nothing. "It may be corrupt."

She continued, her eyes growing weary as she scanned through graphs and charts and proposals that might as well be in gibberish.

"Wait," Dylan said. "Go back to that last folder." He pointed to the screen, read the document name. "Clay Jackson Avimaxx CTIII."

"This document has the same name but with a C at the end."

They compared the documents. One indicating Clay Jackson was in the control group for the clinical trial, the other that he'd been given the drug. Otherwise the documents were identical. Tish noted the signature at the bottom of the form. Elyse had always kept meticulous records, saved every card, letter, receipt, and note that came her way. All scanned or filed in her office. But this was different. Tish could feel it. *Oh Mom, what have you done?* A pit the size of Alaska formed in her stomach.

"We assumed Clay Jackson had the drug," Dylan said, "but what if Saycor didn't want that to get out? Something like that could kill a trial, right?"

"From what I know, yeah."

"It looks like they may have switched him into the placebo group to show his death wasn't related to taking Avimaxx."

"I have to talk to Luke again."

She went through the kitchen, slid open the large barn doors leading to the great room, and there he was, hunkered down in a black leather chair.

"When did you see Mom last?"

Her brother was slamming a ping-pong ball off different things in the room—the wall, the bookcase, the base of a hammered pewter lamp—catching it every time. She asked again, now with more urgency. The ball traveled to the ceiling and back to Luke's hand.

"Friday." Flat affect, no eye contact.
The day Elyse went missing.
"What time?" Dylan asked.
"Five forty, post meridian."
"And you're certain it was Friday?"
Luke ignored the question. Of course he was sure.
"What did she say?" Tish asked.

Luke cranked his head, found his next target, and raised the ping-pong ball. She closed her fist around his hand. "What did she say?"

"I need to throw the ball."

Tish loosened her grip. "Luke, this is important."

The ball bounced from the corner of the window trim, and he caught it effortlessly. Tish was growing impatient, an understatement.

Dylan extended his hand. "Mind if I try?"

Her brother's eyes slanted down and to the left. He was considering. Wasn't he? There was no instruction manual for Luke Duchene. He snapped the ball side-armed like a pitcher releasing a nasty sidewinder.

Dylan stretched long to catch it, then lobbed it against a picture frame, snatching it up before it hit the floor. "How about something more challenging?"

"Tennis trophy, 2012."

A grin from Dylan as he aimed for the bookshelf, hit a bowling trophy instead. "Ouch."

Luke shook his head robotically. "Epic fail."

"Mulligan?"

"Green bowl, in and out."

This was getting tedious. Tish hoped Dylan knew what he was doing. But the fact that he was engaging her brother at all was remarkable, a feat in itself.

Dylan bit his thumbnail, sized up his mark. He let loose and the ball careened across the room, into the bowl, out, and he lunged, collapsing onto the carpet. He waved the ball in the air, then tossed it back to Luke. "That counts."

"She never comes Friday afternoon," Luke said, rolling the ball up and down his arm. "She went straight into her bedroom."

To put the flash drive inside the telescope and then in the safe, Tish thought. "Anything else?"

"When she came out, she said she loved me more than life. I highly doubt that. Without her life, what relevance does love have?"

"Luke, please," Tish said through clenched teeth. "I'm more interested in what Mom did while she was at the house."

"She went out on the dock, threw something in the water. You know, I found her visit very odd. And inconvenient. She was acting strange, and I didn't appreciate the interruption. I guess she got the message because she left."

Acting strange was putting it mildly. Tish took a deep gulp, forged ahead. "Mom may have been acting strange, well, because she's in some trouble. We don't know where she is. We really don't know much at all."

Luke tilted his head at an angle as if the words needed to funnel into his ear, into his brain. "Is she with RJ?"

"No." Though it wasn't a lie, there was no triumph in this truth. Only guilt. But she couldn't tell him about RJ, not yet. One disaster at a time.

Luke seemed perturbed. "You don't need to tell me what you don't know. Get back to me when you have some facts." He tossed the ball one final time, caught it, and left the room.

"What would Elyse have thrown in the lake?" Dylan cupped his fist around his chin in a thinking pose, which would seem like an archaic gesture on anyone else. "And what else did she do while she was here?"

Robert entered the kitchen, grabbed a mineral water from the fridge.

"I hate to ask this—" Tish started.

"Don't worry about it. Go do what you need to do," Robert said. "Luke can stay here for as long as necessary."

A kaleidoscope of feelings sawed through her. Eagerness to find out more about the flash drive. Guilt for racking up favors she could never repay. Even envy at Dylan's handling of her brother in a way she never could.

A call on Dylan's phone eclipsed them all. "Slow down, slow

down. She's what?"

✥ TWENTY-EIGHT ✥

DYLAN shook his head, stalled in a nightmare. "Kate's missing?"

"I went into her room to check on her, and she was gone." The underlayment of primal fear in his brother's voice pulsated. Finn had stared down murderers, fought off drug-dealers, and gang-bangers, but that was nothing compared to this.

"I'm on my way."

Tish reached for her purse. "I'll go with you."

"You should probably sit tight in case your mom shows up. Promise you'll wait for me to get back before you do anything else." Dylan jumped in the car and jammed it in reverse.

He heard her yell, "hope she's okay," watched her grow small in the rearview mirror as he raced toward Riley's Peak.

Streetlights blinked by as Dylan's gut constricted. Kate's young life had already been a windstorm of change. People coming and going, dragging her from one house to the next. Bianca and Finn were finally giving her the stability she needed and then that sawed-off felon, Doyle, showed up.

He pulled onto Chalmers. *Shit.* Traffic was crawling at a snail's pace. He leaned out the window, tried to assess the hold-up and saw three cars on the left shoulder, one flashing blue lights. A fender bender. He could almost hear the conversation, see the finger pointing. People seemed to lose a handful of brain cells when you put them behind the wheel, a few handfuls more after a collision.

As he inched along, he imagined Kate slipping farther and

farther away. Every second counted. Needing an opening, he motioned to the car next to him. *I know you see me, jagoff.* Dylan slowed to catch the eye of the woman in the next car. He pitched his brightest smile with an extra helping of desperation, and she finally let him pull in front of her. Zipping onto the right shoulder, he motored past the line of cars.

Minutes later, he pulled into Finn's driveway.

Bianca was waiting at the front door. "It's Rusty. I just know it."

Dylan let her cry on his shoulder. Felt the familiar pang of having this woman in his arms. "Tell me everything."

"We went to check on her, we let her read for a few extra minutes, but when we went back . . . she was . . . the door was wide open. She'd never leave, never by herself, it was dark . . . and what if—"

Dylan placed steadying hands on her arms. "Slow down, Bee."

He hadn't called her that in a while, not since he thought they'd be together forever. But now, as it fell from his lips, it sounded too intimate.

"I could have sworn I locked all the doors." She reached for a tissue. "What if he somehow broke in? Isn't that what Rusty went to jail for the last time? Breaking and entering? If anything happens to her, I'll never forgive myself."

Dread zipped through Dylan. "Where's Finn?"

"He found out Rusty was at Lost until Gus stopped serving him."

Lost, the seediest bar in town. Dylan had spent many a night there, knew the kind of low-life creeps that made the dive their primary residence.

"Rose has my car," Bianca said. "She's searching around town."

An onslaught of fresh tears streamed as Nutmeg crawled forward. The dog eased onto her haunches and slipped her nose under Bianca's hand. "Rusty must have come in the back door." She corked her fist firmly on her mouth, and ran down the hall. She threw the coverlet off the bed and moved pillows aside. "Her stuffed iguana's not here. She must have it."

"Anything else missing?"

Bianca rifled through drawers, checked under the bed, swung

the closet door open and pushed things aside. "I'm not certain. What if he hides her somewhere? She's only a little girl, and with his past, and—"

"Bianca, stop."

"I know, it does no good to obsess, but I'm out of my mind with worry."

"Can someone come and stay with you? What about Maris?"

"She's still in Peru taking care of her mom."

"Helen?"

"At Stanley's." Bianca tried for a laugh. "But not sure I could handle her third eye chakra right now." She pinned him with a look that shredded his heart.

"We'll find Kate. I promise."

Another promise with the world riding on it. But he'd be damned if he didn't keep this one.

⊰ TWENTY-NINE ⊱

AFTER Dylan left, Tish tried to dam the undercurrent threatening to ooze through the fissures of her façade. She crossed the floor and eased onto a barstool in Robert's kitchen.

He was wiping the sink down with a sponge. "Are you okay?"

When she'd looked into Kate's eyes, it had been clear she knew more than most kids her age, more than many people period. Tish breathed a prayer that she'd get the chance to get to know her better. Was the universe conspiring against her? Sucking up people she cared about one by one? She tried to answer him, but could scarcely manage a nod.

"How about a glass of wine?" he asked.

What she wanted was a smoke, but she tamped down the craving and besides, she was out of cigarettes with no plans to buy more. Maybe the self-denial was a fitting sentence. She could have prevented this disaster with Luke. She could have handled all of it better. "Yes," she said on a long exhale.

Robert uncorked a bottle of Chenin Blanc and poured them each a glass. A series of pans and ingredients appeared on the island, pulled from all corners of the kitchen. A myriad of spices lined up alongside a row of prep bowls.

Here she was on the set for *Top Chef*, and she'd lost her appetite.

Robert plopped Luke's wooden bowl onto the island, gave it a spin. "I have an idea. I'm going to pull out all the stops and whip up his favorite."

"I don't even know what that is anymore." She propped her chin in her palm. "You're not talking about spinach."

"Don't worry. Spinach is off limits in this house. C'mon, you remember. Think about it."

Possibilities pressed the bruised places in her past as he stood there cool and soothing as a vanilla milkshake. A smile forced its way through her funk. "Oh, right. Crab cake summer. Mustard. No remoulade."

That summer had been particularly hot, and they were all in the lake more than out. She remembered noticing Robert's physique for the first time. Wanting to study him, feeling weird. It confused her. He was her friend, more like a cousin than someone she'd ever consider dating. She and Liv had often joked about it, but Liv made them swear none of them could ever date. Ever. Tish agreed, but she had to admit, the thought had crossed her mind. Robert made her laugh, made her feel safe, and at fifteen was already exhibiting impressive skills in the kitchen.

"Did you know that mustard has been purported to control asthma and can help reduce constipation?" Luke had said, as he slathered the top of his crab cake in Dijon.

"That's gross, Luke," Tish said. "And who says 'purported'? No wonder you don't have any friends."

Elyse glowered at her. "Leticia!"

A look Tish was accustomed to. A neon sign that said her mom derived grave disappointment from one child and complete joy from the other.

A clang brought her back to the present as Robert clamped a lid firmly on a Dutch oven.

"What makes you think he'll eat them now?" Tish asked. For a moment, she envisioned crab cakes stuck like magnets to the crisp white walls. But Luke had never broken so much as a toothpick before he demolished the handcrafted telescope today.

As if on cue, her brother plunged through the kitchen and onto a bench seat in the breakfast nook. Her heart buckled at the sight of him. Stubble darkened his already dark features, and the beginning of a mustache snaked across his upper lip. His face had always been as smooth as polished mahogany, shaving once in the morning, once at night. A regimen from their dad. For a split second, she was almost glad he wasn't here to suffer Elyse's absence or to witness Luke's decline. But then, if he were still alive, would either of those things be happening now? His telescope likely wouldn't have become a hiding place for a flash drive like this was some John le Carré spy novel. Clay Jackson's name was in both the drug and placebo groups. Had Elyse tampered with the clinical trial? Tish knew so little about what her mom did, but she knew the woman was wound even tighter than usual when one of their drugs was in trial.

Each sip brought a new wave of uncertainty. She reached out for Robert, and he stopped whisking. "I appreciate all you've done," she said. He gave her hand a squeeze and returned to cooking.

She scooted in next to Luke, searching for words. Flagging courage, she found what she hoped would be the right thing to say. "I'm not going to tell you things will be okay. Maybe they won't. I won't lie to you. But we will get through this."

A new take on her mom's favorite Robert Schuller quote: "Tough times don't last, tough people do." Tish had always resented the relentless push to face adversity head on. What was wrong with falling apart once in a while? Admitting that sometimes life was too damn hard?

She wasn't going to force her brother to handle more than he could. As soon as he was stable—as stable as possible—she would tell him about RJ too.

Luke took in a breath so deep it threatened to suck the air from the room, then let out an elongated sigh. Resignation? Or maybe he was just inhaling the scent of crab cakes sautéing in garlic and what looked like a pound of butter. Was it only two days ago that she and Dylan were discussing the merits of butter? Time seemed to twist and bend like a funhouse mirror.

Robert placed two large platters on the table—crab cakes with a side of angel hair pasta and grilled romaine. Tish grabbed the wine, refreshed their glasses.

Moment of truth. Luke leaned over his bowl and sniffed, hands resting in his lap. He picked up his fork, tore off a chunk of crab cake and doused it in mustard. Closing his lips around it, he pressed his eyes shut. Summoning taste buds or memories? Though she'd probably never know, Tish liked to think her presence, along with Robert's expertise in the kitchen, were working to stave off a meltdown.

"Crab cake summer, the same summer you flipped the kayak," Robert said.

Tish stabbed a piece of romaine. "I've tried to block that one out."

"Stubborn," Luke said.

Tish swiveled his way. "Me? You're calling *me* stubborn?"

A smile lit his eyes. "Like an ass."

Robert nearly spit his food through a laugh. "You could have asked for help. We all knew about your shoulder."

She wouldn't admit it now, or probably ever, but yeah, she'd been stupidly stubborn about that. So positive the kayak wouldn't flip and when it did, she wasn't about to ask for help from either of them, and she towed the kayak behind her to a small cove. It took an hour to right it, but she muscled through, tearing her rotator cuff even more in the process.

That night they'd made a fire in the outdoor pit and Robert "borrowed" some Kahlua from his parents to spike their hot cocoa. She remembered wishing that time would never end. The memories swirled around her, twisted her insides. She could never go back to those carefree summers.

Luke took a final bite of his crab cake, wiped his mouth with a napkin, and rinsed out his bowl. A perfunctory nod at Robert and then Tish before he retreated to the guest room.

"Let me help clean this up." Tish cleared the table and put dishes in the sink. "I meant to tell you, I ran into Ethan Aiello yesterday. Do you remember him?"

"Name sounds vaguely familiar."

"He was one of the athletic directors at summer camp." She bit her lip. "He mentioned Liv."

Robert instantly stonewalled. She'd tried to talk to him about Liv's death before, but he'd always changed the subject.

"Ethan seemed pretty broken up," Tish continued. "Like there was something more to it."

"Something more to what?" Robert asked after a long pause, his tone bordering on frustration.

Tish almost let it go, but it had been eating at her since she saw Ethan. "It makes me wonder . . . if something happened between them."

"Why would you think that?"

"I remember her spending a lot of time with him, signing up for badminton and other activities he was supervising. I didn't think anything of it at the time, but now, looking back, he did treat her differently."

"I highly doubt there was anything going on. Liv was . . . needy, that's all."

He would know better than anyone. Robert and Liv had been more like siblings than friends. They'd been together since preschool and their families were close. At times, Tish had felt twinges of jealousy about their tight bond, wishing she lived in Turtle Cove year-round and not only during the summer. But then in middle school, something changed between her two best friends.

"Did you guys have a fight or something?"

Robert busied himself clearing the stove, wouldn't look up.

"That summer after sixth grade," she said. "You were both acting different."

"That was twenty years ago, Tish." Robert dropped a pot in the sink with a clank. "Why bring all this up now?" His nostrils flared as anger edged his voice. So rare for him. "You know, maybe that's part of your problem. You're stuck in the past. If you were half as interested in the present, we wouldn't have to stuff your brother with crab cakes to keep him from going off the deep end."

He stormed from the room, leaving Tish still burning from the lashing pain of the truth.

∽ THIRTY ∾

DYLAN walked into Lost, the place he'd sworn off for good, and felt himself go itchy, weightless. He'd had a love/hate relationship with the bottle, simultaneously craving the sensation of being untouchable while dreading being held hostage by his own mind and body. Memories unleashed relentlessly, the very memories he'd tried to drown with alcohol.

With each step across the sticky floor, his pulse stuttered at the thought of getting sucked back into his old life. The smell alone made him want to call his sponsor. But he had to find Rusty. Maybe he'd have better luck than Finn now that he was no longer on the force. Cops in bars prompted a certain silent camaraderie, like any loose lips might sink these losers' ships.

The bar was half-dead, typical for a Monday night. A handful of regulars slouched in their usual spots. But what better place to get lost than in a place called Lost? And not so long ago he was part of the crew keeping the dive afloat. Funny how the mind rolled to sea worthy metaphors in this hole-in-the-wall.

The owner coughed out a wet greeting. "Tierny, ya jackass! Never thought I'd see your ugly mug in here again."

"We can't all be pretty like you, Gus. And you know you missed me." He scanned the dark space. The nautical theme that once seemed charming was now old and sad. A rusted-out anchor clamped to the wall. Grayed and ripped buoys, hanging from unfinished rafters. "Place looks like shit."

Gus was polishing a tumbler with a grimy towel. "I miss your cash. Besides, ya livened up the place." He coughed again, wiped a gob of phlegm from his lip with the towel. "Lemme guess. You're here 'bout the same thing your brother was. He only comes in when he's on *official* business. Sure you two clawed yer way outta the same cha-cha?"

Gus was nothing if not crass.

"He's smarter and better looking, but yup."

"Like I told him. Oh-no where Rusty is. But sit, Jackass." He filled the glass with ice, picked up the nozzle, topped it with coke, and planted it in front of Dylan.

"I can't stay."

"Said oh-no where he is, but that don't mean somebody else here can't help ya."

Dylan plopped down on the stool and it wobbled under his weight. Years ago, Gus had remodeled Lost with the cheapest furnishings possible, everything right down to the seating, and hadn't changed a thing since. It was only a matter of time before the entire place disintegrated.

"Dinkus!" Gus hollered to the other end of the bar. "Git your ass over here."

Only Gus could get away with barking at customers this way. Dylan remembered Dinkus. Bourbon, neat, beer chaser. That's how he remembered all of them, by their vice of choice.

"You know that jackass, Rusty Doyle?" Gus asked as Dinkus dallied over.

Dinkus scratched an overly bushy eyebrow with his thumb, brushed off a barstool next to Dylan, and swung his leg over it. "Yeah, mean wit a dekkacards. Cheats. Whattyagittinat?"

"The P.I. here has some questions. Go ahead, Tierny. I got inventory in the back. You ladies getta know each other." He coughed out a laugh and bowlegged his way through a door marked "Jackasses Keep Out."

Dinkus ran a hand through greasy, steel-gray hair. "Hauscome you showin' up now? Ain't seen ya in a cupple tree years." He crossed his arms, buttoned his lips. He was going to need some persuasion.

CHASING GRAVITY

Dylan leaned across the bar, grabbed a bottle of Jim Beam and two shot glasses. "Time flies, huh?" He slapped a twenty down.

It struck him then, what a cliché he had been, maybe still was. The ex-cop, drowning his demons in the sauce. Drying out, only to be tempted repeatedly by the liquid siren.

Dinkus slammed his drink back. Dylan traced a finger around the other shot. If ever he wanted to jump off the wagon into a vat of this stuff, it was now. "I need to find Doyle."

"Gitdahellaht! That good fer nothin'?"

He could spend time explaining, but telling this drunk about his family's private business felt like the equivalent of telling a hooker your aspirations. "It's a family matter."

"Family." Dinkus guffawed. "Prick's happy as a dog with two tails that somebody else's raisin' his kid. Said he never wanted some brat tyin' him down nohow."

Maybe Rusty didn't really want Kate, but if he didn't have her, where was she? "Did he say where he was headed when he left here tonight?"

The old man pressed his lips together, raised a shoulder. He knew something. The worst possibilities burst forward. Maybe it would be easier to kill these mind pictures by taking this shot. Dylan could almost feel the liquid slide down his throat, warm his limbs and whisk away the haunting images. But even if he could cross over and temporarily blot out this current nightmare, taking a drink would only crank up the old reel to reel in the sorry story of his life. He slid the shot toward Dinkus. "Think hard."

He emptied it. "He's been hangin' out at this one room hole over Pizza N'at."

Come on old man, keep talking. Dylan filled the shot glass again.

Dinkus downed it, wiped his mouth with the back of his sleeve. "Thas all I know."

The dullness in Dinkus' rheumy eyes made Dylan instantly regret shoving shots in front of the poor old man when he should have offered to drive him straight to the next AA meeting. Another day.

In the car, he called Finn. "Any luck?"

"Scoured Rusty's apartment and nothing. Guys a pig. That rat hole should be condemned."

Dylan envisioned Kate in a place like that and the idea amped up his resolve. "I got a lead at Lost, may be a long shot, but I'm checking it out."

"Where? I'll meet you."

"I've got this."

"Dylan, we're talking about Kate here."

If swift justice needed to be dealt, there was no need for both of them to have to pay the consequences. "I got this. Trust me, okay?"

The words transported him back. When they were kids Finn had fallen into an abandoned mine shaft and broken his arm, and Dylan had been his only way out. "I'll save you," he'd said, as his little brother bordered on hysteria. "Trust me."

"I trust you, bro," Finn said now.

"Why don't you check out the trailer park where Kate lived with her grandma?"

"I did. No one has seen Kate since Nadya died, and the neighbors said the same. I've got guys canvassing all over. Other than that, I'm at a loss." Finn's voice fractured. "I'm worried about Bianca."

"Go be with her. I'll call you soon."

As Dylan headed to the north side of town, Kate claimed his every thought. Her delight when she first saw her new swing set. The way she could scale a tree like a cat. Her inquisitiveness. "Do you think all spiders are as smart as Charlotte?" she'd asked after they read one night. "I bet they're like angels. Protecting people. Keeping bad things from happening to them."

Parking in front of Pizza N'at, Dylan took the outside stairway to the apartment two steps at a time. He raised his hand to knock, trying to ignore the nasty smell coming from a half-open garbage bag someone had left sitting by the door. Inside, a voice squeaked as if infused with helium, followed by a squeal. Forget knocking. He burst in, called out for Kate, but the scream turned out to be the hyena laugh of Rusty Doyle's booty call, clad only in bra and skirt that barely covered her assets.

Doyle's drunken features scrambled to register surprise as he growled his objections. "What the cobb?"

The hyena hooted a catcall. "Never had a three-way, but if your friend here wants to play, I'm game." She ran her tongue across her upper lip in slow motion.

Dylan ignored her as he scoped out the place, under the unmade bed, pulling back a shower curtain that served as a closet door, looking under the sink. He ended his search in Rusty's face. "Where's Kate?"

"How my apos ta know?"

The woman plopped back on the couch and took a slug of malt liquor as if this interruption was a commercial break. Like she was accustomed to strange men pawing through her things.

Dylan grabbed Rusty by the collar, yanked him close. "Think it over, Doyle. Pretty sure the joint's still got a cot with your name on it."

Sobriety inched its way into Doyle's expression. "Fer cryin' in da sink. I aint done nothin'. But if my little girl's lost, I wanna help fine 'er."

The comment, rife with sincerity, caught Dylan off guard. On some level, Rusty just might care for Kate. But Dylan would see pigs sailing overhead like shooting stars before he let that waste of skin get near that little girl again.

"You work on sobering up. I'll get back to you." Dylan turned and shot down the steps.

Why was it that people who wanted to be parents and watch their kids grow up, like Clay Jackson, never got the chance? Then you had people like Rusty.

Like Rose.

Ready. Fire. Aim. How had things gotten so screwed up? He dreaded calling Finn to report a big fat zero. He rolled down the window, and the brisk night air breezed through the car. Maybe the cold would bring an idea. Instead, it brought the smell of hogs, the "smellamuny" as his buddy Durwood put it.

Durwood was a fixture in the Peak, the local farmer everyone knew, everyone loved. As handy with a mechanic's wrench as he was a pitchfork. On the left, a cupola reared its proud head majestically above the barn made of wood and stone. In a side lot, the junkers Durwood used for spare parts lay in quiet slumber. And near the house, six wooden cut out angels surrounded a chipboard soldier.

Then it hit like a bolt from the sky.

Kate had set out to find her own guardian angel.

THIRTY-ONE

TISH rolled one response through her head, then another. She was equal parts angry that Robert had kicked her when she was already down, and shamed that he'd verbalized the truth about her inability to stay fully focused on the here and now. They needed to hash this out. As she was getting ready to go track him down, he came walking into the kitchen.

"Hey, Tish. About what I said—"

"In the past."

Robert hesitated before a slow smile spread across his face. "Touché."

Without words they agreed that Luke was their mutual priority, and he was doing surprisingly well. He seemed to like having his sister around, although it was a delicate dance. She played cards with him and kept him company, but also gave him space.

Thoughts rolled to her mom and what Luke had shared about her visit the Friday she disappeared. Elyse had thrown something in the lake. The idea pestered like a pebble in Tish's boot. Maybe she also went in the boathouse and left something behind, something that would help Tish figure out what kind of trouble she'd gotten herself into and more importantly find her.

"I need to go out for a while," she said.

"Want some company?" Robert reached for his jacket.

"I'd rather go by myself."

"With all that's going on—"

She raised a hand to stop him. "One of us survived boot camp . . . " She paused, regrouped. "That's not coming out right. I need this time alone. Please."

Robert placed his jacket back on the hook. "I wish you wouldn't, but is there any point in trying to talk you out of it?"

She wrinkled her nose. "Stubborn ass, remember?"

"How could I forget?" He opened the door for her. "Do you have your phone?"

"Got it." She patted her hip pocket and hurried out before he changed his mind and tagged along.

As she jogged, she worried again about Kate but didn't want to pull a Helen, bugging Dylan for answers. He'd call when he knew something. But what was taking so long? She said another prayer that Kate would be found soon. A prayer that echoed one she'd prayed for her mom over and over since this whole ordeal began.

Cooling down in the driveway, she shuddered with an effort to hold in a sob as she looked past the yellow tape surrounding the house scorched beyond recognition.

She started down the hill, her feet easily finding the recessed grooves in the flagstone steps, avoiding the bumpy spots, the way she'd done since she was a kid. Walking the length of the yard, she paused and ran her hand over the river birch near the shore. The nursery said it would take twenty years of cabling to ensure the four trunks held together but Elyse cut the cord after a year.

Tish stood at the end of the dock. "Mom, what were you doing out here?"

Just inside the boathouse, a large flashlight sat on a wooden table by the door. She flipped it on, swung the beam around. She began moving things aside. She opened old coffee cans stuffed with wooden bobbers and jars full of fishhooks. All normal boathouse stuff. Nothing unusual.

Then a voice stopped her in her tracks. "Find what you're looking for?"

∽ THIRTY-TWO ∾

DYLAN parked Finn's car as an alarm blared on his phone. AMBER ALERT lit the screen followed by the description of a boy and the vehicle he disappeared in. If only they had more information on Kate's disappearance. If someone had seen something. He pulled his jacket up over his mouth and nose and trudged toward the barn. How did anyone get used to the smell?

Durwood limped over, rubbing his thigh. Filthy bib overalls, camo hat tilted to one side, bushy beard that must itch like hell in the summer and be home to any number of hibernating parasites in the winter. "Durn mule, Jebediah, used my leg for kickboxin' practice."

Dylan locked eyes with his old friend. "I'll cut to the chase. I'm here because I think Finn's little girl"—here he started to choke up—"Kate is missing and I believe she might have made her way here. I hope to God she did."

"If she's here, we'll find her."

"I'll check the barn."

"And I'll run over these out buildings with a fine-tooth comb."

Without further exchange, Durwood hobbled away at a surprising speed for his uneven gait.

Dylan pushed through the barn door where the jack-of-all trades tinkered on anything with wheels. Mopeds, riding mowers, even an old hearse. If anyone could bring his truck back from the dead, it was Durwood. He was regular machine whisperer.

"Kate . . . Katie-bug are you in here?"

A noise snagged his attention, and he turned to see a bushy tail scoot into the darkness.

His old heap rested next to a burnt orange beater that made his ride look like the homecoming queen. Searching the bed of his truck, he lifted a tattered blanket exposing a rusted-out hole he should have patched a long time ago. He held his breath as he moved to the front, opened the door, and searched the cab. Empty.

"Katie, honey," he called out, unwilling to admit his hunch held no more substance than the dust-motes around him. "It's okay. Uncle Dill will never let anyone take you. I promise."

Then he saw her. Kate, wedged between two bales of hay, feet stretched out in front of her, clutching her stuffed iguana. She wore one of Bianca's fleece jackets over Bat Girl pajamas and fluffy, purple slippers. "I told you to keep quiet," she scolded the iguana. Then to Dylan, "I looked everywhere for a spider-angel like Charlotte, but I couldn't find one."

Dylan pulled her close, stroked her hair. First he dialed Finn, not wanting his brother to agonize one more second than necessary. "I've got Kate. We're on our way. I'll explain everything when we get there." He gave her a squeeze. "Oh baby. You don't need a spider-angel. You have me, and Mommy and Daddy."

She sniffled. "But they're not. They're not my *real* mommy and daddy."

A hammer blow to Dylan's heart, fast and heavy. "Katie—"

"That's what Mr. Rusty said. He said he's my daddy. But he doesn't take care of me." She paused, reflecting. "It got me thinking. Your mommy and daddy should be the people who take care of you, right? It doesn't matter whose tummy you came out or who your daddy was at the beginning. Real mommies and daddies are the ones who love you."

Her words left Dylan dumbfounded. He pulled her onto his lap, linked pinkies with her. "We're family. That's forever." He stroked her hair. "You came in my truck, didn't you?"

"I didn't think Mr. Durwood would mind me looking for a spider-angel. Don't you think this place looks like Zuckerman's farm? Mr. Durwood was talking to Miss Helen right outside my window so I went out the door and I climbed in the back of the truck and now I'm here."

"You must never leave the house without asking your parents again."

Kate's eyes were so big, so full of remorse. "I won't," she whispered.

"All right then. Now, let's go home. Nutmeg's been worried sick about you."

"You mean Bookmark."

"Bookmark it is."

As they emerged from the barn, they saw Durwood limping toward them, his outline lit like a lantern. Maybe it was the outdoor light, but something about the way it danced across his cap suggested a halo. Dylan's eyes teared.

Kate hung her head. "I'm sorry I went in your truck without asking permission, Mr. Durwood."

Durwood slowly lowered himself to his good knee. "That's all right, Miss Tierny. And you can visit my farm any time. Let's just ask Mom and Pop first, 'kay?"

Their Katie-bug had hitched a ride to the only farm she knew to find her spider-angel. What that little girl had gone through to make sure she wouldn't be taken from her new family.

Dylan carried her to the car, strapped her in the back seat. She looked up at him with wet eyes. "Am I in trouble?"

He leaned in, kissed her forehead. "You gave us all a scare. Promise me you'll never leave again?"

She drew an X across her heart. "Promise."

At the house, Dylan stood back as Finn and Bianca crushed Kate between them. Then he saw Rose, ready to make it a group hug. Why was she even here? Why should she be a part of this celebration?

She put her hand on his shoulder. He stepped away.

"It's past my bedtime," he said, moving toward Kate. "Remember what you promised."

She yawned. "Yup."

They locked pinkies again before he headed for the door.

Rose followed him outside. "Can't you stay for a while?"

He kept walking.

"Dylan!"

He swung around. "Really? You think you can show up after nearly two decades and waltz back into our lives like nothing ever happened?"

In her loose-fitting outfit, all billowy and light, she almost looked like the woman he'd called Mom.

"I didn't exactly abandon you," she said. "You had your father."

Bitterness flavored a burst of laughter. "If that logic helps you sleep at night." He got in the car, rolled down the window. "Speaking of Dad—"

"I found out too late to come to the funeral." Her face twisted to a dramatic mask. Always the actress. "You don't understand, I—"

"Save it." He jammed the car in gear and peeled from the driveway.

That woman irked him. The emotional arm wrestling continued.

He dialed Tish to tell her about Kate. The call went to voice mail, and he left a message. Once he got home, he flipped on the TV, scrolled through channels to TCM. Jimmy Stewart was holding Kim Novak close, kissing her as she struggled to get away. He'd watched *Vertigo* a thousand times, but this scene never failed to bring on a wave of dizziness. His own fear of heights coursed through him like a hemorrhage as Jimmy chased Kim up the stairs of the clock tower and watched her fall to her death. The utter desperation.

On any given day, Dylan could look in the mirror and see the same.

THIRTY-THREE

TISH whirled around to find a man in the doorway. Her hands jerked into position, ready to launch a fist in his solar plexus. Then she saw the gun and wished for the second time since she'd been here, that she hadn't left hers in Savannah. "Who are you?"

"Who I am doesn't matter. What should concern you is why I'm here." Said in an almost refined British accent.

A chill scuttled through her. Her eyes darted left and then right. The heavy flashlight hurled at just the right angle might do some damage.

"Planning to bung that torch at my head, are you?" He sneered. "Best think about what's at stake before you do, luv."

As he spoke, a large man appeared outside the boathouse door, half of his body shrouded in darkness. Another step and she saw a woman's arm in his grip. The sight roared toward Tish like a freight train.

Mom.

Their eyes met, and Tish read a multitude of foreign emotions—I'm scared, I'm sorry, help. Her mother—always in control, never a stray hair or ill-chosen word—needed her now.

"Leave her out of this," Elyse said.

"Shut up," the skinny one barked, his bug-eyes popping.

"Where's Luke, Leticia, what happened—"

The one holding Elyse grabbed her face.

"Luke is safe," Tish blurted. Her emotions gathered to a knot at the sight of her mother's face in his angry mitt, her shackled wrists, the white linen suit soiled and wrinkled.

Bug-eyes aimed the gun at Tish's brow.

"Are you okay, Mom?"

Before Elyse could answer, the hefty one barked, "No more chit-chat." While he was plowing through things on the shelves, knocking them to the floor, Tish noticed Elyse working her thumb back and forth inside the zip-tie.

Be careful, Mom. "What's this about?" Tish asked in a voice too loud and too urgent.

"Your mother has something we need," the gunman said.

The flash drive they'd found in the telescope.

"Let me guess," she said, trying to temper her tone. "Something that made you ransack the house and then when you couldn't find it, burn it down?"

"Wasn't us. Maybe the retard left some candles on or something."

She wanted to lunge at him, but assholes would remain assholes whether you kicked in their teeth or not. And there was also the matter of the gun pointed at her head.

All at once, she envisioned what they might do to Robert's house if they found out that's where she'd hidden the flash drive. Or to Robert. Like she needed another reason to feel guilty for dragging him into this. If she'd brought it, this would be over. But maybe not. Maybe not giving it up was the only thing keeping her mother alive right now. She needed to stall. "I have no idea what you want. But even if there was something at the house it'd be burned to a crisp right now."

Tish was rambling, her mouth talking smack while her brain grappled with the problem at hand: How to get away.

Her cell rang.

Keeping the gun trained on her, Bug-eyes reached for her phone with his other hand. He glared at the screen. "Dylan is going to be disappointed that you're otherwise occupied."

She remained silent as he tossed it to his partner, who slammed it to the ground and stomped on it once, twice, three times.

Bug-eyes cast him an incredulous look, shook his head. "You

can't be bloody serious. There might have been something useful on there. Sometimes I wonder why your mother didn't take one look at you and—"

"Leave my momma out of it." He lowered his head like a bull, ready to charge.

Tish angled toward Elsye, hoping the goons would battle it out, providing a distraction.

Something fell from Elyse's hand. The zip-tie. All at once, strength training and hand to hand combat maneuvers coalesced with what Tish thought was their best chance for survival. She granted Elyse a slight nod, so quick it could have been a nervous tic.

The big one backed off and began picking through the pieces on the floor, trying to fuse parts of a circuit board together as the other one hurled insults.

Tish made a bull run at Bug-eyes. She knocked him sideways, and the gun flew from his hand. A nearby shovel became her weapon, and she walloped him on the head while her mom scrambled for the exit.

The other one was too dumbfounded to react as Tish slammed the door behind them. She snatched the paddle off the wall, shoved it through the door handles. Exchanging a glance with her mother she whispered, "Cannonball."

Elyse flashed a bewildered look but obediently ran behind her out onto the dock, and they leaped into the cold water.

Tish had calculated the odds. It was only a matter of time before the thugs would crash from the boathouse, and though the big guy wouldn't last a yard in a foot race, Bug-eyes seemed to be in decent shape.

Sure enough, they hadn't gone far when two figures emerged shouting obscenities. A shot rang out. Tish yanked Elyse underwater. They shed their shoes and swam for their lives.

When they were out of steam and far enough away, they floated on their backs.

"Where is Luke?" Elyse asked between breaths.

"With Robert."

After a ponderous silence, the second set of questions came, this time about RJ.

Tish tried to keep her teeth from chattering right out of her mouth. "We need to save . . . our breath."

The lie of omission burned her tongue but the truth was, they did need to conserve energy to make it to shore and then sprint to safety. At least the physical part of this scenario had a ring of familiarity.

They'd both competed in triathlons. All that was missing in this one was the bike.

∽ THIRTY-FOUR ∾

DYLAN woke with a fire poker lodged in his temple. Memories of brain splitting hangovers after too many nights lost in handles of gin bobbed to the surface. But this was different. A damn tension headache, or maybe a migraine. He rubbed his eyes, squinted at the clock. 5:00 a.m. He'd actually slept through the night. Grabbing his phone, he checked to see if Tish had returned his call. Nothing.

A thought slivered through him. Tish was with Robert.

Why did the image of her with another man slice at him. Why did the sound of her voice, her southern-fringed words, echo in his mind like an ingrained backbeat?

He guzzled a quart of water, showered and ran through the morning routine he'd neglected since he'd been working this case. Fifty push-ups, fifty pull-ups, fifty tri-dips. Better than nothing.

One more time. Tish's cell went straight to voice mail. Again. He was half-tempted to call Helen and tell her to find another P.I. until that promise he'd made reared its ugly head.

After half a pot of coffee with enough sugar to keep him buzzing through the rest of April, he hopped in the 300. He was going to have to start keeping track of the mileage and charge Helen for all the back and forth. Damn, he was bitter.

Turtle Cove or Crestwood? Before deciding on North or East, he dialed Tish again and got the same slap in the face. No matter. Elyse was his charge, the only reason he'd spent the last seventy-two hours with Tish. He needed to find the woman and put this case behind him. Little Miss "I'm running this operation" could call if she needed him.

East. Toward Crestwood and Philip. Still early enough, he might catch him at home. If not, he'd head to Saycor. Time to pay a visit to Gretchen with the mile-long legs and extra front tooth. Based on his first impression, she wasn't the type who would be content just managing the calendar and making sure the coffee was hot and plentiful for meetings. She might be more involved in day-to-day operations than the average executive assistant.

Philip was stepping into a gold Range Rover as Dylan approached. Was the guy trying to compensate for something with a car the size of an M1 tank?

Bypassing pleasantries, Philip said, "What is it you want?"

"Well, I haven't had breakfast yet."

"I don't have time for your games."

"I just have some questions about Elyse," Dylan said. "We need to find her, right? And find out what happened to RJ?"

"I've already told you what I know."

"How did Clay Jackson die?"

Philip shoved his briefcase into the passenger seat, spent too much time positioning it, then turned back to Dylan. "Mr. Jackson passed away from a massive coronary. That it was during a trial for Avimaxx was unrelated and unfortunate."

And was Mr. Jackson in the drug or placebo group? The question would have to wait. Dylan wasn't ready to call Philip's bluff. The guy would find a way to bury details even deeper. "That's why you wrote his wife a check?"

Philip cleared his throat, adjusted his tie. "We're an altruistic company. We help the poor any way we can. And we're done here."

"SOP, huh? Someone cashes in while test driving one of your drugs and Santa stuffs his stocking."

A flash of a twitch below Philip's right eye. "A death during a clinical trial is rare, but not unheard of. I thought you were commissioned to find Elyse?"

"She manages the trials, correct?"

"Yes."

Dylan pictured the forms on the flash drive. Another company was on the form. A bold signature right next to Elyse's. "And all the trials are done at Saycor?"

"We use a CRO, a Contract Research Organization, but that's all public knowledge. You're welcome to consult Google if you have any more questions."

LMC Research. Dylan had seen it on the form.

Philip stepped into his Rover, slammed the door, and sped away.

Maybe someone at LMC might be able to shed some light on the information on the flash drive. He looked at his phone again. No missed calls but a text from Bianca thanking him again for finding Kate.

Wouldn't Tish at least be curious? He got in the car, shoved the key in the ignition. That woman had some nerve, disappearing like this. Doesn't answer her phone, doesn't try to call . . .

Unless there was a reason she couldn't.

∿ THIRTY-FIVE ∿

The Night Before, Monday April 6th

TISH clenched her teeth against a rising panic as she and Elyse found their way through the dark to Robert's house. Looking over at her mom, she realized they both resembled wet sewer rats. Cold, wet sewer rats. First she'd get her mom dry and warm and out of danger of shock before she laid the real shocker on her: RJ's death. If ever she wanted to be somewhere else, be someone else, it was now.

At Robert's, she flung the door open as a prickly kind of energy hummed through her. "We need help."

Robert emerged and flipped on the overhead light, his face set in tense angles as he pieced things together. "Elyse!"

They stood there, dripping all over the entryway rug.

Robert rushed from the room and returned with a stack of bath sheets and a pair of sweats for each of them. Tish wrapped them both in the towels and rubbed her mom's shoulders, her back.

"What happened?" Robert asked.

"Let us get these on and then we'll talk," Tish said.

In the bathroom, no words were exchanged as they snaked out of their wet clothes and draped them in the shower. The dry, albeit oversized, sweats felt good against Tish's still clammy skin. A small consolation in this nether world that had left her shaken.

They returned to the kitchen where Robert paced by the island, strangling a dish towel as if he'd come undone by it all.

"I need to see Luke," Elyse said.

Robert stopped, placed the towel on the counter. "He's asleep."

The blood in Tish's body rushed simultaneously to her head and her feet. What to say first. It was the old chicken or egg conundrum. She decided to gather information before dispensing it. "Mom, Luke is safe. We need to talk about what happened."

Elyse drew the back of her fist to her mouth and held it there for a long moment before dropping onto a bar stool.

The gentle strains of a lone saxophone tipped the background air. The wrong music for the wrong time. Tish pressed the button on the wireless remote and settled on the bar stool next to her mother.

Robert moved to the butler's pantry, grabbed three snifters and a bottle of Cognac. He poured two fingers in each glass and set them on the counter between them.

Tish and Elyse upended their glasses. Tish couldn't remember the last time she had a shot, and here in the space of a few short days she'd had three.

Elyse's gaze turned inward as emotion flickered in her eyes. "I need to get home to RJ. I can fill you in on everything later, Leticia. Once my clothes are dry, I'll—"

"No, Mom." Tish smacked her hand on the island. "I've been worried sick about you. You put our lives in danger." How selfish she felt for talking about her life, even Luke's, before she told her mom about RJ, but she needed to see all the pieces of the puzzle before she could put it together. "Please. Tell us what happened."

"We . . ." Elyse rubbed at her temples.

"This is about what you put on the flash drive," Tish said, trying to coax the painful account along.

"Yes. Evidence that we manipulated the trial. When we found out Clay Jackson died, we panicked and moved him into the placebo group."

Tish's heart tilted as her mind stumbled through the implications, confirming what she already knew and had hoped wasn't true.

"I realized what a stupid, impetuous thing it was and planned to make things right," Elyse went on. "Philip and I fought about it. He's the one who had those cretins grab me. He had to be."

Tish told her about Helen hiring Dylan and how they'd gone together to the Saycor offices. "We spoke briefly with Gretchen."

"I'm thankful you weren't alone in this, that you had Dylan"—she turned to Robert—"and Robert. But didn't I tell you to lay low and wait?"

Tish felt her face heat. "You've got to be kidding. You're going to give me a lecture about how I handled this?"

"No, no, I'm sorry. I can't blame anyone but myself. I'm just glad you're okay. And about Gretchen, trust me, she doesn't know anything. Philip Kelrich wouldn't share something like this with anyone. There's too much money at stake."

No real surprise. Philip would stop at nothing to keep the river of cash flowing in his direction.

"You're hurt." Tish pointed to the gash on her mom's forehead.

"I'm okay. I'm okay now. But the house . . ." her voice trailed off.

"Those guys at the boathouse said they had nothing to do with the fire."

"They did seem surprised to see what was left of the place. And it makes sense. Why would they torch it if there was a possibility the evidence was still there?"

"So they came back with you tonight because they wanted to search the house again?" Robert asked. "By the looks of it, they were pretty thorough the first time."

"They didn't touch the boathouse. I don't think they realized it's ours."

The little outbuilding could be easily overlooked, but it had housed Tish's first sailboat, a reminder of everything good in their lives. Now the only thing standing on the property. "I found the telescope in the fire safe and gave it to Luke, hoping it would calm him down. He smashed it against the wall instead, and that's when we found the drive."

Elyse pivoted toward the back of the house. "I need to see him."

Tish felt her composure slip. She steadied herself. "Mom, RJ—"

"I called him, but he didn't answer—"

"RJ is dead, Mom. He drowned in the hot tub." It was as though the words were hot, burning her tongue, the way she spat them out.

Elyse's face took on a tight appearance as if cellophane had been stretched over it.

"And we don't think it was an accident." Adding insult to injury, rubbing salt in the wound, and any other suffocating cliché that described adding another dimension of heart-splintering pain. "His funeral is tomorrow."

Her mother burst into a full-throated sob, and Tish held her, rocking her back and forth. Robert went to stand in front of the open kitchen window as if to examine the yard blanketed in darkness.

So much of this reminded Tish of her first encounter with Liv's parents after Liv's death. Holding Liv's mom. Liv's dad excusing himself from the scene. Tish swam away from the awful memory. This present situation required action, not rumination.

"Look what's happened already, Mom. Philip won't stop until he gets the evidence, and maybe not even then. We need to get you and Luke far away from here until we can figure out what to do."

"RJ didn't even know what was going on," Elyse said. "Why hurt him?"

"Are you sure he didn't know anything?" Robert asked.

"He knew about Clay's death, but not about switching him to the placebo group. I didn't want to burden him with something I thought we could handle. I wanted him to be able to focus fully on his big opportunity. And now . . ." Elyse grasped Tish's arm. "What about the investigation?"

"They've ruled it accidental," Tish said. "No signs of forced entry, no signs of struggle. His blood alcohol showed . . . well he'd clearly been drinking."

Elyse pressed her eyes shut. "If only I'd been there."

"Mom, you can't blame yourself. The police may not have found anything, but I know this wasn't an accident. You do too."

Robert picked up the glasses, loaded them into the dishwasher.

"I can take you all someplace safe."

Safe. Tish suddenly remembered she needed to tell Dylan and Helen she'd found Elyse. And why hadn't he called her to say they'd found Kate? Unless they hadn't found her yet. Getting ahold of Dylan went from important to crucial. But she didn't know his number. It was programmed into her cell, which was shattered on the boathouse floor. Maybe he had a website. Moving to Robert's computer, she keyed in Dylan Tierny, P.I. but for some reason couldn't bring herself to push enter. If she called him, she'd hear his voice. If she heard his voice . . . She looked up Helen's number and left a voice mail. She owed him that. There was no way around it, she had to let him know she'd found Elyse. And she needed to hear from him about Kate, even though she knew if it was bad news she would come completely unglued.

"I'm not going anywhere." Elyse's voice quivered and hitched. "Until I see RJ again . . ."

"Mom." Tish tried to condense equal portions of compassion and firmness in her voice. "He's not . . . he's not the way he was."

Elyse stood, started down the hall toward the guest bedroom.

Tish followed. "Luke doesn't know yet, Mom."

Elyse sighed, seemed to steel herself against what was coming.

Luke was sleeping on his back, propped up by two pillows, almost in a sitting position. He looked peaceful, relaxed. Elyse sat next to him, whispered, "Luke honey, Mommy is here."

His eyes popped open and a smile warmed his face. "You're just in time. I was having the best dream."

"What about, darling?"

"I was on an archaeological dig but instead of finding bones and fossils, I was finding memories. You were in them."

"I was?" She stroked his forearm. "What kind of memories?"

Tish let herself lean against the door frame as the tension in every muscle fiber of her body eased. Elyse was Luke's favorite woobie, a human security blanket, instantly transporting him back to the comfort of childhood.

"Hmm. There were twenty-four. Should I tell them to you in chronological order?"

"I'd like that."

⸎ THIRTY-SIX ⸎

ELYSE pulled her coat tight to her chin despite the mild temperature. A funeral day should be dismal and overcast. Not a lavender hyacinth reaching for the sun kind of day. Her toes competed for space in the too small shoes, and she could feel blisters forming with each step. Robert had grabbed the wrong pair of black pumps when they'd sent him back to the house. Pumps she'd been meaning to get rid of for years now. There were so many things she'd left undone, so many things she'd meant to do.

She'd wanted to go to the house herself, to feel RJ's presence one last time before he was laid to rest, but Tish and Robert argued it was too risky. The only reason they gave in to her attending the funeral was because there was safety in numbers. Surely those buffoons wouldn't try to snatch her again with so many people watching. How did she get to this point? To this place where it was too dangerous to step foot in her own home?

Now, at the gravesite, RJ's sister, Annabeth, radiated anger beside her. She still hadn't spoken a word, or even acknowledged Elyse. The rest of the family was equally standoffish, and Elyse hoped it would stay that way. Because one word, one cross-eyed look, and ten years of pent up resentment would burst from her with geyser-like force.

Why did they hate her so much, so much more than usual? Did they think she was responsible for RJ's death?

The reality hit like a thunderclap, stealing her breath, nearly knocking her off her feet.

The police had deemed his death an accident, no foul play. But the course she and Philip had chosen was intentional, and foul. And what if RJ had found out they manipulated the trial and confronted Philip?

"May his soul and the souls of all the faithful departed through the mercy of God rest in peace."

She reached for Tish's hand. Something she hadn't done in a very long time. Luke stood across from them. He'd made it clear, he needed to face North. Her son was an enigma. The moment she thought she'd figured out his ticks and tocks, he'd throw her off again. Not a tear for RJ. She'd rarely seen him cry, but his stoic expression did little to mask his inner turmoil. Robert stood sentinel next to Luke. As different as night and day yet somehow connected.

The midday sun glinted off the decorative urn. RJ would have hated the overly ornate vessel. He never wanted to be cremated. But Annabeth didn't give a damn about his wishes, only her own. This was the Annabeth show. They'd all go to the country club for a party "in his honor," complete with pyramids of jumbo shrimp, long speeches from distant relatives, and wall-to-wall images of Annabeth and RJ when they were kids. Elyse wouldn't go. She'd say her goodbyes, and then she, Tish and Luke would be on Robert's plane.

Maybe they could create new identities, start fresh.

Who was she kidding? She'd never be able to live on the run, constantly looking over her shoulder, wondering if those assholes had caught up with her, or if Philip had hired new assholes to track her down. Even if she could somehow carve out a life on those terms, Luke would never survive. She had to make things right, stop the trial, then turn herself in. As soon as her children were safe.

"Thank you, Father, for such a lovely service," Annabeth chirped, her need to be the center of the universe apparent. RJ's parents shrunk into the background, marginalized by her artificial glow.

She looked right past Elyse to a couple behind her. "Please join us at the club." Then to Elyse, "I didn't think you were coming so I didn't include you in the count."

"RJ never expressed an interest in cremation." Elyse's voice was loud enough to be heard, just short of accusatory.

"I considered all the options. I went to the house for his best suit. I looked at all the expensive caskets, but when it came right down to it, it didn't seem very prudent. Someone could wear the suit and ... Why am I explaining this to you? The decision was mine to make. If you had another opinion you should have been here before now."

Elyse opened her mouth to set her straight, but what good would it do? This woman would never see the error in her ways, only others' shortcomings.

With a self-satisfied flip of her head, Annabeth stomped off, her shadow-parents in tow.

Elyse deeply regretted that her last conversation with RJ was an argument, and about Annabeth. She knew he was too damn nice to turn his sister away. Annabeth had nearly died at birth and spent her first eight weeks of life in the NICU. The entire family fawned over her, and she'd been milking it ever since.

Did her rough start give her the right to take advantage of her own brother? To drive a wedge between Elyse and RJ?

After leaving Luke last Friday, Elyse had headed back to Crestwood, calling RJ on the way. "I'm heading home early and—"

"Great. Annabeth wants to talk to us about something. Maybe the three of us could go to Rinaldi's."

"Not tonight. I'm beat. I just need some time with you before I meet up with Helen and Tish tomorrow." *To tell you how screwed up everything is, beg your forgiveness, and hope that you'll bring me a cake with a file in it when I end up in the slammer.* "And I know what she wants to talk to us about. She wants you to cover another maxed out credit card."

"You can't know that."

"Of course I do. And you should too. Your sister's a leach, RJ. I know you somehow feel responsible for her, but she's a grown woman. Time to cut the cord. You know what? I'm going to head to Helen's. She'll love having me all to herself before Tish arrives tomorrow. You and your sister have a nice night." She threw the phone on the seat and gunned it to Riley's Peak.

Now, Elyse put trembling fingers to her lips. "I'm sorry," she said in a firm voice, revenge already replacing regret.

✥ THIRTY-SEVEN ✥

FROM the back of the graveside ceremony, Dylan swept his gaze over the mourners. A few he recognized from Saycor: Gretchen stood erect, unreadable. Mae studied her engagement ring as if seeing it for the first time. Philip? Suspiciously absent. But his surveillance was more about who might jump from the crowd and snatch Elyse again, or worse.

As the priest intoned his benediction and people started to filter out, Dylan caught Tish's eye. She guided Elyse by the elbow, and they moved toward him. "Mom, this is Dylan Tierny. The private investigator I told you about."

Elyse reached out a hand. "Thank you for taking care of Leticia and for all you've done." Her voice didn't waver, despite the circumstances. Something else she had in common with her daughter, in addition to show-stopping looks.

"I didn't do much," Dylan said. "I'm just glad you're all right."

Robert shook his hand. Luke made fleeting eye contact, which was more than Dylan expected.

And then there was Tish. They were locked in some weird stalemate. The last time they were together there was a little more give and take, okay, a lot more give and take. "By the way, Kate is safe."

"Helen told me. Such a relief. I wanted to call you, but I lost your number."

Lost his number?

"My phone . . . is broken."

The ultimate blow off, second only to "I need to wash my hair."

Was this it then? He'd been commissioned to find Elyse, and here she was. But maybe he should stick close and keep an eye out. Grill her about where she'd been the last three days and piece together how it all connected to RJ. Or maybe he should forget all of that and pull Tish into his arms.

None of that felt right. Not now.

On their way to the snaking line of cars, they spoke about the service, the flower arrangements. Dylan's throat itched to say more, but his tongue was lodged deep.

"Mom thinks Kate should keep Nutmeg," Tish said. "If Finn and Bianca are okay with it."

A parting gift, case closed, tying up loose ends. But then Dylan envisioned Kate and the dog and his bitterness turned to appreciation. "I think the whole family is getting pretty attached."

"I'll miss her," Elyse said. "But she really needs the extra attention a family can give."

Dylan anticipated her next line. Now that I'm all alone. Now that RJ is gone. Or . . . now that I'm headed to the state pen.

They turned to the sound of large tires rolling over gravel. Philip. He exited the Range Rover, moved to Elyse, and tried to pull her into a hug. She sidestepped and crossed her arms.

"Was in a meeting and lost track of time. My calendar alert didn't go off," Philip said, his forehead forming a series of perplexed grooves. He didn't like screwing up.

"Hmm. Technical glitches are the plight of the contemporary man." Luke gave a matter-of-fact nod of his head.

"You can pay your respects at the country club." Elyse moved to Robert's car, climbed in. "Just don't bring your friends."

"My friends?"

"The fat one." She paused, watching Philip's eyes widen. "And the Brit."

Her words visibly corkscrewed through Philip, throwing him off balance. These women could take care of themselves. Feeling invisible, Dylan wondered why the hell he'd even bothered to come.

As if he didn't know.

"Tish," he said softly.

She swiveled in his direction. He canted his head toward the grassy embankment bordering the graves, and she met him there.

"Here's my number." He gave her his business card. "And I want you to take this," he said, settling the .45 in her hand. Elyse might have gotten away, but until the cops wrapped up this case, Dylan wasn't taking any chances.

For a moment, Tish looked hopelessly confused, her mouth gaping open. Then something inside her clicked. She stowed the gun in her bag, did an about face, and disappeared in the rental car with Elyse.

Once they were out of sight, Dylan punched the key fob to unlock Finn's car. In his periphery, something moved. He turned and saw a hooded figure moving toward RJ's grave. After a moment, the stranger dropped something near a flower arrangement. He noticed he was being watched and took off. Dylan angled his way across the cemetery, tackled him.

Seth.

"Get off me, man," the kid hollered.

Dylan helped him to his feet. "Why'd you run?"

"You were starin' at me like some creeper. Freaked me out."

"What'd you drop back there?"

Seth shoved his hands in his pockets.

Dylan led him back to the gravesite, reached down and picked up a bill. "A Benjamin? Seems like a lotta money to be tossin' around."

"I ain't no thief," Seth said, adjusting his hoodie. "I found it. Probably from one of those rich bitches, but it didn't feel right to keep it."

This kid was trying so hard to be a thug, from his bad grammar to his droopy pants to the defiant jut of his chin.

"Listen," Dylan said. "I lost my dad too. It sucks, no doubt. But your mom and sisters need you. You've got to be the strong one."

Seth narrowed his eyes. "Yeah, well, maybe I don't want to." He turned and sprinted across the cemetery, leaving Dylan holding the C-note. And for a moment, he saw the teenager he once was. Full of rage, unable to see beyond the moment. Bent on destroying everyone and everything in his path.

◈ THIRTY-EIGHT ◈

TISH looked out the back window, half-hoping Dylan would be following them. She saw only a pixie-looking woman driving one of those smart cars that resembled a toy. Ahead of them, a U.P.S. truck made an abrupt turn down a side street. Robert navigated around it the way Tish envisioned him piloting a plane, all business, reeking of confidence.

Luke sat in the passenger seat next to him, straining against the seatbelt, pointing his nose toward the windshield. "Hmm. He broke the rules."

"What?" Robert looked confused.

"U.P.S. has a rule, right turns only. Engineers map out every route. No left turns. Unless they're in Manhattan."

"Okay, I'll bite," Robert said. "Why?"

"They shaved millions of miles off their route and reduced CO_2 emissions by over twenty-thousand metric tons." Luke looked pleased with himself and possibly U.P.S. for being so savvy. "And everybody knows you're asking to be sideswiped in the left turn lane."

Once again, his fascination with rules and statistics and laws of nature took center stage while unpleasant thoughts about loss were pushed to the back.

Like the time a leak in the garage roof left a rust spot on the fender of his bike. Any other child would have been upset, but Luke responded with his usual scientific jargon. "I'm not surprised, Mom. Oxygen combined with my bike at an atomic level forming a new compound, oxide, weakening the bonds of the metal. One week produced approximately ten percent rust. After week two it will be twenty percent." Spoken like a seasoned professor even though he was only eight-years-old. But the seed of disappointment had been planted, and it grew throughout the day blossoming to a full-blown meltdown when mashed potatoes touched the green beans on his dinner plate. Tish wondered how this new grief would manifest itself. It was like waiting for a seismically active volcano to erupt.

"That Dylan seems to be showing up a lot," Luke said. "I sense something between the two of you, but I can't exactly say what."

Tish couldn't exactly say what either. The case was essentially over, for Dylan anyway, but he was still concerned about her. She'd seen it in his eyes, eyes that watched her like she was a rare bird.

The warmth vibrating her cheeks subsided. Luke plugged his earbuds deep in his ears, and she turned her attention to Elyse. "It's too risky to stay here, Mom, you know that."

"No, Leticia. I'm not leaving. I need to stay and as they say, face the music."

"Stay and you'll soon hear another bagpipe medley." She couldn't believe she'd said that while the mournful strains of RJ's Scotch heritage still echoed in her ears, but how else could she make her mother understand?

Elyse looked her full in the face. "I can't leave now,"—she glanced at Luke to make sure he wasn't listening— "I don't want anyone else to die if the product is flawed. The people still in the trial . . ." She steeled her jaw. "Plus, I have multiple scores to settle." Emphasis on multiple.

Philip and his goons.

Tish let out a frustrated sigh. "But at what cost?"

They argued, avoided naming names, skirting details, voices climbing, words overlapping.

"Mom!" Tish slammed her fist on the seat between them. "Either you and Luke get on that plane or Robert keeps driving."

Elyse's demeanor changed, her passion dying a little under Tish's harsh tones. In that instant, Tish couldn't help but see Liv in her mom. The defeated pleats lining her face.

"How much lead time do you need to submit a manifest?" Elyse asked Robert.

"About an hour."

"I definitely need a few things from the house," Elyse said. "And no argument this time."

Tish thought about Dylan's gun in her purse. If they encountered those guys again, this time she'd be ready. "We'll have to make it quick."

Robert tapped Luke on the shoulder. Her brother uncorked his earbuds and Robert said, "What do you think about trying to catch a meteor shower tonight?"

Luke started swiping and clicking his phone. "The probability of the Lyrid making an appearance is currently higher than average."

"Would be even better from a plane," Tish said.

Robert caught her eye in the rearview mirror, winked.

"Yes," Luke said. "I would be agreeable to that."

Thank God for small miracles. Luke would break schedule for the opportunity to witness a rare star show.

Robert slowed as they approached the Crestwood house, and a hollowed sadness took up residence deep inside Tish. Her mom needed to do this. This could be her last time in the house.

At the front door, Elyse grabbed the hide-a-key from a stone turtle, and for a beat Tish thought about how little she really knew about this place. If they'd known about the key, Dylan wouldn't have had to use his ValueMart card to open the back patio gate. But why worry about that now? Why did her thoughts keep returning to him?

When the door swung open, she half-expected to hear Nutmeg's nails scratching across the hardwood to get to them, but the house was quiet and seemed empty. All the carefully selected furnishings now superfluous. Elyse hesitated in the foyer before trudging upstairs, tears glazing her eyes.

"I'm so sorry, Mom." As if the words were a suture that could repair the deep slash of what had happened here.

Her head bobbed up and down in an almost automated movement. Good thing Luke had insisted on waiting in the car; it would shatter him to see his mother like this.

While Elyse was upstairs, Robert called in the flight manifest. He rattled off the passenger names, but Tish shook her head. "Scratch that last one," he said into the phone, a wary expression taking over.

Elyse returned with a small suitcase in tow. "Some of my jewelry is gone," she said, her rage stampeding into Tish, all but knocking her down.

"The cops and possibly others have been in and out of the house." Tish had no intention of letting Annabeth off the hook, but right now, she needed Luke and Elyse on that plane. She didn't need Elyse taking any side trips.

"I guess she decided she'd get the money one way or another."

"What do you mean?"

"Annabeth. When I left work on Friday, I called RJ and we fought about her. I suspected she wanted another loan. I say loan facetiously; it's not like she ever paid us back a dime for the *thousands* we gave her. I told RJ enough was enough. Not one more penny. She was on her way over, so I left for Helen's earlier than planned." Elyse hung her head. "I didn't even go home to say goodbye."

Annabeth had told them she hadn't seen RJ recently. A lie. And another reason piled on many that supported getting Elyse and Luke out of town.

Back in the car, they were silent except for the occasional grumble from Luke as he talked to himself about whatever was so captivating on his phone. When they reached the hangar they piled out and Robert immediately went to work performing the necessary checks on his Cessna. Tish allowed Luke and then Elyse to board. Robert paused before handing Tish his car keys. As she closed the plane door, Elyse's panicked face appeared at the window, her muffled protests ringing through the layers of metal.

Tish walked away and didn't look back.

∽ THIRTY-NINE ∾

THE funeral had left Dylan drained. Was it the memories of burying his loved ones? Or maybe the grim reminder of his own mortality? Take your pick. At any rate, he needed time to recharge before digging into work or anything else. He plunked on the couch, TV remote in hand, salty snack at the ready.

He'd barely gotten through the credits for *The General* when he heard a rap at the door. Cheeto crumbs tumbled to the floor as he stood to answer it.

Helen thrust an envelope in his direction. "For your services."

Tish found Elyse. Maybe she was the one who deserved the money. "I can't accept this."

Her eyes loomed large. "Accept, you will!" She pressed the envelope into his chest.

For an irreverent second, the way she reversed her words reminded him of Yoda, and he felt like laughing, but she was serious. And refusing Helen would be a waste of breath. When he thought about it, the money would be nice. He had invested his time in all this. Besides, there wasn't exactly a mob beating down the door for his services.

Only two calls since this chaos with Elyse started. In each case, he'd kindly pointed out these matters could be solved without paying a private investigator. A drugstore manager asking to confirm that his clerk was stealing condoms. "Check your surveillance camera, buddy." And a Richie Rich in Beacham Estates wanting a background check on a gardener. "A subscription to

Intelius will be cheaper and give you all the info you need."

He took the envelope, shoved it in his back pocket. "Thanks, Helen."

"I don't know what I would have done if anything had happened to my dear friend."

He wondered how much Helen knew, or if she'd even care if she learned that Elyse had essentially brought this all on herself by manipulating the clinical trial. There had to be more to it though. Philip was an ass, but kidnapping and murder? Annabeth certainly couldn't be trusted. And why was Seth dropping money on RJ's grave? Why was he even at the funeral? Then, of course, there was RJ. Did he know about the incriminating evidence on the flash drive? Dylan almost laughed at the enormity of it all. The pile of suspects. Anyone at Saycor could be involved: Gretchen, the worker bees, even that chatterbox, Mae. They all had something to lose if Saycor went belly up. And Dylan didn't underestimate the power Philip had over people. He'd bet his last dime that at least half of the employees would follow their leader off a cliff like lemmings.

None of it was his concern anymore. And besides, he needed to beat down his personal feelings before they had a chance to surface.

"Have you heard from Tish?" Helen asked, scrutinizing him.

Surface, they did. And then some. The mere mention of her name brought on the vision of her in his doorway, a vision he couldn't scrub from his memory if he tried. Her beauty had him in its grip, and yet it was the kind of beauty you could never capture, even if you could, you couldn't keep it.

"Not a word, have you?"

Something in his tone must have given him away because Helen beamed and clapped her hands together, the multi-colored bangles on her wrists clanging in disharmony. "Forgive my prognostication, but I knew from the moment you two stepped into the same room that you were fated to be together."

Dylan raised his palms in a pushing-back motion. "Whoa. Let's not get ahead of ourselves."

"Well, I do know that they're all together at Lake Anaba. I'm sure they needed some recovery time after RJ's funeral. Such energy sucking rituals. I prefer the butterfly release myself."

Helen had released seventeen butterflies in his dad's honor, the number representing some crazy ass stuff. She peered over cherry red-framed glasses, sized him up, and winked. "But I'd bet my best tea leaves that Leticia would welcome a visitor of the tall and handsome sort."

Dylan blew out a breath. Helen was relentless, a squirrel after a nut.

"Don't dally. Your aura is a better long-term match for her, but don't forget, that Robert fellow is all that and a bag of chips."

That Robert fellow. Mr. Perfect. Mr. Sensitive. Mr. Ever Ready. Tish certainly stretched out that supple twang when he was around. Dylan pictured him clasping her shoulders, offering to rub out the knots. A knot of his own formed in his gut.

"I'll keep that in mind, Helen. And thanks again for the check." He nodded a farewell, popped the door shut, and planted himself back on the couch—legs extended on the coffee table.

Ten minutes later, his phone buzzed.

"You're coming, right?"

Shit. He'd completely forgotten about dinner at his brother's. Usually a welcomed invitation, but Rose's presence bent any chance for a good time into a complication.

"Yeah, hey, I was . . . on my way."

"Save the hay for the horses."

"I haven't heard that in years. It was one of Dad's go-tos."

The line went blank for a moment. "Just get over here."

Dinner was awkward at first, but growing toward a companionable silence. Kate was unusually quiet. Still subdued from her adventure. Bianca and Finn tried to keep the conversation light with a brief discussion about possible baby names, the unpredictable spring temperatures.

Rose refilled her glass, ran her finger around the rim, making an annoying screeching sound. "Dylan, remember when we watched *Rear Window* during that tremendous snowstorm?" Her words flew out as if racing ahead of a "times up" buzzer.

"Not really," Dylan grunted. He gathered his empty plate and thanked Bianca for the meal. "Best chicken cacciatore I've ever had."

Rose carefully placed her fork next to her plate, cleared her throat. She'd dazzled them with chicken cacciatore when they were kids, doling out extra helpings until they'd nearly burst.

"It was amazing." Finn kissed Bianca's cheek. "My wife has been taking cooking classes at Tres Pecora." He patted his stomach. "And I couldn't be happier." Then to Dylan, "How about you and I clean up and let the ladies take a rest."

Why would Rose need to rest? Maybe her legs were sore from all that running away, Dylan thought bitterly.

In the kitchen, Finn filled the sink with soapy water. "What's happening with Tish?"

"Helen hired me to find Elyse. Elyse is found. End of story."

"What about the guys who grabbed her? What about RJ? And the CEO—"

"Kelrich," said Dylan. "That's for the Crestwood cops. I've done my part."

Finn's grilling prompted more questions of his own. What about Annabeth? Did her involvement include more than stealing scarves and jewelry from Elyse? And Turtle House. An accident or arson? As much as Dylan tried to pretend otherwise, he needed answers.

One more question tipped the scales. Was Tish safe?

"Glad Elyse is all right," Finn said, "but I guess that means she'll be taking Nutmeg back. Too bad, a certain feline I know was warming to the idea of sharing the roost."

"Can't believe I forgot," Dylan said. "Elyse asked if you guys want to keep Nutmeg."

"Seriously? I can't wait to tell Bianca and Kate."

Finn tossed him the dishcloth, leaving him alone with a stack of plates as the swirling ruminations about the case returned.

"Are you sure I can't help?"

At the sound of his mother's voice, Dylan rubbed at a stubborn shred of chicken clinging to the edge of the plate until he thought it might shatter.

"And leave the dishes half-done?"

"Dylan Raymond Tierny." Rose's voice climbed to a squeaky

vibrato, reedy, not the way he remembered it. "I'm your mother and no matter what you think of my choices, I still deserve your respect."

He slammed the dishcloth on the counter, choked out a laugh. "You stopped being my mother when you took off and never looked back."

"Can't we put the past behind us?"

"All I know about the past is that I had a mother in the past, and now I don't." He turned on his heel and shot through the living room where he thanked Bianca and Finn. As he opened the door to leave, he heard a tiny voice exclaim, "You're my very own dog now, Bookmark!" He hesitated and crossed the room to Kate, whose nose was buried deep in Nutmeg's fur. He kissed the top of her head.

Outside, he yanked a plastic pink flamingo out of the ground that had been circling the neighborhood as a joke. He hurled it across the yard. That woman infuriated him. Who the hell did she think she was, showing up after all these years, acting like nothing had changed?

Rose appeared on the porch. "At least let me explain."

He kept walking toward the car, then stalled. He didn't want to give her a chance, but his anger and resentment would continue to storm and froth until it overtook him. He didn't need a degree in psychology to understand that. He pivoted. "Enlighten me."

Rose lowered herself onto the porch swing. She motioned for him to join her, but he remained planted. She blew out an extended breath. "I grew up under my father's thumb, powerless to make a single decision, not about my classes, my friends, even my clothes. I remember this one time . . . anyway, I met your dad when I was working at a drive-in. I was hesitant at first, but he was so charming and confident. And handsome!" A broad smile lit her face. "I thought he'd take me away from my father's control, but your dad—"

"Don't. I won't let you say one bad thing about him."

"I couldn't, he was wonderful. Please understand, it was me who messed up, not him. He lived for me and you boys. But because of his job, because of the things he saw, he was understandably worried about us. He'd put away a lot of bad people, and who knew when they'd get out and come looking for revenge? Mack always checked on me, needed to know where I was. I felt . . . stifled."

"So why didn't you try to work it out with him instead of taking off?"

"Looking back now, I would have done things differently." She pulled a tissue from her pocket, blew into it. "But I had these . . . aspirations. My father never saw any value in acting, said it was an excuse to show off. After high school I had the chance to star in a summer performance, and I took it. He was furious. I never regretted it though. For the first time, I felt alive. Then I married your father and had you boys and didn't act again until I did *The Glass Menagerie*." She huffed out a sigh. "But you were probably too young to remember."

Dylan did remember. He also remembered watching the Irving Rapper film version, where Jane Wyman played Laura. The two of them sat on the couch, mammoth bowl of popcorn between them, licking the salt off their fingers. Movie time with Rose was his best childhood memory.

He sank down next to her.

"When you were fifteen, and so independent, I decided it was time to pursue my passion. I heard about an open casting call in New York for *Hedda Gabler*, the play I'd done after high school, and I thought it was going to be my big chance. Your dad and I argued. He was worried sick about me alone in the city, but he finally agreed to let me go for the weekend. I didn't get the part. But being up there, well, I was hooked. I felt like if I just kept trying . . . I ended up staying longer, a week turned into a month, and eventually I followed some actor friends to California because there were a lot more opportunities there."

Dylan thought about Mack, his obsession with TV. Had he been hoping to catch a glimpse of the only woman he'd ever loved? "Why didn't Dad ever tell us?"

She settled her hand on his, then pulled it away when he stiffened. "I don't know." She shook her head. "I just don't know."

"And why didn't you come back? Or at least keep in touch?"

Rose looked away for what seemed like another lifetime as Dylan held his breath, waiting for the answer to the question he'd harbored for years.

"I was ashamed."

"Of what?"

"I failed. Miserably. I never got more than a part here and there as an extra and all those scenes were eventually cut. I ended up waiting tables and sleeping on couches. I was even in a shelter for a while."

The vision of his mom, wandering the streets, homeless, tore at him.

"But you could have come home, we wanted you home."

"I don't have a good answer. I knew I'd made a big mistake. Then I met a nice man, an older man, and we . . . he took care of me."

Dylan wanted to ask why she needed another man to take care of her. She had a husband. She had two sons who adored her. But what good would it do now?

Looking into her eyes, he saw the woman who'd held him tight during scary movies, the woman who encouraged him to chase his dreams, the woman who laughed at his dumbest knock-knock jokes. Years of questions melted away leaving clarity in their place.

⚜ FORTY ⚜

ANYONE looking through Robert's windows would wonder about the crazy doing burpees, mountain climbers, and single arm push-ups, but Tish didn't care. Strong body. Strong mind.

Plus, she needed the distraction. She could still feel the heat from her mom's anger when she realized Tish wasn't getting on the plane. Part of her wished she had a way to check in with Elyse and part of her was relieved neither of them had phones. Robert said he'd call the house phone when they got to the little beach house in Maine, a condo he shared with other pilots. He'd been going there every year around the same time in the spring for as long as she could remember.

She moved into the kitchen, downed a glass of water, and launched into a series of stretches. She couldn't help but feel strange about being here alone. It reminded her of a novel she'd read where a character in the same situation ended up snooping through drawers, polishing off the leftover ravioli in the fridge, and rearranging the furniture in the living room. But she knew Robert too well to be curious. Now given the same opportunity at Dylan's . . .

The doorbell rang and Tish bulleted for the door to find him standing there.

In a 180 degree turn from his funeral attire—in which he'd pulled off a surprisingly sophisticated look—he now sported a Nike sweatshirt, faded jeans and sandals, the kind of sandals men wear in sleek ads for Puerto Rican rum.

When they'd parted earlier at the funeral, she'd been so certain she didn't want or need to see him again. But now, with that off-kilter smile and those eyes she imagined getting lost in forever, Tish decided one more taste wouldn't hurt.

"Hey." Dylan stepped inside.

"Isn't it a little early in the season for sandals?"

"My sneakers are in the wash."

"I'm guessing you're here for the debriefing."

"I am."

"Up for a walk? Just Desserts puts real cocoa beans in their milkshakes. If we hustle we can make it there before they close."

Over milkshakes, she brought him up to speed as they continued around the lake. Dylan filled her in about his conversation with Philip regarding LMC, the company that ran the Avimaxx clinical trial.

Before long, they stopped at the lot where Turtle House had been. Part of the stone fireplace and a blackened foundation were all that was left. Twilight had given way to full darkness, and they walked the length of the dock. Dylan inhaled deep. "I've never seen stars like this."

"You know, they say in a few thousand years the Big Dipper's mouth will be completely open, but that won't really matter to us, will it?"

She hadn't meant to sound so philosophical, so pessimistic. She crossed her arms, rubbed them. The breeze off the lake held a hint of a chill, and Dylan wrapped himself around her. She didn't move, had no desire to move.

"It's hard not to think about my dad," she went on. "He called the night sky nature's majesty."

"You were really close, weren't you?"

Hot tears lined her eyes, and Tish worked to keep them at bay. She thought about a comment a woman had made at her dad's funeral, 'Sometimes God takes a lamb so the sheep will follow.' A clutching began in her chest and congealed in her throat.

She felt his hand wrap around hers, her fingers wriggle into his.

"It sucked watching him suffer through chemo—the nausea, fatigue, pain. It was horrible, and I couldn't do a damn thing to help him. The only thing that seemed to give him peace was being here, and he insisted on making the trip from Savannah every summer even though he felt like shit." She leaned further into Dylan, his nearness a ballast against the painful memories. "The summer he died, he'd sleep most of the day, but then at night, he seemed energized. Mom would prop him up with pillows on this bench with us on either side of him, and we'd sit goggle-eyed, soaking in the sky for hours. If we blinked, we'd miss the chance to wish on shooting stars . . . we all had the same wish."

At thirteen, she had been old enough to comprehend the horrible thing that had happened to their sweet little family, but too young to realize the permanence of their loss. Too young to realize how much she'd miss her dad in her adult life, how she'd suffer the phantom pangs over and over, wanting to ask him something only to be reminded that she couldn't.

The stars glowed bright in the velvet canopy above. "I'm a little jealous of them. They're so sure of themselves, so stationary. That something as simple as gravity could hold them in place—"

"No one is completely grounded. The best anyone can do is to find something to hang on to when the earth splits open to swallow them whole."

They moved to the bench and Tish slouched back, feeling Dylan's strong arm supporting her neck. "The night before he died, Dad reminded us of the stars he had named for us. 'Whenever you feel sad, Featherweight, look up until you don't feel sad anymore. We'll always be together.'"

"Does it work?"

His eyes begged to understand, and he brushed his lips over hers, a prelude to a kiss. Her heart ratcheted from flutter to pound as her sadness peeled away.

A wash of relief.

The sensation of being grounded and soaring at once.

✦ FORTY-ONE ✦

DYLAN spent the morning responding to emails, organizing files, backing up his computer. Trying, and repeatedly failing, to keep thoughts of stargazing with Tish from ruling his day. He read through a few relevant and not so relevant articles on his tablet. The latest: a judge had ordered an employee to give up his Twitter password when the company suspected him of libel. He'd never understand why people trusted their secrets to Cyberspace. Anything you put out there was destined to come back to bite you in the ass.

He'd left Tish at Robert's last night half-wishing he'd stayed, half-eager to leave on a positive note. She'd opened up to him, and the intimacy of their conversation nearly rivaled the feel of her lips against his.

Dylan talked himself out of calling and back into it several times before dialing Robert's number.

"Ready to finish this?" Tish asked, before he could get a word out. Her open and eager tone erased all his herky-jerky second guesses. A far cry from the battles they'd had when she first barged into Helen's, hands pressed into perfect hips. He was eager to solve this case, but there was more, he was chomping at the proverbial bit to see her again.

"Want me to come get you?"

"I know it's a trek for you, but Rent Rite picked up the Sebring. Pretty sure I'm on their blacklist now." She paused. "Guess I could use one of Robert's cars."

Robert. The guy was certainly there for her. "On my way."

Thirty minutes later, Dylan pulled up to Robert's house. Tish was outside, leaning against a black Maserati. The way the morning sun fell across her face, the determined set to her jaw, put a sharp bright edge on his desire. He hopped from the 300, moved to her in three long strides, and leaned in to give her a peck on the cheek, but some invisible alchemy brewing between them prompted him to slide his hand behind her head and drill his mouth into hers. *Stop.* Did he really want to lose all control? He cleared his throat, kissed one cheek, then the other, lingering against her skin. "This is okay, right?"

"Almost a requirement in some cultures." Her voice growing more elastic now, stretching to open.

His stomach gave a funny twitch, and he went in for more as she stood there expectantly. Without thinking he swung open the door, eased her onto the seat and squeezed in beside her. This thing between them would not be denied. She threw her hands around his neck, pulling him toward her, matching his urgency. A clash of tongues, hands, steering wheel and gearshift ensued, until the windows started to fog. They tore at each other at a feverish pace, and he had a hazy, almost subliminal vision of them climbing out of the car, their clothes in tatters. Somewhere in the middle distance, a car door slammed and the more evolved neurons in his brain reconnected.

"Bad timing?" In a last-ditch effort, he ran his lips down her neck to rest at her bare shoulder where her shirt had been knocked askew.

"The worst." She straightened, collected a sleeve from here, a collar from there, set them back in their places.

Dylan pulled in a breath, but his heart still raced and his mouth still tasted Tish. This was an appetizer, a tantalizing sampling of what the future held, and he knew a part of him would count the minutes until the next course. And best of all—she wanted him too. But that would have to wait.

They'd dialed back to normal by the time they reached the LMC building. It was squat and wide. A nondescript gray box to Saycor's palatial complex. Bare bones landscaping, minimal signage, economy cars in the parking lot. He imagined Philip pulling in, looking down his nose like he'd stepped in dog shit.

"A tech named Vanessa Harrison signed off on the forms," Tish said as they neared the main entrance. "Let's start with her."

A woman with hair scraped into a bun so tight it made her look permanently agitated stepped from an alcove at the side of the building. "I'm sorry, but did you say Vanessa Harrison?" She notched her chin toward the other side of the building. "That guy over there... Tony Mixler... you should talk to him."

A man sat alone at a concrete picnic bench, hunched over a chess set, glasses perched at the end of his nose.

"Tony Mixler?" Tish asked.

He moved a white pawn forward. "Depends on what you want."

"We're here about Vanessa Harrison."

Tony studied the board, selected a black pawn, let it hover. After what seemed like minutes, he settled it on the diagonal square.

"We're looking into an issue regarding Saycor. We were hoping to talk to her."

Tony tapped the top of a white knight, but didn't move it. A thin groan, maybe a laugh, escaped him. "The company's funny that way. They want to work the life out of ya, but then when the life is finally out of ya, they can't wait to give your desk to somebody new." He shook his head. "Sorry. You look like nice people."

The whirligig of the last few days may have jarred Dylan's neurons, but Tony's implication registered.

"Are you saying..." Tish was on the same page. "Vanessa passed away?"

A muscle bunched in Tony's jaw. "That's right. Car accident."

The tech who'd signed off on Clay Jackson's trial form, dead?

"Did you know her well?" Dylan asked.

Tony shifted on the bench, angled toward them. "We were supposed to be married. In August. A quiet shindig, you know, we didn't have a lot of money. Then Vanessa gets this big windfall from some rich aunt. Said we'd have champagne at the reception instead of a kegger. Even went out and bought a brand spankin' new Jeep Cherokee."

Another neck-jerking spin. *Stop the ride, I want to get off.* Dylan watched the poor guy stare at the empty seat across from him as if his fiancé was still there, contemplating which piece to move.

"I'm so sorry for your loss," Tish said.

"The accident was on April third. Six days after she got the car. Six days."

Tony didn't spare any details. Maybe sharing, even with strangers, eased some of the pain. So Vanessa went on a spending spree on the twenty-eighth, three days after signing off on the clinical trial form. In a way, Dylan felt guilty about taking further advantage, but they needed information. "Any possibility we could speak to this aunt?"

"The money was from her will," Tony said. "Didn't think of it until after, but I knew Vanessa going on fourteen years and she never once mentioned a rich aunt. Never even heard anything about a funeral either, just one day she has all this money to burn."

"So you never saw the check?" Tish asked, in lock step with Dylan.

There was no aunt and no inheritance. Only Saycor. And one helluva incentive plan.

"Nope. All I know is, it doesn't matter now." He scrubbed at a tear with his thumb. Turning back to the board, he moved a black bishop into a compromising position.

The idea of this guy, playing chess alone stabbed at Dylan.

As they turned to leave, Dylan noticed Tony pick up the white queen and zig-zag over the other pieces on the board before he returned it to the exact same spot.

❧ FORTY-TWO ❧

The Day Clay Jackson Died, Wednesday, March 25th

ELYSE hung up her phone and fell back against her chair. It might take a minute for the reality to sink in, but she didn't have a minute, she needed to act. She hustled into Philip's office, waiting an impatient handful of seconds while he ended his call.

"You saved me." He shook his head. "That guy could talk the ears off a brass monkey."

"One of the Avimaxx trial participants had a fatal heart attack." Cut right to the chase. No time to sugar coat.

Philip arranged his face in an expression void of emotion, his default.

"We have to stop the trial," Elyse continued.

Philip took his time reorganizing the items on top of his already tidy desk. He always measured himself by a yardstick of control, and that's what he was doing now. "If we stop it, we're done."

"Did you forget about the two participants admitted to the hospital last month? It's not like we have a choice."

He rocked back in his chair. "There's always a choice."

She stared at him, waiting for a magic wand to come flying out of his ass.

He scraped at his temple with an index finger. "The death couldn't have anything to do with Avimaxx. Whoever it was, was in the control group."

"You know we don't know that, Philip. It's a blind trial."

"That depends."

"What are you saying?"

"You know exactly what I'm saying. We need to get LMC on board."

He reached for his phone, and Elyse pressed a hand over his.

"You can't be serious. We can't switch someone into the other group after the fact."

He grabbed her hand and squeezed. "You believe in Avimaxx, don't you?"

She jerked away. "Of course, but three SAEs mean we should take a step back."

"Serious adverse events happen in drug trials every day, Elyse. You know that. This person would have died with or without the drug." His eyes hardened. Come hell, high water or the threat of leaches, he'd get his way. "We lose everything if this gets out, Elyse. All the work, the late nights, the sacrifices, down the crapper. Are you prepared to go back to square one?"

After her husband, Frank, died, and they'd lost his income, she'd alternated feeding the kids rice and beans and peanut butter and jelly for dinner, bought them clothes at the thrift shop, and obsessed over medical bills and the increasing price of gas. She'd slowly put that epicenter of hell behind her, and she couldn't go back. She just couldn't. Over forty million people suffered from anxiety, and those were conservative estimates. Avimaxx could help so many. With the exception of a few rashes and some headaches that could be attributed to anything, the prior trials were problem free. Philip was right. People got sick and even died in drug trials every day, most would have suffered the same fate without the drug. She needed to focus on the end result, on all the people who would benefit.

"Make the call," she said.

Two hours later Vanessa Harrison from LMC was in Philip's office. She reminded Elyse of that girl in school who was only a make-up and wardrobe overhaul away from pretty. Glossy hair, enviable skin, a great figure, but she lacked the knowledge of how to make it all work for her. And that thick wad of gum she always chewed . . .

Philip seated Vanessa in the smallest chair in the room. Classic manipulation technique. He was well-versed. Intimidation was his way of taking the pulse of any situation, and his two fingers were practically on the girl's carotid artery. He squinted and scanned her face. "You confirmed Clay Jackson got Avimaxx, not the placebo, right?"

"Yes."

"So, then we need to make the switch, and you agree to that based on what we discussed."

Vanessa shifted her gum back and forth before she spoke. "But . . ." Her expression was a collage of fear, anxiety, and then as if somewhere in her head a light bulb clicked on, hope. "It will be cash?"

He circled his desk and perched on the edge, towering over her. "I'm sure you'd rather pad your wallet than Uncle Sam's."

An almost imperceptible nod, more of a twitch than a yes. "I still have some school debt, and then there's the wedding."

"It'd be a relief to pay off your student loans and have enough left for a nice reception, wouldn't it?" Elyse found herself jumping on the bandwagon. She laid a hand on the arm of Vanessa's chair. "You're doing the right thing. Avimaxx is a good product."

"And all I have to do is move Clay Jackson into the control group?"

A warm smile replaced Philip's stony veneer.

Vanessa rose from her seat but didn't speak for an interminable stretch. It was like an awkward ceremony where the bride is having second thoughts and can't bring herself to say, "I do." Then finally, "Okay, I'm in."

Elyse leaned against the credenza, braced herself, and let out the breath she'd been holding for the last two hours.

⁕ FORTY-THREE ⁕

Wednesday, April 8th

"RJ, Clay Jackson, and now this Vanessa," Tish said as she walked alongside Dylan back through the LMC parking lot. They say death comes in threes, but in the war she'd seen that number multiplied—exponentially. It wasn't safe to think they'd reached the max here.

They settled into the car. Dylan stacked his hands on the steering wheel, overlapped them, lost in deep reflection.

"What now?" she asked.

"We need something on Philip, but I'm done talking to him. The batteries on my bullshit detector are completely fried. I'd like to snoop around Saycor some more. After hours. So we wait."

"There is one other person we should check out, if not rule out," Tish said.

"I'm listening."

"Annabeth lied about seeing RJ Friday night."

"Have to say, it wouldn't break my heart to see that one behind bars."

"Wouldn't mind that either. And even if she's innocent as far as RJ is concerned, I'd like to call her out on a few other things." Tish felt her voice rising as if on a musical score, the old twang creeping back in.

"I can think of a million better ways to spend an afternoon."

Dylan's smile was tantalizingly off-center. It made her go fizzy inside.

Her imagination skipped along beside him. This man could monopolize every afternoon, and she suspected she'd never be happier.

"So, what's next for you?" Dylan asked. "When this is all over."

"Back to Savannah."

He slid his hand along her jaw. "If you can work me in, I'd like to take you on a proper date before you leave." He paused. "Candles, soft music, maybe a pizza, with extra onions of course. Or if that's too tame, how about twilight parasailing, then a walk with only the moon to guide us."

Now her heart was threatening to beat right out of her chest. "Sounds perfect, but—"

"I'll take sounds perfect," Dylan said with a smile. "For now." He put the car in gear, pulled from the LMC parking lot.

After a short drive, they wended their way through Briarwood, parked in front of Annabeth's. Tish took a moment to survey the property. If an ocean view had somehow been available in Crestwood, she had no doubt they'd be looking at gradients of blue instead of the gentle slopes of a lushly landscaped golf course. The unit was one of the smallest, but an elegant wrought iron door distinguished it from the others. She'd seen one installed on one of those rehab shows and they didn't come cheap.

They rang the bell, twice, and Annabeth finally opened the door, her face screwed into a what-the-hell-do-you-want grimace.

Tish had always dreaded encounters with RJ's sister, but she had a feeling she might enjoy this one. "Do you have time for a little chat?"

Annabeth's jaw was working, but no sound was coming out.

"We can wait until you find your tongue," Tish said.

"There's nothing to talk about."

Tish dropped into a fancy metal chair on the porch, crossed her legs. "Oh, I think there is."

Dylan sank into the opposite chair.

Annabeth huffed and reluctantly motioned them in. "You two are made for each other. Equally infuriating."

They stepped inside. The interior was small but right out of a page in House Beautiful. Annabeth wasn't talented enough to stage this herself. The whole place reeked of interior decorator. How did she manage that on unemployment checks and alimony? A generous brother, that's how.

"Why did you tell us you hadn't seen RJ 'in a while' when in fact you saw him the night he died?"

Something on Annabeth's wrist glistened. Elyse's tennis bracelet. "We argued that night. That was it. If you think I'd ever hurt my brother, you're as insane as I figured."

"But why lie about seeing him?"

Annabeth crammed her fists in the pockets of her long cardigan. "I don't expect you to understand, and I certainly don't owe you an explanation."

"You know what? You don't owe me an explanation. But one phone call, if I remember your words correctly, and I can—"

"What do you want from me?"

"Still wondering why you'd keep the fact that you were at RJ's the night he died to yourself," Dylan put in.

"I don't really see how it's pertinent."

"Everything related to that night is pertinent."

Annabeth bit into her bottom lip. She turned to Tish. "Your mother shoved her nose where it didn't belong. She didn't want him to lend me money."

Tish shook her head. "Lend?"

"I really don't care what you think." Annabeth dabbed at the corner of each eye. "I love my brother, and I hate that the last time I saw him we argued."

For a moment Tish felt something, not pity, there was too much history for that. Empathy? If anything happened to Luke she'd be devastated, and if their last interaction had been an argument . . . If she could capture a picture of Annabeth's soul it would be a dark smudge with poisonous tentacles, but Annabeth would be a fool to kill the only man who seemed to be able to put up with her.

"He tried to smooth things over the way he always does, this time with leftover pizza."

"Pizza?" Dylan asked.

"From La Bella. Price will eat anything, but I won't touch that cardboard crust."

"You had no trouble touching my mother's things. Starting with that bracelet."

Annabeth ripped the bracelet off and plunged it into Tish's hand.

"We'll wait while you gather anything else you might have *borrowed*," Tish said. "You know my mom keeps scrupulous records. It would be a shame to have to involve the authorities."

A tinkling of wind chimes split the thick air as the back sliding glass door opened, and Annabeth's son tromped in, one arm plastered in a neon blue cast.

"Don't forget to take your shoes off, Pricey." The boy entered the foyer, sneakers still in place, one shoelace hanging limply, unknotted. Annabeth settled a loving hand on his shoulder, apparently unconcerned that he'd ignored her request.

He grunted. "What're they doing here?"

"They were about to leave."

"Yup, we're on our way," Dylan said. "As soon as we get what we came for."

Annabeth stormed off, leaving Price playing video games on the couch. Minutes later, she returned, arms crossed. "Here's the scarf your mom let me *borrow* weeks ago. It's all I have." She uncoiled it from around her neck. "Satisfied?"

Elyse and Annabeth didn't exactly swap lip gloss, do each other's nails, and have pillow fights. "Hardly."

But trying to wrangle whatever else Annabeth might have of Elyse's was a waste of time. The visit hadn't been a total loss. Tish felt pretty certain Annabeth didn't have anything to do with RJ's death.

Back on the road, neither of them spoke for a long while. Dylan was the first to break the silence, and they agreed Annabeth was selfish but not murderous.

Tish's thoughts turned inward. Her family's safety rested squarely on her shoulders. She asked for some music, and Dylan flipped on the radio and perused the stations. All at once, Tish found herself mouthing the words, wanting to move with the beat to a song she hadn't heard for quite some time. Plumb's "I Can't Do This." But the chorus, the endless repetition of that line, caused her lungs to close and dark shadows to swim before her eyes.

"Stop the car." She needed control over something. Everything. The earth needed to be still.

Dylan turned off the radio and pulled over to the shoulder. She burst from the car and flopped onto the grass to keep from caving in on herself, willing this rise of panic to pass, but the haunting lyrics, her sense of helplessness, catapulted her back to Iraq.

The smell was the worst—the stench of diesel, dust, and death. After seven months in Baghdad Tish knew it would stay with her forever. It stole her appetite, but she had to eat to keep up her strength. She forced down the last bite of chicken and rice "stew" and shoved her plate away.

"Yo, Duchene," Sgt. Tacks shouted from across the chow hall. "How do you do it?"

She stood to leave, refusing to acknowledge the creep who'd been harassing her for months.

"How do you eat like a dude and still look like a chick." He licked his smirking lips.

Give it a rest, she wanted to say. I can pop a cap in your skinny ass from the other side of camp . . . in a sandstorm.

"Screw you, Tacks." She felt eyes sear into her back, pinpricks of hatred as she deposited her tray and left.

Maybe the smell wasn't the worst of it. Maybe it was guys like Tacks who could never accept a woman standing shoulder to shoulder with them in combat. She and Liv were outcasts, expected to earn the 'right' to be in the military day after ass-busting day.

In their tent, Liv was sitting on her cot facing the wall, bent slightly forward.

"Tacks was a real comedian again tonight. You missed the show."

Liv didn't respond.

"Hey." Tish saw through the murky, shadowed light that Liv was holding her gun. Her cheeks tear-stained. Nose raw. Tish moved toward her, held out her hand.

"Don't take another step," Liv said in a harsh whisper. "I can't do this . . . I can't pretend like it didn't—"

Tish watched in disbelief as Liv lifted the muzzle. For a moment, they were kids again, in a dark pup tent. Liv held a flashlight under her chin, trying to impress with the most gruesome ghost story. But this was no summer camp tradition. This was real life. What happened next played out in painful slow motion as Liv locked anguished eyes on Tish.

Now with Dylan by her side Tish began to cry, big throaty sobs that left her gasping for breath. Her lips trembled. She fought for air as her stomach tightened and her lunch threatened to reappear.

Placing a hand on her back, Dylan began to rub in circles. "Whatever it is, I'm here."

His tender words, his touch, calmed her racing pulse. "I lost my best friend in Iraq. It was my fault."

He brushed the hair from her eyes. "Tell me."

For several petrifying moments she considered keeping the terrible account to herself, burying it once again as she had so many times before. But burying the horror of that moment was a tactic that was eating her from the inside out. She surrendered the whole story, and it came flying out like demons in a long overdue exorcism—Liv's struggle to make it in a world she wasn't equipped for, Tish's fruitless attempt to keep her afloat, the slow motion suicide that she'd tried to stop, the image that played over and over in her mind. Again and again, ad infinitum.

Dylan's arms cinched tighter. Arms she wished would never let her go.

✥ FORTY-FOUR ✥

DYLAN stroked Tish's cheek, cupped her face in his hands. "Liv made the choice to end her life. You weren't responsible." They were sitting in a grassy patch near a small park. Anyone passing by might think they were lovers stealing a moment.

She closed her eyes, nodded. Her body sagged in his arms, as if weighted down by a heavy coat. A coat with guilt woven into the lining and filling the pockets. Dylan knew that coat well. He'd worn the damn thing for more years than he cared to remember.

"I can't say I know exactly what you're going through," he said, "but I can relate to battling those demons. Take it from me, they never completely go away, but you find a way to live with them."

Her eyes slayed him, searched his expectantly.

"I was involved in a high-speed chase, back when I was a cop. It didn't end well." He rubbed at his neck as if the past had taken hold of each muscle fiber and squeezed. "I thought the bottle was the answer. A lot of people got hurt."

When she didn't respond right away, he thought he'd blown it. They were two completely different situations. Who was he to insert his own drama into hers, to compound it?

"I'm sorry for what you went through," she said.

"For what it's worth, I've found a way to cope ... without alcohol."

A parade of women passed-by pushing baby strollers, all clad in head to toe spandex, alternating squats and lunges while cheering one another on.

Dylan stood, pulled Tish up with him.

Her determination resurfaced as a stiff resolve passed across her face. "I promised I'd take care of Luke."

"And you will. You are."

"A day of reckoning for Philip."

"All signs do point to him being involved."

She ran a hand over the bulge in her purse.

The gun he'd given her. He had little doubt she'd use it. Tish was the most capable woman he'd ever met, and he imagined her in Iraq, getting things done, taking crap from no one. Conversely, she had the softest skin, the most tender lips . . .

They moved to the car, got in.

"He's covering his tracks," Dylan said, "but there has to be something he's forgotten."

"Something that ties him to those assholes who took my mom or something that links him to RJ's death. Or what about Vanessa? That couldn't have been an accident."

"Probably not." It was like one of those convoluted math story problems where bogus information was tossed in to throw you off. He'd have to go through this case line by line and cross out the supplementary info. "Saycor's got a security system, but I might have a way around that."

"This isn't RJ's patio gate or the fire safe. You'll have to step up your game." She laughed. A sound he'd never get enough of.

"Watch and learn. But we can't go until the office is cleared out."

She seemed to be picking through a minefield of options. "No sense sitting around here."

"I'm game for just about anything as long as there's food in my near future."

"You may not want a full stomach where we're going." She directed him toward the highway and they headed south.

This sounded interesting. In some ways, it didn't matter where she was going. He'd follow her anywhere. The awareness that he was falling in love slammed into him. But soon she'd be going back to Savannah and his life would return to deciding which channel to watch and which sugary cereal to eat. Her instructions tunneled through his thoughts "turn here, a little bit further, slow down."

She finally directed him to stop. "This is it."

"There's nothing here."

Tish tilted her chin upward, her expression dead serious. "The tallest in the world at one time."

"Oh, no. Uh uh."

She bulleted for the bridge, shimmed up the stone support, and her foot located the bottom rung of the truss.

Dylan slowly opened his car door. "C'mon, Tish. I'm not going up there."

She turned. "Scared?"

"It's just that getting hit by a train—" *Or plummeting to an untimely and painful death.* "—has never been on my bucket list."

"I promise we won't get in its way." She continued to climb. "You'll love the view."

What was that about following her anywhere?

He hoisted himself over the rock that was the base of the bridge, put his foot in the first opening.

"Don't look down." Her voice was already getting too far away from him.

He kept his eyes trained on her backside, and she was right about one thing, he did love the view. Tish had a tush to end all tushes. Tish's tush. Was his knee-locking fear turning him into a complete cornball? "Wait. Let me catch up."

She stopped as he closed the gap between them. He was two rungs away, close enough to touch her, when his foot slipped. Terror flooded through him.

"Are you okay?" A reprimand masquerading as concern.

They finally reached the metal framework, a narrow platform about twenty feet below the bridge itself. Tish swung over, sat down, and indicated the spot next to her. Looping his arm through and white-knuckling the side rail, he eased down. She wasn't holding on to anything, only sitting there with her hands on her knees. This made his palms sweat.

She reached over, patted his thigh, and he felt his whole body flinch. "Relax," she said, like that was a viable option. "Pretend you're at home watching your favorite old movie, stuffing your face with oreos."

He focused on the horizon, the smell of the fresh air and the silence. He had to admit, a certain peace came over him at the wide expanse in front of him, the uneven wall of scrub pines. A large bird, maybe an eagle, rose from the treetops and soared into the distance.

"I never get tired of seeing that," Tish said, cupping her palms and blowing into them.

"You're cold." Dylan reached for her hands, enfolding them in his own, amazed that he was no longer clinging to the bridge for dear life.

"It gets a little breezy up here, but there's no better place to think."

"What are you thinking right now?"

"Liv and I used to come here a lot in the summer." Her words etched with a hint of gloom.

"A good thing?"

"The best. My family spent every summer since I can remember in Turtle Cove. I used to complain about leaving my friends in Savannah, but the summer I met Liv, that all changed. You know how sometimes someone comes into your life and you just click immediately?" She snapped her fingers.

He did. Even with the rocky start, he knew Tish would claim a piece of him, eventually all of him, one way or another.

"Besties ever since," she continued.

He ran his thumb across her hand.

"Robert loved it up here too."

At the mention of his name, jealousy came knocking. He held tighter to her hand, as if that might keep her from choosing someone else.

"But after a local boy died falling off the bridge, they didn't want to climb it anymore. I still came by myself though."

Her words dwindled to silence. She chewed the inside of her lip, her mouth pulled to the side. "I need to put it behind me once and for all." She cinched her jacket around her. "The more pressing problem is Philip. Not that I really know him, but those two goons at the boathouse don't seem like the usual type he'd hang out with."

"Maybe there's a side to Philip you haven't seen."

"Show me someone who doesn't have another side."

How he wanted to ask to see hers, to see every side of her.

They sat some more, absorbing their surroundings—the crisp air, the sky a palette of peaceful blues—until Tish spoke. "How'd you do it?" She asked. "Work on roofs?"

"Well, first I haul up a boatload of shingles, then I chalk it off—"

Tish wagged her head from side to side. "I mean with your fear of heights."

Admitting his short-comings didn't come easily, especially not with her. She was the kind of woman who might just bring out the best in him, and he could feel himself wanting to be someone she could respect and admire. "When I was sober enough to work, buzzed enough to take the edge off, I could have dangled from a hundred-foot tower and played a fiddle. But once I stopped drinking . . ."

A distant whistle sounded, and Dylan did the unthinkable, he looked down. Panic crawled like a living thing beneath his skin. Had his subconscious considered jumping as a good option to escape the approaching train?

"You're going to feel a little vibration," Tish said. "Hold on."

He linked one arm through the rail, curled a foot around it too for good measure. The train rumbled closer, and his arms went weak in their sockets, his legs liquefied. Tish leaned into him as a smile, eager as a child's, spread across her face. The sight of her trimmed the crust off his fear. Grounded him.

The sound above intensified to a thundering crescendo as the bridge began to shoot hundreds of jolts through them. Dylan imagined this is what it would feel like if a tornado combined forces with an earthquake. But it lasted only a few seconds. Then all was still. Calm. He worked his tongue against the roof of his mouth. Dry, metallic, like the steel around him had infiltrated his body. Though it shouldn't have been at the top of his to-do list, he desperately wanted to kiss her. The thought of them losing themselves in the moment and falling headlong to their deaths descended like a leaden rainfall, but this inspiration would not be denied. He pulled her close and exchanged his fear for a moment of pleasure.

"We should go," Tish said. Spoken in a whisper.

Disappointment mingled with relief. He'd be more than happy to have two feet on solid ground but didn't want the moment to end. Would they have this opportunity again? Uninterrupted time together?

As they drove, Dylan noticed how the grass looked greener than before, the sky bluer. It was as if Mother Nature had dumped a heap of Technicolor, amping everything up to its best and brightest. He stole glances at Tish. He'd known her for a few days, but it felt like he'd known her his whole life.

But he was getting ahead of himself. He needed to wrap up this case.

In the Saycor parking garage, Dylan stopped next to a lime-green VW bug. He opened the passenger door, nabbed a key card from the cup holder. "Philip needs to do a better job training his employees if he wants Fort Knox security."

"How—"

"On Monday, I saw the owner of this car grab a suitcase and jump into another car muttering something about hating week-long road trips. When we walked by, I peeked in and noticed the key card and that beautiful unlocked door."

"Nice work, maybe you're more talented than I thought." She smiled a bright smile that made her lips even more appealing, though he hadn't thought that was possible.

Dylan hiked his eyebrows in a suggestive dance. "Tip of the iceberg, baby."

Once inside Saycor, Dylan marched straight to Mae's desk, pilfered through her top drawer, and found a set of keys. Tish waited patiently while he tried three on Gretchen's door before finding the right one. In her office, he slid a chair under a vent close to the ceiling, stood on it and removed the cover. Sure enough, a camera, capturing his every move. "Would love to get a look at what's on these tapes. We should check out Philip's office, see if we can hack into his system."

Tish was sliding books from the bookcase, flipping through, putting them back. "He's likely spying on everyone, not just

Gretchen. That's probably how he found out Mom had the flash drive." She picked up a notepad on the desk and a pencil from a caddy. She ran the pencil over the paper, shading a blotch.

Dylan moved to her, looked over her shoulder. "Good call. Sometimes the old tried and true is just the ticket." He read Vanessa Harrison's name and address aloud.

"Friends?"

"Or Gretchen wrote it down for Philip."

They turned to a sound in the hallway.

Speak of the devil.

"I didn't really peg you two as trespassers." Gretchen's lips thinned to pale blades, masking that extra tooth.

"Guess you knew a little more about Elyse's schedule than you let on," Dylan said.

Gretchen pulled a gun from her coat pocket, pointed it at them.

Tish's eyes flicked to her purse on the chair. Dylan inched over, blocking Gretchen's view.

"Don't move again." She waved the gun at each of them.

"You were responsible for Vanessa's death," Tish said.

"She was about to ruin everything. I've worked too damn hard."

"I get it," Dylan said. "All the years of sacrifice. Hours and hours in the office. Catering to Philip's every whim. It had to be brutal."

A wisp of movement from Tish as she reached for her purse.

"Stop!" Gretchen demanded. "You aren't half as clever as you think." She indicated the purse. "Give me that."

Maybe this one wasn't a lemming after all.

⊰ FORTY-FIVE ⊱

Friday, April 3rd, Five Days Earlier

VANESSA stood in Elyse's office doorway wearing a distressed look that matched her outfit: A floral print skirt an awkward three inches below her knee and a wide-shouldered jacket the eighties wanted back.

Elyse waved her in. "What's wrong?"

Vanessa shoved a hand in her pocket, came out with a piece of gum. She unwrapped it deftly, folded it in half, and placed it on her tongue. "I'm not sleeping. I have constant heart burn."

"It's done," Elyse said. "Put it behind you."

"I can't. I even had a dream last night that Mr. Jackson's family came to my house and those three little girls just pointed at me and bawled."

"You're over-thinking, Vanessa. All we did was make sure that this unfortunate event didn't hold up the clinical trial. Clay Jackson's death was unrelated to Avimaxx."

"We don't know that for sure, do we?"

They didn't know a damn thing for sure. But that was all part of the risk/reward in this business. Elyse had spent hours trying to convince herself. All for the greater good. "Nothing is ever absolute."

Vanessa shook her head, dropped into a chair, stretched the gum over her tongue as if to blow a bubble, but didn't.

"Remember, a lot of people will benefit from this drug," Elyse continued.

"I want to give the money back. I bought a car, but I can sell it."

"We can't undo this," Elyse said, tone rising.

"It was a mistake—"

"No. The trial ends with a careless oversight like that. Think about it. If the testing company doesn't know which participants had the drug and which had the placebo how could they be expected to run a clean trial?"

LMC might have their neck on the chopping block, but Elyse certainly knew what was at stake for Saycor. They'd sunk close to a billion already heading into Phase III, and if they quit now Avimaxx was dead in the water, and the company would soon follow.

Silence weighed on her shoulders, screamed in her ears. Finally, Vanessa spoke. "I know LMC is running the trial. Why do you feel you need to remind me?"

"We're out a shitload of money, true, but you'll never be trusted again."

Vanessa slid her phone from her pocket and lifted it above her head, trophy-style. "You'll be out more than money." Her voice had taken on a different tone, a threatening tone.

"What are you talking about?"

"I've been recording classes and meetings since grad school. It's easier than taking notes."

Paralysis set in. What the hell?

"I recorded the conversation in Philip's office when you convinced me to move Clay Jackson to the placebo group." Vanessa jabbed at the screen, and Elyse's words rolled through the speaker. "We wouldn't suggest this if . . ."

Vanessa spat her gum into the wrapper and popped another piece into her mouth, chomped a few seconds until it became pliable. "I racked up a ton of debt putting myself through college and grad school. You'd think I make a lot of money with an education like that, but I don't."

A vein throbbed in Elyse's temple, threatened to explode.

Vanessa stared at her, eyes wide, shifting her gum from one side of her mouth to the other.

"You're blackmailing us?"

"Your words, not mine." A sharp-fanged rat had swallowed the once mousy creature. Vanessa rose, started for the door. "Talk to Philip."

"Vanessa, we can't—"

She was gone.

Elyse wildly tapped a pencil on her desk and prayed for calm. When that failed, she snapped the pencil in half, jumped from her chair and race-walked into Philip's office. Gretchen stopped filing, looked up.

"He's at a lunch with the investment bankers," Gretchen said. "I don't expect him for at least another hour. Is everything okay?"

Elyse braced her hands on the back of the chair as the walls of Saycor crumbled around her. "I'll try his cell."

On the way back to her office, Mae intercepted her. "That weird chick from LMC left this when she was signing out. No offense, but you smart people can be so scattered sometimes. And what's with her outfit?" Mae handed over Vanessa's phone, turned and scooted to the reception desk as if suddenly realizing she had to get back to her post.

Elyse stared at the gift in her hand. She could end this here and now. No one else except Philip knew about switching Clay Jackson to the placebo group. That was the beauty of a controlled trial. Few people knew who was in what group.

Maybe they could survive this.

If Vanessa hadn't backed up the audio file.

If.

FORTY-SIX

Wednesday, April 8th

A chill wrinkled through Tish as Dylan unfurled the Glock, held it within Gretchen's reach. She extended her arm, but drew her empty hand back with a staccato flick of her wrist.

"Put it on the floor . . . kick it to me." Her voice hitched. This role wasn't routine for her, and Tish didn't discount how wrong it could go. A person with nothing to lose could be every bit as dangerous as a well-trained soldier.

Gretchen squatted, picked up the Glock, dropping it in her cross-body bag without losing eye contact. Keeping her gun trained on them, she shoved Tish's purse in the bottom drawer of a filing cabinet and kicked it shut with her heel. "Now let's go." She paused, as if formulating her plan on the spot. On the other hand, maybe she was thinking about capping them both now just to get it over with. She led them from the office, down the stairwell and out the back entrance of the building to a silver sedan. "Get in, you're driving," she said to Dylan.

Under a dim street light, Tish noticed a dent and series of long claw-like scratches on the front bumper. Was the smash and run Gretchen's M.O.? Had she hired help to run the Sebring off the road? Was hers the last face Vanessa saw?

Tish had sensed Gretchen's dogged devotion to her career, even admired her for it. She was the type who turned down Sunday brunch with friends to make sure she approached Monday morning with half the day's itinerary already checked off. But Tish had honestly never imagined hostage taking—or murder—as line items on her project plan.

Dylan eased behind the wheel, Tish slid in next to him. Gretchen tossed him the keys from the backseat, breathing heavy as she positioned the gun at Tish's back. "In case you have any detours in mind."

Tish listened as Gretchen placed a call. "It's me. Meet me at Walnut Hills Park . . . I, well, I really think you'll want to see this." Then to Dylan, "Take the back way."

As they drove into the thickening darkness, Tish's thoughts swirled. Had Gretchen been the mastermind all along? Was she calling the bug-eyed Brit or the big guy or both to come help her with the finishing touches?

When they had driven deep into the park, Gretchen instructed Dylan to stop.

"If you tell us what's going on, we can help you figure this out," Tish tried.

"All I need to figure out is how to keep you quiet."

In the distended silence, questioning glances volleyed between Tish and Dylan until two beams of light came into view.

A gold Range Rover.

Gretchen waggled the gun. "Get out . . . slowly . . . I'm not afraid to use it."

This whole scene was almost comical, clichéd to say the least, like Gretchen had a *Holding Hostages At Gunpoint For Dummies* next to the stack of management books in her office. But then, maybe she did. Maybe she'd been planning this, researching how to commit the perfect crime until her eyes nearly bled.

Before opening his car door, Dylan said, "I've seen these situations go from bad to worse too many times, Gretchen. How about we put the stopper in before we're all circling the drain."

Gretchen pressed the gun into his shoulder. "Not. Another. Word."

They poured from the car as Philip exited his and opened the passenger door.

A figure emerged and the fear Tish had tried to tamp down came gasping to the surface. Her heart pounded beneath her ribs. In the bright stream of headlights, she saw a dot of shaving cream under his left earlobe next to a square of toilet paper where he'd nicked himself. Luke, hands tied behind his back, eyes flashing with terror.

She started to move toward him.

"Don't," Gretchen snapped.

"Where's Elyse?" Tish asked.

She'd only just found her mother. How was she asking this same question again?

"I don't know," Philip said. "Your brother showed up in a cab, ranting about how she couldn't go to jail."

Luke must have overheard them talking through Elyse's predicament. How had Tish been so naïve to think he would miss a beat? Or had Elyse broken down when they were on Robert's plane and confessed everything?

Her brother's eyes shone big and round. He didn't deserve this. He'd never hurt anyone.

"Why is he tied up?" Tish asked.

"For his own safety. I didn't want him jumping out of my car. He's lucky I didn't tape his mouth shut too. He was babbling the whole way about the comparative properties of gasses and solids."

"Because he's nervous."

"Particles in a solid are tightly packed," Luke started up, "with a regular pattern, but on the other hand—"

Tish caught his gaze. "Remember when you were little and the story about Jesus on the cross gave you a stomach ache?"

"Mom told me to recite the 23rd Psalm in my head."

"Try that now, okay?"

"This is sweet, really," Gretchen interjected. "But let's get down to business."

"What business?" Dylan asked. "You and your boss going to knock us off like you did RJ and Vanessa? Then what?"

Philip focused on Gretchen's gun as if for the first time. "What did you do?" The words barely escaping lips pressed tight.

"What I always do." She straightened as a look of pride winged her face. "Behind every great leader is someone willing to dot the I's and cross the T's."

In Philip's presence, she had transformed into the picture of efficiency, Siri in the flesh.

Philip scraped his fingernails over the crown of his head, stopping to clutch a fistful of hair, genuinely shocked. "Vanessa? And RJ? He didn't even know about switching Clay Jackson to the placebo group."

"I didn't kill RJ. But when I heard that little bitch blackmailing you and Elyse, I knew what had to be done." Gretchen's expression held a note of petulance that stopped short of an eye roll.

"I didn't think anybody knew about the bugs, the surveillance cameras," Philip said.

All the sneaking around, spying and deception. For what? Money? Power? Did it even matter? Right now, Tish had one priority: her brother.

Philip expelled an extended guttural moan, and Tish envisioned the wildlife in the surrounding woods running for cover.

Gretchen's bag, holding Dylan's gun, held tightly across her chest. Tish could tackle her, wrestle the one from her hand if she knew Philip wasn't armed, but she couldn't be sure. And with Luke's hands tied behind his back, he'd be an easy target if this went south. She wished for a conduit into Dylan's thoughts so together they could formulate a plan. At that moment, he turned to her, stealing glances at Philip. *He's more with us than her.* At least that's what she thought he telegraphed her way.

The army had trained her to think and act within a matter of seconds. No vacillating on the next move, no freezing in place. No questions asked. But this was an entirely different animal. This was personal. Her own brother had been pulled across enemy lines. Her actions could get him killed.

Before she could make her move, Luke took off, lumbering toward the woods in an awkward hands-tied-behind-his-back gait.

Gretchen wheeled around, fired. The high-pitched after-ring echoed through the air. Tish opened her mouth but wouldn't let herself scream, because if she did . . . she might never stop.

⊷ FORTY-SEVEN ⊷

SAVE Luke first. Dylan sprang into action, but Gretchen grabbed Tish around the waist to keep her from racing after her brother.

Tish wrenched her arm forward and back, landing an elbow in Gretchen's gut.

Gretchen doubled over, and Dylan jumped in, snagged the gun. He pointed it at her, swiveled it to Philip.

"Time out," Philip said, shooting his arms in the air. "This has gotten way out of hand."

Dylan swung the gun back to Gretchen. She was slumped against the car, fixed in place, as if reality had come up from the ground below, coiling around her, constricting like a boa. He tried to dislodge the bag from her, but she held tight.

"Give it to him!" Philip demanded.

She unwound the strap, gave up the purse with leaden movements.

Dylan handed it off to Tish. She pulled out the Glock, held it on Philip.

"Listen, I swear, you don't have to worry about me," Philip said. "Go get Luke."

Dylan stood there for the space of a dozen rapid heartbeats, deciding what to do. But the answer was flashing neon on Tish's face.

"Give me your keys," he said to Philip.

Philip tossed them, and Gretchen's eyes followed the arc

without turning her head.

Sticks and leaves crunched under foot as Dylan and Tish ran through the woods, shouting for Luke. His fingers curled around her hand, gripped with the surreal possibility that it might already be too late. If something happened, how could he bend the rest of his life around letting this woman down? He could have handled Philip and Gretchen, especially Gretchen, he'd certainly done his time with crazy. And he felt confident that he and Tish would have come out on the right side of this.

If they weren't the only ones making their way through this knothole. Tish's brother added a deep wrinkle, a hitch he hadn't counted on. Didn't Tish say that Robert had flown Elyse and Luke somewhere safe?

"I don't hear a thing," Tish said, layer upon layer of fear stratified in her voice.

"Luke!" they shouted in unison.

"Maybe we should split up," she said.

"And have all three of us lost in the woods?"

"You're right . . . I . . . damn. I hate feeling so helpless. What if he was hit?"

"I don't think he was." What he didn't want to say was that they would have a seen blood trail if he had been shot. "Let's stay on this path. He'd follow the main one, right?"

"Not necessarily. He may rely on a constellation or the Pythagorean Theorem or the growth patterns of the brush. I just don't know . . ." Her words melted into a panicked groan.

They slowed to a trot, alternately calling out and listening for a response until they came to a clearing and there he was, back to them, chin lifted to the sky. Rope still around one wrist, the other free.

"Thank God, you're okay," Tish said, moving toward him.

Luke pivoted and backed away like a frightened animal. Tish lunged, but it was too late. She screamed. Dylan shot to her side. Peering over the steep embankment, they could see him clinging to a tree hovering above a deep ravine.

And a stream filled with jagged rocks.

"Are you hit?" Dylan aimed his question downward.

"I . . . I don't think so."

"Hold on, Luke," Tish said. "I'm coming."

Dylan's hand closed around her wrist. "It's slippery. You'll fall too." He ripped off his shirt. "Give me your coat."

She handed it to him and he tied the arms of his shirt and her coat together. "Anchor to that tree and hold tight." He gave her one of the ends. Standing there, T-shirt clad, peering downward as if into a shark tank, he felt a complicated mix of valor and trepidation. "Here's my phone," he said. "Give me some light."

He pointed his feet in the right direction and forced them to go. Swallowing his panic, he tested a branch and lowered himself down as Tish held a death grip on the coat.

It would be a helluva lot easier if he didn't have to look down, but he had to find the trustworthy places on this risky terrain. He found a spot, tried it with his boot, and it gave way an inch or two before it held. A vibration of fear bellowed through his body as he puzzled over his next move. There were rocky formations and spindly weed trees jutting out here and there, the trick was finding the dependable ones. And the true test would be making it back up this embankment with Luke in tow. The thought only bullied his confidence. What was that called? Zen. He needed to find some, pronto. *Relax*. Which might have worked if he hadn't botched his next step and found himself hugging good ol' mother earth.

Tish's voice came from what seemed like a great distance. "Are you okay?"

"I'm all right," he said, spitting dirt from his mouth.

Luke was two feet below him, hands wrapped around a branch, reciting something in a robotic tone. "The letter E is absolutely the most common letter in the English language, followed by T and then A. As far as numbers, ten is more common than—"

Dylan extended his hand as if coaxing a wild animal. "Grab on."

"No."

Luke's hands were petrified to the tree. Dylan was familiar with this kind of immobilizing, crippling fear.

"It's okay," Tish yelled down the steep slope.

Dylan knew better than to reach out and grab him. Luke took a step, transferring his hand to a low hung branch. A loud crack.

Dylan braced himself to watch Luke go tumbling down the ravine. When he didn't, Dylan gave a brief letting-go kind of sigh. "Buddy, you don't mind if I call ya buddy *now* do ya?" Inside he was a trembling mess, but he forced the fear from his voice, trying to replace it with a little humor. "We're kind of in a jam here, and I need you to take my hand. See, I'm not crazy about heights. Never have been. I'd sure appreciate it if you had my back."

Luke latched onto Dylan as the branch broke off and went crashing into the rocks below. After a duet of deep breaths, they made their way upward, using the same hit and miss method Dylan had used on the way down.

Tish started toward her brother, stopped. "Guess we've both reached our quota."

He eyed her quizzically.

"You've had enough touchy-feely stuff, and I've had enough of you scaring the crap out of me."

"Deal. But it's rare that the fear response elicits an actual bowel—"

"Stop." The panic that had been squeezing Tish's throat departed, making space for a desire to laugh and cry at once. "I get it."

Tish turned to Dylan. "Thank you."

And it might have been a pleasant place for a happy ending, if they didn't have Bonnie and Clyde waiting for them on the other side of the wood.

Philip and Gretchen leaned against the Ranger Rover, their breath floating up through the night chill in two parallel streams of vapor. Philip steeped in a strenuously stoic air, but the woman beside him was toast. She had given it all for the company, but whatever she was trying to attain—status, money, power. All gone. Had something in her past set her up for this? Maybe she'd been raised on dreams that she could do anything, have anything. Or the opposite.

Analyzing this crazy would have to wait.

Tish settled Luke in the car before returning to Dylan.

Philip took an obvious distancing step from Gretchen. "I honestly thought Mr. Jackson's death was a fluke, or a one in a million outlier that wouldn't make a difference in the long run. We had to move him into the placebo group to keep the trial going. Do you realize how much we would have lost if we hadn't?"

A rhetorical question. Philip didn't want answers; he'd already justified his actions, and now he wanted to scrub his soul.

"We convinced the manager of the clinical trial at LMC to make the change," he continued. "Vanessa was the only one who could do it. Then she panicked, or, I don't know, got greedy. I didn't find out she'd tried to blackmail us until I saw the video footage. When I heard she'd had a car accident I was honestly"—he coughed as if the words stung his throat—"well I'm not proud of this but I was relieved. All I had to worry about was Elyse and that flash drive."

"So you spied on my mother."

"I've been screwed a lot in the past." He rubbed his forehead. "I would never hurt her. I had a guy follow her to get the flash drive. That's all."

"Guys," Dylan said.

Philip cocked his head. "I don't understand."

"There were two," Tish supplied.

His face grimaced in confusion. "I only hired one. I'd . . . well, I'd used him before, and he got the job done. Plus, I was desperate, in a hurry. If this got out . . . I've never met the guy in person. He had a British accent." Philip's whole body sagged as he puffed out a breath. "Sounding so B movie now, but it all happened so fast."

"Yeah well, they forgot to send in the stunt doubles before they nearly killed us trying to run us off the road."

"That wasn't supposed to happen. I just told them you were looking for Elyse and they needed to keep an eye out for your car."

"You had other options," Tish went on, and even under the blanket of night, Dylan could see that she was balling her fists.

He placed his hand over hers, squeezed. *Let him bury himself.*

She squeezed back.

Philip spoke now in a different version of his voice, where elucidation and lament coalesced. "He must have thought there was bigger money to be made from what was on that flash drive than what I'd promised him. He was only supposed to search her, search her car. Not freaking kidnap her!"

Greed. The sin that could turn even the whistle-clean into complete dirt bags.

"What about RJ?" Tish asked.

"I had nothing to do with that, I swear," Philip said. "He was my best friend."

He turned to Gretchen.

After a convulsive shake of her head, she said in a throaty monotone, "I don't know anything."

"Those same guys, then?" Dylan asked.

"I never mentioned RJ. I had no reason to think he even knew about the flash drive, and that's all I was after."

Dylan angled an appraising look his way. "As far as we know, you were the last to see RJ. That will get the cops' attention."

"He was very much alive when I left. I had another appointment and have people who can vouch for me." He hesitated, but then as if realizing the barn door had already swung open and the animals were running free, he spilled the rest. "I'm in a biweekly poker game. High stakes."

"IU with TD," Tish said.

"Illegal underground. Terrance hosts it."

So if Philip didn't kill RJ and Gretchen didn't—he'd be shocked if she possessed the upper body strength to hold a man under water, no matter how drunk he was—who did?

The question rolled around like a skeeball until it dropped solidly in the hole.

⸙ FORTY-EIGHT ⸙

A whisk-me-through-Oz tornado was spewing debris around Tish's brain, which made it difficult to gain her balance.

"The guy called himself Macbeth," Philip had said, before the police carted him and Gretchen away. "Here's his number, but I doubt it's still valid. I don't know the other guy's name. Like I said, I didn't know there was another guy."

Amazing how forthcoming the once tight-lipped CEO had become when his lies could no longer mask the truth.

After Luke retreated to Robert's guest room, his new comfort zone, Dylan, Tish and Elyse held a pow-wow.

"How did Luke end up back here, Mom?"

Elyse gripped her glass of wine, stopped short of taking a sip. "Helen would say I brought this all on myself, that Karma's a bitch," she said with a sad laugh. "But it seemed like the harder I tried to make things right, the worse they got."

"I know a little something about that," Dylan said. His voice was kind and understanding, and Tish felt her heart warm.

"I thought everything was fine," Elyse said. "Robert and I talked over coffee this morning while Luke was listening to NPR. About how either Philip or I would end up in prison, or maybe both of us, but if he had his way it would be me."

"And Luke picked up every word."

Elyse favored her with a slight smile. "I should have known better. Then Robert left for the store to pick up groceries, and I was just so exhausted, I fell back asleep. Luke left; took a cab to the bus station. By the time Robert returned and we searched all over town, we figured he was half way to Philip's."

"It's over now." But this was far from over, they both knew that.

Elyse took her glass into the kitchen, rinsed it out, then started for the back of the house. "I need a hot shower."

When she heard the bathroom door shut, Tish leaned closer to Dylan and spoke softly, so Luke couldn't hear from the other room. "You're probably ready to forget all this."

"Still the matter of RJ."

"They'll probably reopen the case. I'm sure the local police will have it covered."

Dylan flashed that sideways grin that had knocked her on her butt the first time it made an appearance. "Trying to get rid of me?"

"I can't pay you, and Elyse isn't in a position to either, given what's coming down the pike for her."

A muscle bunched in his jaw and made her instantly regret the words.

"I don't need to get paid," he said. "Let's just say, I'll sleep better knowing this is resolved."

"I think we all will."

"As I see it, we have two choices. Tell the cops what we know and let them handle it, or dig up everything we can to put the guy away for a long, long time and hand it to them on a silver platter."

"You sound like you know who did it."

"Don't you?"

She narrowed her gaze at him. "You're the Private I."

That smile again, a thousand watt, blinding. He tapped both her shoulders. "I now dub you my apprentice." A slow wink. "Probationary status of course."

"Lead the way, boss."

Twenty minutes later, they were at Pizza La Bella. "Need to make a pit stop," Tish said, already halfway to the restroom. If she didn't, she'd be headed for a serious bladder infection. Pausing before the mirror over the sink, she glimpsed her own reflection.

She pushed a limp wisp of hair from her eyes and said, "It's all right, Featherweight." Her dad, still in her head. Always in her head.

Back at the front, Dylan was arguing with the guy behind the counter.

"It's not like I'm asking to see the corporate personnel records, which by the way, yours is going to contain a nasty letter in about a week," Dylan said.

You'll catch more flies with honey. Her dad again. Tish approached, armed with her best magnolia-infused southern charm. "It just hit me. Theo James. You know, the guy in *Divergent*."

The kid looked confused, but she had his attention.

"I bet you get that a lot. You could be his twin!" If she squinted and canted her head at a forty-five-degree angle, there was a passing resemblance in the eyes. She remembered a Buzzfeed headline: "Is Theo James a Mythological God?" She stole a glance at Dylan. Theo wasn't the only one.

A softening in the kid as he considered the comparison.

"We only need to see the logs for one night," she said.

He nodded and disappeared into the back office.

Dylan let out a long, low whistle. "Impressive."

She shrugged, which prompted him to wag his head in disbelief. "You don't even realize what a genius you are, do you? Not to mention downright gorgeous."

As a blistering heat spiked up her neck, the manager returned with a one-page print out. "You didn't get this from me."

Tish pulled an imaginary zipper over her lips then shifted her attention to finding the Crestwood address. Mushroom, green pepper, and sausage delivered at 10 p.m.

Directly below that, the evidence they needed in twelve-point courier font.

❧ FORTY-NINE ☙

AT the Jackson house, light from the street lamp glanced off the picture window, and behind the blinds, Dylan caught the profile of a figure sitting at the kitchen table. Maybe he should have insisted on doing this alone. Tish had been through enough hell in the last few days to last a lifetime.

He knocked.

The figure rose and dragged to the door.

Dylan half-expected Seth to make a run for it like he had at the cemetery, but he backed away and resumed his spot at the table. "Not surprised to see you."

The thought of a kid, on the cusp of adulthood, with nothing in front of him but a prison sentence, tore at Dylan. But that sympathy faded with one glimpse at Tish trying to hold it together.

The house was too quiet. Mrs. Jackson didn't appear to be home, or those three little munchkins. Dylan closed his eyes against the thought of them quaking in the aftermath of all this.

"We have some questions," Tish said.

Seth crossed his ankle over his knee in a casual pose, but there was a weariness in the set of his shoulders. "I'd offer you a Coke or something, but we're out."

Dylan hauled a chair from the table for Tish, sat down in the one next to it. They circled the checkered tablecloth as if waiting for a home-cooked meal.

Looking through his ex-cop goggles, Dylan could see the kid

was processing things, maybe inventing lies.

"We know you delivered a pizza to RJ Corman the night he died," Dylan started.

Seth sucked his bottom lip between his teeth and bit down hard, wiped his hand across his mouth. "Yeah."

"What happened that night?" Tish asked, showing remarkable restraint for someone sitting across from the person who might be responsible for RJ's death. "I need to know what happened to my . . . to my dad."

"Mr. Corman was pretty wasted. He gave me the alarm code when he called in his order, laughed about it, said he didn't want to leave the comfort of his hot tub."

Mr. Corman. Dylan noted respect in the kid's tone. "Go on."

"When I got there the music was loud, and no offense, but Mr. Corman kind of started dicking me around, and I'd already had a long night dealing with assholes. Usually he's real nice, but like I said, he was feeling no pain. Made me bring him his wallet from the kitchen. He laughed again when he realized the pizza was already on his charge card. He pulled out a wad of cash and peeled off a dollar. Handed it to me and laughed some more. I didn't know if it was on accident or he was trying to be funny. Then he said, 'just kidding' like he was the funniest man on earth. He asked me if I wanted a drink. I told him I was working; told him I wasn't even twenty-one yet. Then he drunk-whispered, 'I won't tell if you don't.' When I told him I needed to go, he handed me a hundred-dollar bill. As hammered as he was, I thought maybe he thought it was a ten, so I said, 'are you sure?' He just made this drunk-clown face and fanned the rest of his cash in front of him. 'Take it. I'll make lots more dealing drugs.'" Seth's hands clenched on the table. "He just kept laughing and laughing."

"None of that sounds like RJ," Tish said.

"Take it or leave it."

There was no way to tell if the kid was solid, embellishing, or downright lying. Dylan's hunch was that he was being truthful. He knew firsthand how the lack of inhibitions could make people shit-faced stupid.

"So what happened next?" Dylan asked.

Seth's gaze hopped between them. "You wired or something? Guess I shoulda asked that sooner. Probably doesn't matter anyway though."

Dylan shook his head. "No sir."

"It was never my plan, what happened. I actually liked Mr. Corman. He was always a good guy, you know?" His lips stretched in a sad smile.

"Did you drink with him?" Tish asked.

"Naw, I left." Seth ran a finger around the curve of his jaw. The kid probably hadn't even been shaving long and here they were suspecting him of killing a man. "It didn't bother me at first. I chalked it up to Mr. Corman being blitzed beyond belief. I drove around, even delivered a couple more pizzas. But taking that big tip from him started to feel like stealing from a kid or somebody who didn't know any better, so I went back when my shift was done. I let myself in, and I was going to give back the money. I had a speech all planned too. About what a jerk he was, how he shouldn't flaunt his cash like that. Not everybody is rich like him. The old man was a prune by now, and still acting a fool. He said, 'you're back' like I was his long-lost friend. I looked around at his fancy schmancy digs, his waterfall with the lights, his super expensive empty booze bottles, even his suede or cashmere slippers or whatever the hell they were by the hot tub. Then he says, 'hey I was kind of an ass before, wasn't I? Sorry, but it's been a rough week. A guy in one of our drug trials died.' Matter-of-fact, like that. He didn't know he was talking about my dad. He knew me as the pizza guy, not the kid whose dad died from one of the drugs he and his wife were peddling. Not the kid whose mom was going to wonder how to put food on the table while he sat around roasting in a hot tub with a big wad of cash in his hand. I pushed him under the water so I wouldn't have to listen to him say anything more. Held him there. I was only going to teach him a lesson, let him feel what my dad must have felt like when his heart gave out. Scare him a little and then tell him that was my dad he was talking about. I swear I didn't hold him under that long, and then he . . . stopped moving. I freaked out and got the hell outta there."

Tish folded her arms across her stomach as if feeling a sharp pain. "And the fire at my mom's house on Lake Anaba?"

"Your mom is the reason my dad is dead. Her being the manager of drug trials and shit or whatever. And it didn't seem right, Mr. Corman dying when they were all guilty. My life was over either way. I googled her and got her address. I broke a window, set some rags on fire under the water heater."

"And Mr. Kelrich?" Dylan asked.

Seth stared out the window. "I'd eventually get him too."

Irony on steroids. Here they were keeping this guy from going after the one who got this disastrous ball rolling: Philip.

∽ FIFTY ∾

SETH'S confession ricocheted through Tish as she ran a bare foot over Robert's carpet. She bit down hard on the ice in her mouth. Despite a history of disapproval regarding Tish's aggressive relationship with ice, Elyse made no protest.

Dylan had dropped her off at Robert's after they'd taken Seth to the police station. He'd gone willingly, ready to face the consequences. She'd forgive him one day for what he'd done, but she'd never forget. And for a sliver of a moment, she even felt sorry for him, for his need for revenge that had forever altered his life.

And she knew all too well how a split decision could haunt you forever.

Elyse dabbed at her eyes. The torrent of tears unleashed upon learning about RJ's final hours had stopped, but the morose mood hung thick and heavy in the room, like a tent weighted with monsoon rains.

Maybe a different topic would help. "I still can't believe Luke took a bus," Tish said with a long slow shake of her head. "I didn't think there would be enough disinfecting wipes in existence for him to ride a bus."

"I remember the first time he took a cab on his own when he moved here. He wore a surgical mask and told the driver it was the only way to ward off airborne illnesses in germ-ridden places. He got dropped off a mile from his destination."

Tish fell back against the couch. "That's huge. Why didn't you tell me he was making this kind of progress?"

"You haven't exactly been easy to communicate with . . . especially since Iraq. When I do get ahold of you, it's like you can't wait to get off the phone. That's why I thought this weekend would be good for us."

"It might have been . . ."

"If I hadn't screwed things up. And cost RJ his life." Tears continued to stream down her face. "I'll never forgive myself."

Tish ran a reassuring hand down her arm. Her mom would punish herself enough for both of them. "You didn't kill him, Mom. Seth did."

"I need you to do something for me."

"What is it?"

"First thing tomorrow morning, I'm going to the police. I've no idea how this will play out. If they determine Clay Jackson died because of Avimaxx"—she sucked in a lungful of air—"there could be prison time."

Tish had been preparing herself for this eventuality, but hearing her mom say it, watching her pained expression, broke her heart. In a role reversal where Tish had now taken the reins, she should know exactly what to say. Still, no words presented themselves. There was nothing she could think of to put her mom's fears at ease.

"I won't deny I'm scared out of my mind," Elyse said. "But if I know you and Luke are okay, it'll make things a lot easier."

"You don't have to worry about us."

"Can you stay with him?"

"No."

Tish turned to find Luke, in the doorway. "No," he repeated. "No one needs to micromanage me. I'm no one's subordinate." Each convincing syllable perfectly rounded, emphasis where it naturally should rest. She'd never admired him more.

She and Elyse rose in tandem, rounded the couch and embraced Luke. A Bible verse memorized in summer camp came barreling back to her. "A person standing alone can be attacked and defeated, but two can stand back-to-back and conquer. Three are even better, for a triple-braided cord is not easily broken."

If ever they needed to hold together, it was now.

"No more," Luke said, breaking away. "Hugging has never been in my wheelhouse. It's time for you both to respect that."

At least some things were back to normal.

He retreated to another room, and Tish grabbed a Sancerre from the wine fridge.

"I'm going to enjoy this while I can," Elyse said with a dubious laugh. "Doubt they serve this in the slammer."

"Not funny, Mom."

"Joking about it keeps me from turning myself inside out with anxiety."

"I can stay in town as long as you need me."

"You being here would bring me comfort, but honestly now that I think about it, I'd feel too guilty. You've got your own life to get back to." She canted her head in a question. "Unless of course there's another reason you want to stay in the area."

Tish averted her gaze.

"Dylan is . . . how is that Helen puts it . . . 'All that and a bag of chips'?"

He was the whole chip aisle. In fact, the only guy she'd ever met that made her curious, no, eager to follow that fine invisible thread into her future. But the timing was wrong. She had no job. Emotional baggage up the ying yang. Savannah was the only thing that made sense right now.

"If you don't need me, and Luke wants to go it alone, I'm going to go back home, okay?"

Elyse leaned back and examined her with the intensity she usually reserved for her work and then softened. For the first time, Tish felt like her mother was really seeing her. "Anything's okay with me as long as you're happy."

And here they were, after all this madness, finally reaching some hybrid of agreement. Sharing a perspective. Seeing each other, and that seeing truly wasn't about magnification after all, putting flaws under a lens and watching them loom large. She thought about her dad's tutorial on the telescope's ability to gather more light than the human eye, its light gathering power.

Maybe a shorter word for that was love.

⊰ FIFTY-ONE ⊱

DYLAN convinced Tish they needed to meet and was surprised when she suggested Turtle Cove. No matter how much she loved lake sunsets, it must be hard to walk past that shell of a house. Legs dangling from the dock, they had front row seats. She'd told him she wanted to see one more before she headed back to Savannah.

The sun was still about a good fist from the horizon, holding its own against the thickening twilight. When she turned her head to study him with a send-off look that he recognized, he couldn't stop himself from swiping her bangs away from her eyes. And that was enough to make him fall apart.

An air current above held a red-tailed hawk, hovering, calling out, screeching.

Say something to her.

Tish tucked her hands between her knees, rocked forward and then back to a rhythm he wasn't a part of. She was drifting away from him, and there didn't seem to be a damn thing he could do about it. It was like she couldn't wait for April to be over so she could tear off that calendar page, wad it up, and throw it into the trash. Never to look back.

A cloud insinuated itself over the sun, but not in an ominous way. It seemed like a partnership, a connection. And Dylan reminded himself, sometimes cloudy skies produce the most spectacular sunsets. He wiped his hands up and down his jeans. "It'll be a long process, but given what your mom's been through, being kidnapped and all, they might go easy on her."

"Hope so."

He listened for the things she didn't say, rifling through a few details in his mind. Elyse would likely serve time. There would be some rough days ahead for her, stressful days, endless days.

"What will you do now?" he asked.

Tish pressed her lips together until they turned white. "Go back to Savannah. Get a job. Lord knows we could use the money."

We.

"Mom could lose the Crestwood house," Tish continued. "She wasn't even on the deed. RJ put Annabeth's name on all his stuff as beneficiary a long time ago and never got around to changing it. I suppose he thought he had plenty of time."

There wasn't an ounce of complaint in her voice, and he knew she'd do what she had to. Any woman who had suffered through boot camp, the horrors of war, and witnessing her best friend kill herself could certainly find her way around some financial setbacks.

"But why Savannah?" he asked. "Crestwood has jobs. Turtle Cove has jobs. Hell, even Riley's Peak has a job or two left." How could he be suggesting this to an almost stranger? He'd known her for less than a week. The disdain between them was now a distant, unfathomable memory. They'd come a long way from the first morning at Helen's. So how was it that this was all coming down to geography? "I'm sure your mom and Luke would like to have you around," he tacked on.

The suggestion hung in the air for a while as her eyes stayed plastered on the horizon. "Riley's Burger?" She was doing an excellent job of distancing herself.

All at once, Dylan grew hot in the face. His body, as if it belonged to someone else, went ridged. And yet he wanted to feel her thumping heart against his. He wanted to touch her, hold her, but there was this barrier now.

He spread his hands. "Was any of it real between the two of us? Because it sure felt like more to me."

Tish slowly circumnavigated the questions, and her hesitation pulled on Dylan. Did she need to think about it?

Arcs of pink and then blood orange blazed across the sky as the sun dipped behind the tree line, and it was as if all his senses were doubled, hell tripled, as he watched delight seep into her face. He could not remember ever seeing a more pleasing combination of features on a human being.

"It was real," she whispered.

"Then stay, damn it!" He turned her to him.

She squirmed away and rose to her feet. "I can't."

She left him sitting on the edge of the dock, his body aching with the burden of being alone.

❧ FIFTY-TWO ❧

WHILE Elyse was meeting with her attorney, Tish fumbled her way through the pantry in Crestwood, trying to locate coffee filters. They'd somehow avoided Annabeth for the past two days, but it was only a matter of time before she'd barge in with a locksmith in tow. As Tish moved a box of granola bars aside, the doorbell rang. She felt a flare of excitement that dissipated when she opened the door to find Ethan Aeillo. At the sight of him, an unwelcome torrent of emotions spread through her. She'd convinced herself the drama with Philip and Gretchen was the last bullet point in her personal hell, but no, here was another.

"Hello." Ethan's tone was too casual, too light and airy for the truth she saw in his eyes.

Tish said nothing, although a string of profanities fell heavily through her head, dropping one after the other like giant dominoes.

"I thought you might be here, and I was afraid you would leave before we had a chance to talk."

The door creaked open, and he slipped inside. It was time to get this over with, but Ethan was a flesh and blood representation of the past, and the past was something she'd struggled so long to avoid.

He glanced toward the kitchen, maybe looking for a place they could sit and chat. No, she didn't want to sit and chat. He could stand, and she hoped he was uncomfortable. Then he'd say what he came to say and be out the door and she could get back to denying that anything inappropriate ever happened between him and Liv.

Ethan wouldn't make eye contact but looked in her general direction. "I live with this every day. If only . . ." His face scored into a thousand segments of regret. "I started trying to help her when she was sixteen, maybe seventeen. But when she was in her twenties and still skirting around the issues, saying something bad happened when she was thirteen, I told her to get professional help."

His words were needles, and Tish the pincushion. As her muscles tensed against each prick, she could feel herself beginning to shake, and Ethan moved forward, presumably to comfort her. She held up her hands. Ethan couldn't help consoling the inconsolable. It was his thing. But he'd given up on Liv. Had she done the same?

What happened when Liv was thirteen? That summer things between her, Liv and Robert seemed different. Awkward. Elyse had always called teenage girls shape-shifters. You never knew which creature was going to show up. Tish had chalked Liv's behavior up to that, but had she missed something?

And why had Ethan become so interested in *helping* Liv when she was sixteen? It was around the time her mom had complications after surgery and almost died. Had he swooped in then with a ready ear, strong comforting arms . . . Something more? Tish's throat closed up at the thought.

Ethan shook his head sorrowfully. "I didn't think I could help her. She never really opened up about what happened beyond obsessing over something that she said was all her fault."

The thought burned a hole in her conscience. What kept Liv from telling her best friend about something so horrific that it haunted her more than a decade later?

The emanations of Ethan's tortured words should have eased his pain, but he looked as horrified as ever.

"I thought she was just reaching out for attention," Ethan said. Tears were falling now, and he wiped the end of his nose. Tish unraveled a sheet of paper towel from the roll and handed it to him. "She told me I was the only one she could talk to. Then when I heard . . . Maybe I could have helped her. How am I supposed to live with this?"

The question, the sharp tip of a knife that had settled between Tish's ribs the moment she'd seen Liv's desperate eyes, the gun in her hand. A question she feared she'd never be able to answer.

※

The deepening pallet of the sky through the apartment window in Savannah reminded Tish she'd wasted a whole day not doing what she came here to do. Her stomach gave a nervous lurch and she rubbed at the bridge of her nose. How had they accumulated so much stuff in the short time they were here? The storage closet was veritably spinning with boxes holding memories she'd worked hard to anesthetize.

She opened the first box, scrutinized the contents with the zeal of a woman possessed. She *would* do this. A jumble of Tish and Liv's things, things she hadn't bothered to sort after Liv died, mocked her. There was a reason she hadn't dealt with any of this, but time hadn't helped as she thought it would. In some ways, the passing of time only made it worse.

"Ghost Tour." Tish ran her fingers over the leaflet as her mind drifted through a blur of events. Liv had thought they needed a break from working all the time and bought tickets with money that should have been earmarked for gas. A native of Savannah, Tish had been to all these tourist traps, but maybe she couldn't blame her friend for wanting to experience the nation's most haunted city firsthand. "We can take the trolley. It'll be fun." Tish could hear Liv's clipped northern accent as plain as if she were here in the room.

Tish plunged deeper into the box. Salt and pepper shakers from the diner where they worked, a mug that said "Messy hair, don't care," a curling iron. She was a heartbeat from picking up the phone and calling someone, anyone, to come and get it all, when something caught her eye. A text book. *The Story of Literature.* Tish opened it, read the name on the inside cover: Jason Ludwig 6B.

Leafing through, about halfway a yellowed newspaper clipping stopped her. She swept the clipping aside and the title of a poem, "Funeral Blues" by L.H. Auden, loomed. She read the poem to the last line, "for nothing now can come to any good." A bold slash of black added below it for emphasis.

Tish opened the folded newspaper and read:

> Local residents are mourning the tragic death of Jason Ludwig who was found dead at the base of the Shawnee Bridge, Wednesday April 5th. Detectives believe he was walking the bridge alone when he was startled by an oncoming train. Jason was a sixth-grade honor roll student at Erie County Middle School. His parents, Rachel and Bode Ludwig, and brother Harry, will lay him to rest on Friday.

Tragedies in small towns take on a life of their own. Everywhere she went in Turtle Cove that summer people were still talking about Jason Ludwig. He was such a smart boy. He would have made something of himself. He was so good in science. Maybe doctor material. The whole town was awash in sadness for what could have been. He'd been in the same grade as Liv and Robert, yet when Tish asked about him, they said he was just some kid. They weren't particularly interested in talking about the subject others couldn't seem to digest. Yet Liv had kept this newspaper clipping about his death. Why?

Two days later, Tish paced, fighting the rocks of apprehension that made her arms and legs burdensome. She and Robert had agreed to meet at the small coffee shop near the Savannah Airport. They'd worked out the logistics, and for some reason she felt a need to be on neutral turf. As she wore a path into the sidewalk, she considered their history. Friends for over twenty years, but in the last few weeks she felt like she barely knew the man.

A gray SUV pulled to the curb and Robert stepped out. He was dressed in crisp jeans and a blue blazer, which would last all of five minutes in the Savannah heat. It was only May, but the humidity had been off the charts that week.

After a stiff greeting, they went inside and ordered iced coffees. They moved to a small table in the corner, exchanged the usual banal catch-up questions. How have you been? What's new? And on until Tish was about to burst.

"I need to know about Jason Ludwig," she said.

The name made him grimace. "Why do you insist on living in the past, Tish?"

"Because it's the only way I can make sense of Liv's death. It's the only way I can move on."

He sighed. Seemingly torn between a need to keep the past secured under lock and key and giving her the closure she needed.

"Liv and I were there that day."

Tish had had her suspicions. The way Liv had shoved the newspaper clipping in the boy's English book certainly meant something. But hearing Robert admit it cut like a knife.

"We went to the bridge after school every day we could, just Liv and I. Jason kept pestering Liv to hang out, he had a crush on her. It was my idea to invite him along. I told him he needed to prove his love to Liv." His voice remained calm, but his eyes conveyed the pain he must have felt all these years. "I was just a stupid kid, Tish. We all were. Just kids."

"How did it happen?"

"We were climbing the bridge, the way we always did. Liv and I had done it so many times we honestly didn't have a second thought about it. Jason was nervous but determined. Liv told him to turn back, that we'd meet him when we came back down, but he persisted. Then, when it was clear he wasn't giving up, we both urged him on. Liv started joking that she'd kiss him if he made it all the way up."

Tish could imagine the scene. Liv's silky hair blowing in the wind, her round eyes beckoning him to follow. Lithe, tanned limbs, bordering on womanly capturing his full attention. For a beat, Tish felt Dylan beside her, the thrill of his lips devouring hers as they sat on the same bridge. Just as quickly the thought vanished as the reality of what happened all those years ago settled heavy in her chest.

"When he was almost at the top, he slipped." Robert's last

words forced out in a cracked whisper.

Tish's eyes began to well with tears. She'd never met Jason. Her circle of summer friends didn't extend much beyond Robert and Liv, but hearing the details made her heart hurt. For Jason, for his family, for her best friends. Then the anger started to bubble. If Robert had known this all these years, known that it was torturing Liv, why hadn't he said anything? Liv could be alive.

"We panicked. It was a long fall. He was . . . we were certain. We were kids, just kids," he repeated.

"What does Ethan have to do with all this?"

"Liv never told him. I made her swear she wouldn't. No one could know but us."

Ethan must have felt so helpless, trying to counsel her when she'd give him nothing to go on.

Tish wanted to scream at Robert for his part in this, for hiding this all these years. But she fled the coffee shop instead.

In her car, she gripped the steering wheel and burst into tears. Sobs that tore at her lungs, her throat. For the briefest moment, a thought passed through her. She needed a cigarette. But the idea brought on a surge of nausea. Those days were long gone. She grabbed a tissue from the glove compartment, blew her nose and wiped her eyes with a fresh one.

Minutes later, Robert rapped at the window. She got out, leaned against the car. He started to speak, and she raised a hand for him to stop.

She vacillated, not sure what to say. Finally she spoke. "Liv's at peace now."

Layers of sadness, guilt, and regret peeled away. She'd always wonder if she could have done something different, but maybe like grains of sand relentlessly irritating an oyster, something good could be gleaned from this. She plucked that pearl from its shell, a new understanding.

જે

Three months later in Savannah, Tish opened the door to find Dylan. The sight of him was as familiar as swallowing, as comfortable as a hammock but as alarming as the boom of an unexpected firecracker. Tish felt a crimson rash running up her neck, racing to find her cheeks.

"Did you really think I'd let you go?" His question hung between them long enough to drape the room in silence, a silence that held them in place until moments later when they entwined in each other's embrace.

She backed him to the couch, lowered him there. Her hands moved to his chest and began to part his shirt, button by button, peeling it back over his shoulders. Stalling, she traced her fingers over the ink outline coiled around his arm. It was decidedly a bee filled in with an intricate design. Upon closer examination, she saw butterflies scattering, one morphing into the other.

Dylan snatched her hand, laced his fingers through hers, and held it to his chest. "Ever see one of those crazy staircase drawings?"

"Escher, right?"

He caressed her face. "You never cease to amaze me."

"I didn't realize you were that into art."

"I'm not."

"Well, only two reasons I can think of to get a tattoo, for yourself or . . ." A loud discomfort filled the space between them, and Tish wondered if she'd crossed a line.

"Bianca loves Escher's art for its symmetry," Dylan finally said.

"You loved her, didn't you?"

Dylan didn't speak for another long moment. "After we broke up, and especially after she and Finn got together, I wondered why I'd ever gotten the stupid tat in the first place. I thought it might be awkward if I ever had my shirt off in front of them, if you know, we took Kate swimming or something. But having it removed would have been like denying my past. And there's no going forward without remembering my past, if that makes sense. Sorry to get all philosophical. To answer your question, I did love her."

She felt a twinge of something, maybe jealousy, followed by an ache in her throat. She swallowed hard. "And now?"

He clutched his fingers tighter around hers, pressed the back of her hand to his beating heart, and angled a grin at her. All his previous grins had been warm ups for this one, and she was stunned to her core. "How can I put this?"

He leaned in, kissed her softly. "I want you to understand." He kissed her again, deeper, with a gravity that let her know she was the only one on his mind, in his heart. His touch made her forget. It made her remember. It gave her strength. It left her weak. Complete, but wanting more.

Tish was quiet, pensive.

"What are you thinking?"

She canted her head, raised up on an elbow, and gave him a long appraisal. "About how convincing you can be. And about your next tattoo. Maybe an army boot? Or an onion?"

Dylan crooked his arm around the back of her neck and pulled her to him.

"I love you." Spoken before his lips reached hers. She hadn't even felt her mouth shaping the words and she couldn't believe she'd said it first. She'd never said it first. She'd never even said it to anyone outside her family. His echoing response, spoken with a smooth balance of conviction and affection, brought on a squeezing sensation in her chest, a burst of emotion, and she held on just in case this wasn't real.

But this was real. And she'd known it right from the start. There was a gravitational pull whenever he was around, a feeling that she'd known him all her life, a knowing deep in her center. Maybe her soul.

They should be together.

❧ FIFTY-THREE ❧

Turtle Cove at Lake Anaba, A Year Later

DYLAN'S mind tripped back to his first glimpse of Tish, clad in leather jacket and tight jeans, and thought about the woman gliding toward him to Lady Antebellum's "I Run to You." In a simple, yet elegant gown, Tish was a stunner to beat all stunners. Her bangs finally swept away from those arresting eyes, held in place with a cluster of shiny gems that flecked bronze in the sunlight. High-heeled boots peeked out from under a flowing, cream-colored dress. Boots. He never thought his bride would wear boots. But she was perfect.

If he could peel his eyes away from the most beautiful woman he'd ever imagined, he'd see his best man, Finn, standing next to him. Bianca, Tish's choice for Matron of Honor, Kate, the flower girl who'd done such a fine job splashing magnolia petals down the path to the archway beside the lake. Tish's landlady in Savannah had shipped them overnight so Tish could have a touch of the place she loved on her wedding day. Tucker was there, Dylan's Jager-drinking best bud since high school. Of course, Luke and Robert. Rose, Elyse and Helen, standing close together, three of the strongest women on the planet. Rose beaming, little Mack, squirming in her arms. A momentary hollowness at the thought of his father missing this, missing meeting his grandson, his namesake, but then pure joy. His father was still with them, always would be, and the family was reunited and growing.

Everyone important was here.

As Tish stopped on her mark, Dylan saw her take a steadying breath, and he reached for her hand.

Ethan Aiello, the marriage officiant, cleared his throat. Somehow, his being here completed the circle.

Dylan thanked his lucky stars, or maybe Tish's lucky star, the one her dad had named for her, that he was in the right place at the right time when Tish came along. Though he'd had his doubts about what he was doing at Helen's that cool spring morning, now he knew why. Nothing ever felt so right.

"Love has brought us together." Ethan's voice was deep and decisive. "The love of two people transcends all things."

Dylan fogged through the rest, his heart beating wildly. Before he knew it, Finn was nudging him, handing him the ring. He reached for Tish's hand slipped it on her finger.

*

The coolness of the band circling Tish's finger was at odds with the warm tears sliding through her eyelashes. This was actually happening. She nearly burst into laughter. Dylan's pale green eyes seared into hers as she felt her skin go splotchy. The cool rush of breeze off the lake was a welcome reprieve. Maybe no one would notice how this man in front of her made her weak and strong at once.

Dylan wore an understated gray suit, but there was nothing casual about his demeanor. As she watched the grin spread over his face, she knew that he'd never been more serious about anything in his life.

A constellation of joy and peace and contentment had replaced Tish's anxieties. There would be bumps in the road ahead, but she'd rather travel a bumpy road with this man than a smooth road with any other.

The evening was balmy with pockets of cold as the sun set in a rebellion of pink, red, and orange across the lake. With the help of Dylan's old work buddies and signing a zillion mortgage papers in blood, construction had begun on the house, the house they would call home, and possibly one day raise children in. Luke would live with them for as long as he wanted. Dylan's idea. The two had become something of an item, spending large blocks of time together.

A glimpse of her mom boosted her assurance. Elyse would be okay. She'd made a mistake, paid for it. Community service and a hefty fine. It could have been a lot worse, but she had cooperated and thanks to a DA open to bargaining in exchange for information to help put Philip, Gretchen, and the kidnappers behind bars, she was a free woman.

Tish heard Dylan's vows breaking through, begging her to join him in this moment, a moment that was the first of many to come.

And at Ethan's prompting, she heard herself say with alarming clarity, "I do."

About the Author

WHEN Nancy Smith and Cat Trizzino met in an online writers' group, their individual styles blended to a shared vision. Though they live in different states, Nancy in Michigan, Cat in Maryland, their passion for well-crafted stories makes the physical distance irrelevant. Tempeste Blake is the result of their combined voices, an author who writes grab-the-tissue-box, heart-in-your-throat romantic suspense and loves to throw her characters into the deep end to see if they sink or swim.

Thank you for spending some of your precious time in Riley's Peak. Please stop by www.tempesteblake.com to chat about the story, characters, or whatever. And if you'd like to share your opinion in a review on Amazon or Goodreads, well, there's a double dose of good karma coming your way.

Acknowledgments

FOR their insightful comments and feedback, we wish to thank Michele Brant, Rebecca Shepard, Patti Shepard, and Doug Willner. John Herrmann for sharing his knowledge about clinical trials. We own any errors in that area. Our family, friends and fellow authors for their unfailing support. Our husbands, Randy Smith and John Trizzino. You miraculously keep us grounded while encouraging us to soar.

Also by Tempeste Blake

℘

CHASING SYMMETRY

"A steady, rewarding build ... a vibrant cast of characters." ~ Kirkus Reviews

"*Chasing Symmetry* is a must read novel and Tempeste Blake is an author to watch!" ~ Jen Thomason, *Dandelions Inspired*

"Brilliant, exciting, keeps you guessing until the end." ~ Mary K. Ruple

℘

A sample of Chasing Symmetry, the first book in the Riley's Peak series, follows.

CHASING SYMMETRY

ONE

SOMEONE had been trying for the perfect shade of red—a blend of crimson and cadmium speckled the floor in a careless array.

Bianca envisioned one of her students rushing into the supply room, oblivious to the paint dripping from a hastily sealed container. Understandable that cleaning up wasn't a first priority. A college student's life is led by a higher power—hormones.

She moved into the storage room to fish through a bin of rags, squinting in the dim light. All she wanted was a little more light, not a studio renovation. It was an ongoing battle with Chet, the custodian. He'd flicked her a requisition form, his standard rebuttal, and she'd filled it out, twice. If he didn't change the burned-out bulb tomorrow, there was always Miller's Hardware.

Back to the mess at hand, she squatted, rag suspended. But upon closer examination, this wasn't paint. The odor was cloying. Familiar. She followed a trail snaking from under the supply cart, nudged the cart aside, and gasped.

A woman sat slumped against a stack of canvasses, head lolled back, legs extended like a large doll, arms reaching out in an unsettling symmetry.

Lifeless eyes frozen in horror.

Bianca's gaze slid over the woman's gray uniform, the splattered blood. Terror built, a scream that wouldn't come. She scrambled to her feet, lost her footing, and toppled against the shelves. A basket of yarn slammed down, and she clawed through the unraveling skeins, tangling them in her hair.

Her voice returned in the form of a low keening.

She had one foot out the door, but a sound, a muted gurgle, drew her back. Moving closer, she placed shaky fingers along the woman's neck. A pulse—thready, but there. Or was that her own pulse vibrating through her fingertips? Bianca held her breath, checked again. Her heart climbed up her throat and lodged there as she positioned the body for CPR. Please, oh please, help me remember how.

She tilted the woman's head back and saw the source of all that blood, her right temple. Pressure. Apply pressure. She clamped the rag over the wound, pinched the nostrils to start mouth to mouth, stopped. Hadn't they changed the rules? What were they now? Compression only? Placing her palms on the woman's chest, she pushed. Twenty? Thirty? With each compression, her voice cracked in a whispered demand, "Breathe. Breathe. Breathe!"

In an instant of suspended time, Bianca realized the futility of her efforts, but she couldn't pull herself away. Again, her fingers reached for the neck. Nothing. Damn it. Nothing!

Her cell. She bolted to her feet, slapped her pockets. Where...? A tendril of ice seized her spine. Something rooted her in place as a thunderclap of self-preservation boomed.

Whoever did this has a gun.

Made in the USA
San Bernardino, CA
01 February 2018